I HEARD LENIN LAUGH

Also by Martin Sixsmith

Moscow Coup: the Death of the Soviet System

Spin: a Novel

MARTIN SIXSMITH

I HEARD LENIN LAUGH

MACMILLAN

First published 2006 by Macmillan
an imprint of Pan Macmillan Ltd
Pan Macmillan, 20 New Wharf Road, London N1 9RR
Basingstoke and Oxford
Associated companies throughout the world
www.panmacmillan.com

ISBN-13: 978-1-4050-4121-8
ISBN-10: 1-4050-4121-8

1 3 5 7 9 8 6 4 2

A CIP catalogue record for this book is available from
the British Library.

Typeset by SetSystems Ltd, Saffron Walden, Essex
Printed and bound in Great Britain by
Mackays of Chatham plc, Chatham, Kent

'All our lives we fought against exalting the individual, against the elevation of the single person, and long ago we were over and done with the business of a hero, but here it comes up again: the glorification of one personality. This is not good at all.'

V. I. LENIN, MOSCOW, 1920

I HEARD
LENIN
LAUGH

PART ONE

HELLO. AND pleasure for meet you. My name Yevgeny.

Yevgeny, it is true. But my friends they call me Zhenya.

For you, this hard to understand. But for us Russians, very easy.

Someone in Russia called Aleksandr, his friend call him Sasha. Nikolai, they call him Kolya. And everything seem normal.

Also, my name Gorevich. But this important, as you probably see later in my story.

So please remember name, Yevgeny Gorevich. I explain later.

Now, where I was born? In Vitebsk.

And when? In very first year of Great Patriotic War. So, 1941 of course.

You want to know about Vitebsk?

OK. Start thinking about famous painter, Marc Chagall. Now you see Vitebsk: it got cows flying over roofs of houses playing violins and green sheeps smiling very large.

All right, only joking.

Some more name affairs for you now: you know what Chagall mean in Russian? It mean 'I strode, you strode, he strode'. And that Chagall, he strode pretty fast right out of Vitebsk and right into Paris.

No one here blame him much. If you see Vitebsk and you

3

see Paris, you understand why. Strange to say, nobody in Vitebsk ever know Chagall back then. He was here and was gone.

In those days, corrupt cosmopolitan (meaning Jewish) decadents been not using much popularity in Soviet Union. They got to go to West to be popular, and get very famous and rich in Paris, London, New York.

But we all been staying right on a spot in Vitebsk. Government in Moscow and local party guys, they all telling us we real happy and 'no other land in world where man can breathe so free' etc.

But strange to say, I – Yevgeny/Zhenya – was not so very happy.

And why?

The reason you see as I recount you my story.

So, coming back to that old Chagall, one thing he get wrong: too many violins.

But one thing for sure he get right: all those huts with wood walls and straw on roof.

Absolutely.

And I been living in one hut like that.

Myself – Yevgeny/Zhenya – and mother, Tatiana.

You asking about my father? OK, I tell you. But only later. Because my father, he too will be important in this affair.

Now, what the first thing I remember in my life? Actually I don't remember for sure what this is, because I am pretty old now with memory going to the worse (sixty-five years old, as you sure to be calculating if you can do mathematics plus you also know what is our year right now).

But one thing I do remember when I am small child and living in petticoats of my mother, as we Russians use to say.

Maybe I remember it, or maybe I just remember my mother telling it.

But I think I remember it, because later it been pretty darn important to me.

First, you got to understand Great Patriotic War just been through Vitebsk and, among other items, Patriotic War mean many broken windows.

Consequently, when I was tiny child, not all houses and huts in our town been having any glass in the windows. Lots having just boards.

But our house was having glass, and my mother she proud of it.

So that crow was pretty important to her. Why? Because that crazy damn crow, he decide he want to break our glass and let a wind and snow in our kitchen.

Every morning, we hear him. Bang, bang, bang. Then some screeching. Then more bang, bang, bang.

Me, I was pretty little and this crow he pretty big, and I am real scared lying there in my bed.

Funny thing is, this crow always undertake his banging just as sun arising and start to shine on our windows.

And my mother she can't figure it out at all. She get up every morning when she hear the crow and she wave and yells for scare him away.

But he just flap his big wings and fly up real kind of lazy into his tree.

And when my mother get back into bed and gets warm again and sleepy, damn crow start all over again: bang, bang, bang and screeching and squawking.

And I am scared, so I get in bed with my mother and she tell me not to worry and everything be OK.

But every day he keep coming back.

Every day, my mother see him bang into our window and drop like dead to ground. But then he shake himself little bit and get up and undertakes it all over again.

And this is just madness! That crow, he flying straight into our window and smashing himself to the pieces!

So why he doing this?

That what I want to know.

But my mother she cannot tell me. She just worried that damn crow going to break up our windows and leave us cold and wet and shivering.

So she goes down a road to see Mr Finkelstein the kulak (we only call him kulak, of course; he isn't really one, or else he be getting purged long time ago).

Anyway, Mr Finkelstein he likes my mother (as I find out later, this especially because my father not there) and he say her: 'Madame Gorevich, you want I come and shoot that damn crow?'

Well, my mother is pretty sad for hear this and she feeling sorry for the crow. But Finkelstein say, 'No, my dear, I will get out my very big gun and I come and wait with you in your bedroom for little while. And then I shoot him.'

And my mother say OK, but she pretty unhappy about all this arrangement, including especially the very big gun.

So next day she take me and we go to see Dr Astrov (maybe I getting this name wrong, but I think you know what I have in the mind) who know everything about nature and forests and crows and so forth, and who also much younger and nicer than old Finkelstein.

And she tells that doctor whole story and she ask him my question: why this crazy damn crow is doing such crazy damn thing?

And young Astrov think for the little while and then he tell my mother: 'Mrs Gorevich, this what I think. That crow very, very sad.'

And I see my mother give a little nod and looks at him straight in his eyes (which are very dark and brown and full of his soul).

'That crow is sad because he lost something very important. He lost the partner of his life.'

And my mother is looking and looking at him while he is speaking, and he say, 'I think that crow lost his true beloved mate and now he is yearning for her pretty bad. And when he is yearning, he comes over to you house because you got the glass windows. And when the sun arising in the morning over the forest, those windows they start looking like little mirrors. And the crow, he look in those mirrors and what he does see?'

I can see my mother looking in that doctor's eyes like mirrors right now, and she ask him, 'I don't know, doctor, what he does see?'

And Dr Astrov says, 'Well, Mrs Gorevich, he see the reflection of himself. But, because those windows maybe a bit dirty, this image looking little bit blurred to him and probably he don't know exactly . . .'

But my mother is not for having any of this and she tell the doctor, 'No, doctor, my windows all clean. Everything in our house is clean.'

But doctor just smiles and say, 'All right, let's say it because this crow not seeing too well, ever since he been trying for knock his own brains out. And instead of realizing that he seeing himself in you windows, he get to thinking he actually glimpsing his lost partner and she is there in some different other world just on other side of that glass. And when he see this, he is real full of *toska* and more than suicidally desperate to see her again.'

Now, excuse me please. You probably notice already that my English pretty darn good, so maybe you wondering why I just left that word *toska* like it sound when we say it in Russian. Well, that is because even I cannot think of any word for translate it to you: *toska* means you are real full of sadness and complete desperate, just like that crow is, and – if I think about it – just like my mother is too, because when she hear that doctor mention *toska*, she just sighs and give the little *vskhlip* (which I guess is similar like a sob, but much sadder because it is like your whole soul is pouring out all it feelings through this little sound in your throat and maybe also some tear in your eyes).

Anyway, Dr Astrov is still talking and he says: 'So that old crow, he don't care what he does to himself, like smashing himself on a window and cracking his head open and so forth, because all he care about is getting into that other world on other side of the glass where he see all his happiness and his fate. He just don't understand it is an illusion and that maybe he can never get there.'

And I can see right now that my mother is not going to let old Finkelstein get out his very big gun after all and that crazy damn crow is pretty darn safe for coming at our house and smash himself on our window any time he like, because my mother is thinking pretty much those same thoughts which the crazy damn crow is thinking, and she starting to like that crow almost as much as she like the young doctor.

So I am resigning myself to lots of screeching and squawking in the mornings every time that sun arises, and on way home from doctor's place my mother don't say too much except maybe 'thanks God' and so forth, and she holding me real tight by the hand and her eyes looking far away somewhere . . .

*

And next morning, round about seven o'clock because it October now and sun arising pretty late, we both in bed and hear that crow sitting on our fence and squawking away before starting his usual kamikaze affair.

And then that usual bang, bang, bang on the window.

But this time I hear my mother is not getting up to shoo him away, and I guess she just lying there imagining pretty much those same things which going on in the crow's head, or else maybe thinking about that young Dr Astrov, when we hear the terrific big unusual bang followed by terrible awful squawking and sudden smashing glass; and then squawking stops all of the sudden and just little bits of glass are tinkling like shiny piano notes on the kitchen floor.

And everything go quiet, like a church at midnight with the corpse lying waiting in its coffin to be buried.

And my mother and me both lie there and no one want to go in that kitchen because we both pretty darn scared.

But then I hear my mother getting up and go through, and I hear her scream real loud so I run in to be with her and our whole floor is covered in broken glass and that big black crazy crow is lying in the middle of it with his neck all broken and bent, and blood all round him and his eyes open and staring right up at the ceiling *like he's seen something he wanted to see and he's found something he'd long been seeking for.*

In the end, of course, I can't tell you for sure if that crazy bird had got to the place where he been wanting to go, but that night I dreamt that big flocks of black crows are chasing me and next morning, you know what, I found myself kind of missing him and not hearing him banging away on our window.

And I guess my mother is missing him too, because she just sit there and stares out of the other window (Mr Finkelstein already come and boarded up the broken one).

And all through my life, and especially now I am in here and age sixty-five, like you know, I start hearing that damn crow squawking in my brain every time I get sad and lonely. And when I hear it, I know it always means I am about to get the *toska* pretty bad.

Anyway, I guess what you actually wanting to know is how I got to speak English so darn good, whereas in old Soviet Union they tended to figure this is dangerous and capitalistic language and no one allowed for learn it properly unless they all members of Party and all checked out for trustiness and so forth.

Well, since you wanting to know, I tell you.

And this bring us to very important fact about my life.

It is my mother who been teaching me to English.

And why?

To answer, I tell you first about my life as a youth.

As a child, I Zhenya was unhappy. And I not meaning just usual Communist unhappy where everybody get pretty blue – except top Party guys, of course, who all got big Chaikas for drive around in and special shops for buy the food and maybe some caviar on Sundays and Moldavian pink champagne.

No, I mean more than that unhappy.

And since I will be telling you all I remember, including bad bits, first bad bit comes at schooldays.

In Vitebsk, school back then is a muddle.

After Great Patriotic War, the education in Soviet Union all been disrupted and needing massive Stakhanovite effort to get going again, and straight away it gets infected by spies and enemies of the people and revanchists.

Uh-oh, bad times must be lying ahead.

And just in case you having problems understanding this, please remind yourself how all things been largely different back then. For instance, there I am at school learning to read and doing it pretty good. First lessons we learn stuff like 'cat' and 'table' and 'chair', and everything looking fine.

I go home to my mother and reading her stuff out of my book, which is green and pretty worn out because it already being used before Great Patriotic War and only dug out of cellars couple of years ago.

And I like reading to my mother, because when I get stuff right she always smile and give me little kisses, and when I get things wrong she just smile anyway and puts her arm round me.

So I am reading her stories about little Misha and his cat and how they always get to play in a meadow and help with harvest and so forth, and everything happy. And my reading is getting better and better, and I start growing up into fine youth and future builder of socialism.

But then one day, Misha with his cat – or maybe it someone else being hero of the stories by now – meets an enemy of the people who is unmasked as Menshevik lickspittle, and I get home and read this to my mother and she don't smile at all.

She asks me to show her this book and she read it herself and then she get that sad look that worries me pretty bad.

And I say, don't worry, Mama, that Menshevik lickspittle sure not going to make any trouble for us.

And I am right, of course, because in next lesson we learn how his secret plotting gets exposed and the competent organs come to deal with him, and it is pretty fine adventure and we boys all like this story pretty good.

But I can see my mother still not happy and she just sit there and smiles, but not a real smile if you know what I mean. Kind of sad smile.

So next night, I read her other story from my reading book to cheer her up.

I wish to recount you that story right now, so you can laugh also and highly appreciate it. It concern that period straight after Great Patriotic War, when Soviet people begin working under Five Year Plan.

One day, a schoolteacher been telling his pupils about the Plan and all wonderful new houses, cinemas, streets and parks, electric trains and so forth it going to be producing. So those boys get very excited and they discussing this great thing on the way home from school.

'I would like go to bed tonight and wake up not tomorrow but after five years so I can see everything at once,' say one boy.

'No,' say another boy, 'that not too interesting. I would like to see how great Soviet nation is building all that.'

'And I,' say third boy, 'would like to do all that with my own hands!'

Well, this is great story and it making me fill up with pride, but even so my mother only smile and pat on my head.

And she still seem pretty unhappy and just go off to the piano in our living room and start playing and humming some song with title of 'An die Musik' written in strange letters on it cover.

Anyway, Olga Borisovna, our old schoolteacher with dirty nails and legs having the big swellings round the ankles, says I am a smart kid and reading better than anyone in class, including even Vova Smirnov.

Pretty soon I am first who can spell Trotskyite hyena, imperialist hireling and all those other big important words without making any single mistake.

And I can see Vova not very happy about this.

Vova (excuse me just one moment for one more name affair: Vova is same as Vladimir or Volodya, but only for his friends to call him this), he gets pretty mad whenever he think somebody trying to overdo his own efforts.

This is because everybody know Vova's Pa is old Mr Smirnov, chairman of the kolkhoz (which is to say big collective agro-kombinat farm where we all live and work happily together) and also candidate member of Vitebsk Region Raikom.

And so important he is that everybody usually just let Vova be best at everything. Otherwise why risk making old Smirnov mad when he can decide most things just like God, who we don't believe in or, rather, like Glorious and Wise Leader, who we do believe in?

I give you for example.

Vova and me playing football in same youths' teams, both for school and also for collective farm. And both playing attacking role.

So sometimes it come to an action in front of the enemy gates and I am in perfect position for score the goal. Wham!

But what? The coach he say me, it is better always pass the ball to Vova so he can mark the goal, and I ask to coach, even if it mean our team is not scoring?

And coach, he kind of sigh and look upwards and say: yes, even if it is so.

OK, I say, I am the good boy and know my socialist duty, so I agree and always I am making pass to Vova Smirnov instead of making the goal, and generally everyone happy. But when it come to matters of reading and writing, old Olga Borisovna the teacher seem to forgot the rule about Vova, and in particular she forget to tell me always I should make some mistakes.

So in fact I don't.

And therefore the matter is that Vova Smirnov is not

number one in the reading and spelling affairs, and that number one is me, Zhenya.

And whole school know about this and soon start talking and maybe even laughing somewhat at Vova and pointing him and say he certainly not the top dog when it come to spelling Bukharinite deviationist and so forth.

Well, Vova he laugh a little and pretend we still great friends, even though his eyes saying something different and his lips look little bit pressed together when he see me in the corridor.

And then things go to even worse.

For first of May which, as is known, is workers' holiday and also name day of our glorious kolkhoz, Olga Borisovna decide there going to be special jubilee celebration, for show what our school been achieving and what children all been learning. And she say she want to choose very best reader for declaim the special story or two at this celebration, in front of all parents and families.

Now, I can see problem looming here, and looming in my direction!

From the one sides, I know best reader is me and I pretty proud of this; but from the other sides, I know it better be Vova who do the declaiming because if not, there likely to be big retribution and it probably be me getting retributed.

I got to decide what to do.

Maybe I tell Olga Borisovna I don't want to do no declaiming?

Or maybe I tell her I feel sick and can't go to her celebration?

But no. I don't do nothing.

Except start learning that darn story she wanting me to read out on first of May.

And you know what? I can still remember that story word after word even now, more than half of century later.

You want to hear it?

It is story about sheeps and a wolf, and this is exact how I been reading it to whole kolkhoz all those many year ago:

'Once on a time, big wolf see some sheeps feeding in a field. And he wanting to eat some of them. So this wolf he make a plan. He put on skin of a sheep and goes in that field his self. And he able to kill many of them. Shepherd cannot recognize his enemy because the wolf has put on skin of a sheep and he look like a sheep. "Why so many of my sheeps always disappearing?" ask the shepherd to his self. He never lost no sheeps before, so he getting pretty angry. "I going to catch that thief," he say. "And then I get the thick rope and I hang him." But still, one by one, those sheeps continue to disappear. When at last more than ten sheeps disappeared, the shepherd he gets real watchful. So he walk about in the sheeps night and day, and he watch them real careful. And one night he see a sheep who is not moving around and eating grass like sheeps do. "That is not a sheep," he say; "that is wolf in sheep's outfitting. That is the enemy who kill my sheeps!" And shepherd take the rope he bring with him and quickly throws it round the wolf's neck. Then he take him to a tree growing nearby and he hang him. Two other shepherds coming close to that place and very much surprised to see a sheep hanging on a tree. "What this all mean, comrade?" they ask him all surprised. "Is it possible you hang sheeps?" "No," answer the shepherd, "but I hang wolves when I catch them, even when they dressed in a sheep's outfitting." When those two men understand their mistake and see that shepherd is saying true, they tell him: "You quite right, comrade. Most dangerous enemies are those pretending to be our friends."'

OK, so everyone understand pretty quick what this story actually all about and everyone nodding and smiling, though maybe not Mr Smirnov and his wife, who is big and fat with the very red face that look real angry with me because I am doing this socialist reading ceremony instead of her Vova.

These sort of tales all pretty good and pretty easy for understanding, especially in light of those old days when Soviet state is very constantly under threat from many enemies and spies in all crafty disguises.

I know, and everyone know, that they mainly designed for putting up the wind of any degenerate, revisionist, opportunist, intriguer, parasite, speculator, petit-bourgeois provocateur, formalist, saboteur, deviationist, shirker, idler, social-fascist, demagogue, traitor, wrecker or Zionist agent which happen to be in earshot of me while I am declaiming. (Oh yes: all that big list of enemy of the peoples and other bad guys pretty familiar to us all back then.)

And everyone in that audience get the points pretty good, so there is lots of applause and everyone standing up and cheering and so forth, mainly because nobody want to get spotted sitting down in case people think they also degenerates themselves and start to take actions against them.

And my mother stand up and give a little smile, but kind of modest, like she is just happy for her son but not anything else, in case any Smirnovs watching her. Those Smirnovs get up and clap too, but it look to me like they not really enjoying to do this, which is little bit worrying for myself.

And it don't take very long for me getting proved right.

In school next day, Vova Smirnov comes and say to me, 'Well done, Zhenya. You declaim pretty good, just like one of our big

Soviet poets. And, by the way, you coming to play football for kolkhoz team next Sunday?'

And I say 'Sure' all unsuspecting and pleased that Vova not too mad with me any more. And he just smile.

But when it come to Sunday, that is when I find out what he really got in mind for me.

At first, the game start pretty well. We playing against Marxist-Leninist philosophy class from Vitebsk Gymnasium (just for letting you know, in Russian this mean like an academic place, not the athletic one), and they got all their brains in their heads but not in their feet or anywhere else useful for football, fortunate for us.

When they get the ball, it seem like they debating thesis, antithesis, synthesis and so forth before they deciding what to do with it!

But we all pretty good at taking the deterministic view of history and we sliding right in there to steal it off them before you can say dialectical materialism.

So we soon making all the attacking, but just cannot get the ball in their gates.

Then come the opportunity of goal, and enemy defence all slipping up in the mud, while I run round them all sharpishly and carry the ball to just ten metres from their kipper.

And this kipper – very big fellow with massive gloves on the hands and flat cap just like Lev Yashin – come bearing toward me.

But I am so cunning as a fox and pretend to pass to Vova, like as usual.

And enemy kipper gets fooled.

He start turning against Vova, because he figure the pass always go to Vova and I am never shooting; but this time, my psychological ploy is victorious, because I just keeping the ball and actually shoot the goal. Wham!

I am lying in the mud all triumphant and happy. But first I see our coach not looking too happy.

And then I see Vova running toward me and saying real loud 'Great goal, Zhenya, well done', but he seem to slip up in the mud next to me and lands real heavy on my leg which is still outstretched from shooting goals, and snap! goes my leg; and youch! goes me; and 'Oops, sorry!' goes Vova real loud.

But then real quiet he says me: 'That does for you, class enemy! Now I settled your accounts, degenerate adventurist!'

So I understand pretty quick that his so-calling slipping in the mud is even better ploy than mine was, and my leg been well and truly snapped with fully calculated intent.

Then the coach come running over and see my fibula bone all sticking out through the skin and he start sicking on the ground, which is real reassuring for me, and making me feel pretty sick too.

However, life has great and wise leaders in all situations, and old Mr Smirnov, Vova's Pa who is chairman of the kolkhoz and also candidate member of Vitebsk Region Raikom, comes up to take control of the situation, looking all concerned for me, but also smirking little bit secretly. And he start ordering people about, like 'You there! Pick this boy up!' and 'You, get that jersey and wrap it round him leg bone real tight!' and so forth.

And I am telling them 'No, no, no! No picking and no wrapping! This hurting me too damn much!' but old Smirnov insisting the whole time and nobody dare to disrespect his commands because they all too scared.

So I get lifted and carried – bump, bump, bump; ouch, ouch, ouch – all the way to Smirnov house.

And when we get there, old Smirnov he say, 'Get out some

vodka, pretty damn quick!' to him wife and whomever around there.

Well, you better remember that I am just the young boy at this stage of my life and never drunk anything except milk and *kvas*, and maybe little bit of beer which I been finding in a bottle someone left on the sidewalk, but I never told nobody about this because I am pretty unpartial to the taste and anyway it made me feel ill.

So I am saying, 'Uh-oh, not for me, Mr Smirnov', but then I figure out I am just the decoy here and he pretty much wants that vodka for his self. So he starts insisting, 'No, you need to drink this, son, for keeping all that pain away 'till Dr Astrov get here.'

But I can see he is pouring me out one glass and pouring his self out ten glasses.

Anyway, for making this tale shorter, I drink one vodka glass and it make my throat burn and I am coughing and going red around my face.

But old Mr Smirnov is drinking his vodka more like *voda* (which is Russian word for water) and never looking any different.

And Vova (who is not speaking me too much whatsoever, because I guess he feeling pretty ashameful of what he done to my leg) decide he want some vodka too, and I can see he got some practice drinking this stuff because he just grin when he swallow it and gets to look just like his father, all happy and full of humanitarian impulses.

Also, for some reason, Dr Astrov is taking really long time to get to that Smirnov house and during this inbetween, more and more vodka getting drunk by everyone except me, who is still hurting pretty damn bad in the leg region.

Eventually, Mr Smirnov's humanitarian impulses start taking

over and he get very expansive in the friendliness and humour department, and start telling all sorts of jokes, supposingly for cheer up my spirits but really because he and Vova both pretty happy they revenged themselves on me for disrespecting them.

These guys are real drunk now and wanting to be smart and humorous, but I am not drinking at all and mentally remembering those jokes they both telling.

Such as very old one about Soviet newspapers, What is difference in between *Pravda* and *Izvestiya*? Answer namely that no news in *Pravda* and no truth in *Izvestiya* (sorry, but you needing to know *Pravda* in Russian mean truth and *Izvestiya* mean news).

And when Vova hear word *Pravda*, so he start telling funny story of a man who goes to his doctor for complaining about pain in his bottom region. And doctor examine this and exclaim: 'Ah yes, I see the problem: you got big piece of paper stuck up there in your butt', and patient say 'Pravda?' to which doctor reply, 'Nyet, *Izvestiya*!'

(OK, I explain: if you say 'Pravda?' in Russian it mean either newspaper *Pravda*, or it mean 'Is that true?', and joke is funny because in old days of 1950s people in Russia all having to use newspaper for wiping off the bottoms because toilet paper constant *deficitnaya*, meaning there isn't any.)

Actually, that joke is making me laugh a lot and even forget for couple of minutes about the leg pain, but I see maybe it not so funny for you who not speaking Russian too good. And then Mr Smirnov, wanting to tell better joke than him son, start saying, 'So tell me, what is difference in between capitalism and Communism?'

Well, everybody go quiet when he say this, because now he starting to tread on the breakable ice.

But old Smirnov is pretty red around the face by now and sweating from vodka, so he say, 'I tell you! Under capitalism, as is well knowed, it is the exploitation of man by man; whereas under Communism it is complete the opposite!' And old Smirnov he start laughing so loud that he never notice everyone else being real silent and looking little bit worried on their faces.

Then at that moment Dr Astrov arrive and old Smirnov stop laughing and start pretending to look concerned about me, whose leg bone still sticking out through his skin and whose face not red, but very, very white.

So Astrov look at my leg and says, 'I going to do something now, Zhenya. And maybe this hurt you little bit', and – *ookhty! bookhty! fookhty!* as we say in Russian – he been guilty of very big understatement there! I maybe sixty-five years now, but never in this long life anything ever hurt me as much as what Dr Astrov did to me then (except maybe things been hurting my heart more in following years, but never my body so much).

But, honour to that doctor, he sure fix my leg, because that fibula bone is going right back inside my skin and start looking bit straighter again, and then he tie the real tight bandage round it, with long stick inside to keep things in they necessary places, and he say to me: 'Now these *kolkhozniki* will carry you back home on this door which they unscrewed off it hinges, so you not getting bumped around on the way. And I come with you and explain your mother what happen and what she must to do for look after you, because you must stay at home and not go to school for at least six weeks.'

Well, I am real glad Dr Astrov is coming with me, because I know my mother get so worried about me she sure to fall aweeping and maybe even swoon; but I also know that if Dr Astrov there, the reason for her swooning maybe not totally just because of me! And anyway if she is swooning – for whatever reasons – then top medical services will be right on hand for treating her as required.

In fact, everything turning up OK, because from seeing Dr Astrov my mother is getting so concerned with fixing up her hair and straightening out her dress and offering him some fresh *tvorog* with jam and tea, that she not even noticing extreme severeness of my condition, which – to be fair – is now looking not too bad, because the broken bits all hidden under a bandages.

And after giving me hot glass of sweet tea and putting me into bed, I can hear her fussing about Dr Astrov downstairs and sounding real pleased when he say he going to look in every week till I get better and telling her to keep me warm and sitting still until that bone get fully healed.

And that night as we are putting out the lights, I tell my mother that old Smirnov been giving me alcohol for drinking, and she just laugh her tinkling little laugh that sound like a small bell or slender bits of glass falling musically on the floor.

But when I ask her what is difference in between capitalism and Communism and tell her what old Smirnov say is the answer, she is not laughing at all but just tell me to keep quiet and never ever repeat that foolish old man's foolish joke.

Well, I am sleeping pretty bad of course, because pain is squeezing my leg bone and vodka still whirling round inside my head bone. But I am also thinking pleasantly of six weeks away from the school, which seem pretty much like the eternity, and of things I can be doing in those weeks, excluding football of course, but including lots of book reading, which is my next favourite thing, and getting to play piano better, because we got an old royale downstairs that my mother is very proud of and plays real good herself, and when I playing on it she always say I sure am gifted for the music and one day she be sure to tell me just where that old piano really came from, but not yet because I am still too young to know about important things like that.

So I am pondering about this and I fall asleep just before the sun starts to arise.

And when I awake it is already midday and my mother is there sitting on my bedside and wiping my forehead with the cool cloth.

I sure loved my mother in those days, and even now I got to tell you that I love her still, all these years later and even though she is gone from this world, God rests her soul. And reason for that deep loving is because now I understand we all pretty much just a part of our parents, and our mother and our father – if we know him – made us into what we are. So if we love ourself we also got to love them too, because they are continuing to live on in us.

This is something you may understand or you may not understand, but you will understand it for sure about me, Zhenya Gorevich, if you come with me to the end of my story.

And do not worry if you love your mother too, by the way, and therefore you thinking this story going to get pretty darn sad right from here onward, because it is not. I still got plenty good things to tell you, many of them including my mother and her continuing life in this world, before we reach the end of our road.

And although I cannot guarantee everything being happy and humoristic between now and then, I sure doing large efforts to keep it hunky and dory, except for those times when the *toska* sadness comes through and I just can't do nothing to stop that black crow squawking into my life.

Anyway, that morning my mother say to me, 'Zhenya, I am real sorry you broke your leg, but one good thing it mean you going to be here with me for six weeks and we can start doing those activities we always been meaning to but never get around for, such as training you much better on playing piano and also reading all so many books, and maybe even doing some paintings or writing poetry.'

And I say to her, 'Mama, you been reading inside my brain, because I been thinking exact the same thing'; and she give me her big hug and say, 'Zhenya, I love you, little son', and turn away just for a moment because I think she got a tear in her eyes, like mothers do.

And in those next six weeks, my mother been as good like her word.

For the start, she go to see Mr Abel, who live in one room of big old apartment house at other end of Vitebsk, far away from kolkhoz, and ask will he come see me and teach me piano.

Now, Mr Abel is Russian, but he also a German. Him great, great, great, great uncle (or something) come here for teaching Catherine the Great to play Bach on a harpsichord, which been all the raging in those days.

And for many decades all those Abel generations becoming pretty good Russians and living up in Sankt Peterburg and not doing harm to nobody. But when it come to Great Patriotic War they all suddenly very dangerous.

So Stalin he say to them, 'Get out of here, you former Germans! I am ordering competent organs to take you away somewhere you can't do no sabotage or undermining the will of Soviet people, like maybe out in deserts of central Asia!'

And, guess what? Seems Mr Abel got lost on the way, because for sure he been expelled from up there in Leningrad (one more name affair for you, but I suppose you all understanding this one) and came ending up for living not in central Asia, but right here, just up a road from us.

At first, he been pretty sad of leaving city of Great Peter, Window on the West and Venice of the North. But I guess he got to like old Vitebsk, because he never been complaining, never try go back, and got pretty fat down here after all those years. Everybody in Vitebsk know The German, as we call him. Everybody know he play the piano and also teach to young boys. But some people thinking there something little bit wrong with Mr Abel.

And guess what? I got to find out what that something is.

On first day, he come knocking on our door all polite and charming to my mother, and say, 'So this is young musician? This is new young Rubinstein and new young Paderewski?' and so forth with other such nonsense.

And my mother very smiling to him and giving him the cup of tea with sugar, and also agreeing to pay him one rouble for each lesson, which seem pretty darn expensive to me. Then my mother show him our piano royale and Mr Abel say, 'This is fine piece of music apparatus, Mrs Gorevich, having the foreign provenance. Will you tell me where you got it from?'

But my mother say him, 'No, Mr Abel, I will not tell you. This is apparatus belonging to our family. I play on this piano many years and son Zhenya pretty good musician too.'

But Mr Abel say, 'I will be the judging of that, Mrs Gorevich. Please you now do us an honour of leaving me alone with young Mr Zhenya and I start teaching him the playing.'

So my mother smile and say, 'Of course', and I get left alone with Mr Abel, who is turning out to have pretty strange methods of teaching, but I tell you more about that in a minute.

At first, he get out his battered old music case with leather all worn and handles all broken and start rummaging around inside.

And then he say, 'Ah!' and pull out some sheet music all tattered and torn, with corners all missing where piano players been turning over the pages for twenty years or maybe even twenty generations since Great Catherine, who knows?

And I am thinking, this going to be marvellous special music and I play it just like great pianist Sergei Rachmaninov (who we actually not supposed to admire in those days because he been class traitor to his people going off to live in decadent capitalist Hollywood and writing schmaltzy music for schmaltzy movies).

But, guess what? Mr Abel must be thinking I am just complete nincompoop starter for piano, because he give me couple of puny études by Czerny, including 'Mr Czerny's Burden' (ha, ha, ha), which I been learning like three year ago and can play easy as piece of pie or slice of cake.

So I just sniff up my nose and play those études like sight reading with no mistakes whatsoever and about *molto allegro* speed instead of *andante* like they actually being marked.

Mr Abel look at me and sort of stroke my hair with approving, and say: 'Well done, little man. You sure are a *molodets!*' (which is Russian meaning pretty good fellow).

And then he makes more rummaging and pulls out some more tattered and torn sheets. This time, he give me that old Mozart C Major sonata, but – real annoying – only slow movement, which anyone can be playing.

So again I play it from the sight reading, again with no mistakes, but this time just at real tempo which old Mozart been recommending.

And Mr Abel sure seem pleased with me, because he comes putting his hand on my neck and start stroking it down inside my collar, all warm and friendly. And when is he talking, he seems little bit out of breath like following the cross-country run.

Now, I think you all starting to guess what special teaching methods Mr Abel is employing, and also probably what that wrong thing about him which I mention you earlier.

And just in case you didn't guess yet, I better tell you what he ask me to play next: passage from very famous Liebestraum in A flat by Liszt, where everything getting very excited toward the end.

Actually, I suppose my playing of this one maybe not so great, because I only ever seen it one time before. But Mr Abel sure seem to like it: he come standing behind me with left hand on my neck and getting all agitating while I come to that big crescendo.

And just when I get there, he really start squeezing me and making loud noise like sort of sigh or maybe a groan. And then he say he just going to sit down for a minute and think about my beautiful playing.

When she hear things all go quiet, my mother come into the room and find Mr Abel sitting by the window and me still at piano staring at the keys, not daring to turn around. My mother been listening to me play through the walls and she say straight away to Mr Abel, 'So, my Zhenya pretty good pianist after all?' and Mr Abel just give the little grunt and appears all smiling, and my mother say, 'Excellent then. I expect you next week at same time', and Mr Abel make the little bow, straighten up his cloths, and walk little bit stiffly through the door.

So that is end of my first lesson.

Meanwhile, my mother announcing that she going to get the art master from Vitebsk Gymnasium to come and teach me painting. But, judging after such Mr Abel events, I tell her pretty quick this is not so great idea and maybe just one teacher is enough for now, so perhaps she can teach me the painting herself, seeing as she pretty good at it and always making pictures of beautiful flowers in vases standing on a window sill and so forth.

Well, my mother is pretty happy to hear this, because she understand that her son loves her and want be with her, so she says, 'Yes, Zhenya, this is real good idea. I will get the *General Third Course Book for Young Artists* and we study and paint together.'

Now, this Third Course book got to be pretty darn good because I see it got the introduction by Great Leader and Wise Teacher his self, explaining what painting under socialism got to be about, like for instance it say the only style we all got to paint in is great socialist realism, '. . . which faithfully reflects glorious Soviet reality of workers and peasants ennobled by labour and thankful for liberty which Soviet socialism under guidance of the Great Teacher has brought them'.

And that book all packed full of illustrations for showing exactly what Great Leader and Wise Teacher got in mind, such as lovely pictures of tractors and combine harvesters in very large wavy fields where wheats all looking full with health and not riddled with usual crop rot, and women driving machinery looking very beautiful even though they got extreme large bicep, and villages where sun always shining and so forth.

Then for town examples, it show the beautiful paintings of factories where everybody look happy and working real hard like a Stakhanov, with lots of red banners on the walls and sometimes maybe Stalin or Lenin visiting them, making big speeches with two arms waving upwards and maybe shaking off a worker's hand or so forth.

For being helpful to young artists, it also give the long list of stuffs we maybe want to be painting, such as Young Pioneers

Helping with Wheat Harvest, or Socialist Emulation at Work in Classroom (I not so sure what that one all about), cheerful May Day parades, Great Lenin as Revolutionary Child, or Stalin Meeting New Generation of Socialist Youth.

Now, this book make me think quite a few things. First, I am thinking those paintings all very lovely and beautiful with real bright colours and so forth, but actually not looking much like real life. For instance, in those pictures you don't see no horses with the bony ribs poking out through they backs and you don't see no tractors all broken up with wheels missing or trying to harvest wheats that all been drownded in rain and mud, or people frowning and scowling and fighting, or even no drunken peasants and workers lying on side of a road and freezing to death like old Semeon Semeonich last winter because he been drinking so much vodka he can't even feel it been getting cold to about forty degrees of frost.

No sir, none of that such stuff in *Third Course Book for Young Socialist Artists*!

But then, on the other hands, all those painters got to be pretty good artists, because they all won Stalin Prizes and Lenin Prizes and some of them even People's Laureate of Culture and other good things.

So I ask my mother why no one painting actual real stuff which we always seeing right here in reality life in Vitebsk? Or maybe we living in the only town in Soviet Union with this reality going on, and everywhere else actually resembling to beautiful paintings in that book?

Well, my mother look at me with her little sad smile, like she thinking this boy got a lot to learn, which I sure did, and actually I was about to start learning it. Because when we start making our paintings, even with all that good advice and guidance from *Third Course Book*, my stuff is turning out pretty darn bad. All the Socialist Youth fellows in my pictures are looking unhappy and glum with cloths all in rags, like we actually seeing here in town, and old folks all looking gloomy and worried about harvest or quotas or Five Year Plan or some such, not to mention houses with no glass in the windows and flocks of black crows in the fields and peasants drinking too much vodka, and no sign of Great Lenin or other Great and Wise Teacher whatsoever, because they never actually been in Vitebsk so far as I know.

And when she see my paintings, my mother just look the same way she did when I been telling her old Smirnov's joke about difference in between capitalism and Communism. And she try to explain me the way that Art happens, involving complicated stuff about real reality – which we really seeing – and other different realities, which only Art can show us.

Like, for instance, when she paint her picture of flowers in a vase on a window sill, she can see the real reality for sure, which maybe involving some few leaves having the bit of slug blight and some petals being little bit faded and limping, but then she is using her Art to ignore all this stuff and actually paint those flowers looking very perfect and very lovely.

So I ask her: is that what all these People Laureates and Stalin Prize artists been doing when they are painting socialist realism reality?

And she say maybe so.

But she also tell me not to get too angry or upset about this, because Art is pretty powerful thing and can do real important things for us, even if some people are using it for purposes we not always agreeing with.

And then she start telling about something called 'higher reality' which we all got to aspire upwards to, but can't always get into because maybe we been exiled from this higher reality, which is actually our birthright and our promised land, but now it got a bit lost or something.

It take me quite a while to figure out what she been talking about.

But when I look back now, I think my mother just decided I was growing up and needing to learn some pretty important things. And for some reason, she decided I need to learn them all at once.

Because next thing I hear, she been enrolling me at the Vitebsk Chess Association and some bunch of those students coming round for special evening at our house, where they going to practise speed chess with me and get my playing up to top quality standard real quick.

And so they did.

At first, whole thing looking like the disaster. Those students are red hot chess players and first game I play with them going just like this:

Student: e3

Me: g6

Student: Qf3

Me: b6

Student: Bc4

Me: a5

Student: Qxf7

Me: Oh shit, this looking like a checkmate!

(And it was).

I been feeling pretty stupid after that, but those students all real helpful, especially after my mother been giving them big glasses of *kvas* and plate of *pirogi*.

They all telling me how to advance some special prawn to stop getting beat up in five moves next time, and then they playing eight more games with me that night, and when they leaving they give me whole pile of match sheets full of special moves explaining this defence and that attack and tell me I better learn them because they coming back for more *kvas* and *pirogi* next week.

And all the time, my broken leg been getting better and stronger, but when Dr Astrov come every week and ask me how am I doing, I just make the little grimace and tell him things still pretty bad, doctor, and I cannot walk or stand on this bad leg and it still needing several extra weeks resting up in the bed.

OK, I tell you two reasons for this pretending.

One, I know my mother likes that young doctor always coming to visit our house and she spend lots of time baking cakes for him and also choosing her best dress and combing out her hair for about two hours before he arrive, so I figure I can make her happy by being sick for as longer time as possibly I can.

And two, I also myself enjoying being home and learning all this new stuff with my mother that I never learn before at school. Talking of which, schoolteacher been sending me home-work to do for whole time while I am off sick.

And, OK, I am doing this homework.

Mainly I like lessons about great Soviet inventions and all other good things USSR and socialist inventors been producing, which are making us envy of all mankind. It make me real proud to learn about achievements of our motherland and what great nation we Russians are and how lucky for belonging to such country where man breathe proud and free.

But later on I been hearing maybe some of these things actually been invented in capitalist West and not in USSR and maybe many affairs they been telling us in those days are turning out not too true or real; at least not if we talking about real reality, although all completely true if we talking about Soviet realism reality.

Anyway, much more interesting than school learnings is all the stuff my mother been teaching me during this sick and recovering period.

Mr Abel keep coming to our house and turning out not such the bad guy, although my mother is always sitting in that piano room while I am getting my lesson now, and he is actually pretty good musician and knows much about music both in Soviet places and in capitalist West.

So I am getting my love for piano from my mother, and also certainly getting love for reading and writing from her too. In all the years I know her, which are very many, that darn lady never stop reading even for one moment!

She is writing lots of stuff, too, although she never showing me this, because I guess that is her special world and she not sharing it with other people. Even now I remember her favourite writers.

Turgenev, Chekhov, and for sure more than anyone – Pushkin.

When I am little, she always been reading Turgenev novels, with titles like *On the Eve*, or *Rudin*, or *Fathers and Children*. And while she is reading them, she often been recounting me what they all about.

Rudin, for an example, is story of a hero who comes to visit family estate of a heroine somewhere deep in the great Russian countryside. This Rudin fellow looks pretty handsome and romantic and coming straight from the big city, so bringing all the latest political developments with him, such as secret doomed revolt against tsarist tyranny, need for self-sacrifice, steadfast courage, romantic idealism, unswerving manhood etc.

And guess what? that lovely heroine pretty quickly falling in love with Mr Rudin and soon they both swearing the undying constancy and faithfulness even until death and so forth.

So my mother looking pretty happy at this part of her reading.

But later I see from her face that things not turning out too well. I see her frowning and wiping off her eye a little, so now I am guessing that tragic developments been unfolding. I am assuming this little provincial lady – this *baryshnya* as we been calling her in old feudal days – been letting down our hero and trying to chicken out of all those pledges and death pacts.

But I am wrong.

Surprise, surprise! it is Mr Rudin turning out as a weakest link, and our *baryshnya* being ten times more stronger than he ever been! After making all those promises and boastings of eternal love, that so-called former hero now comes aweeping and apologizing and asking if maybe they can just agree to call things off after all, while that poor *baryshnya* got to hide her tears and tells him to forget her and go and do great deeds, if he can.

And then she just bites her lip and lives all the rest of her life never breathing any word of the pain and sorrow which are constant filling up her breast for ever more.

What for a tragic outcome!

And I can see my mother is pretty upset because she just sitting and cries by the window (which been repaired by now, following that previous crow episode), and that night we are not eating our dinner until very late, '. . . long after the virgin moon already risen in the fresh spring sky to cast its silvery light on sins and frailties of all mankind and illuminate the sadness which lurks in the heart of every woman everywhere.'

And when she is recounting me this *Rudin* story while we are drinking our tea, my mother got to keep stopping and biting her own lip till she can continue. And I see now that she feels pretty deeply for that *baryshnya* and she is pretty disgusted with the weakness of men, even including so-called heroes.

So that night when I am lying in my bed, I make a sacred, secret vow to myself that I never will be weak like a Rudin and never make a woman sad like he did. In fact, I am deciding right then and there that whenever I find the woman which I truly love, I am never going to fail her and never let her down and nothing ever can stop me being united with her, even if I got to carry out all the mighty labours of great *bohatyr* hero Ilya Muromets to be with her (actually, at following stage in my life I am nearly regretting that last bit, but you will be finding this out later on).

As for my mother, I think she done so much reading in her life that at the end she got to know all great monuments of Russian literature by heart, especially by immortal Aleksandr Sergeyevich, such as 'Bronze Horseman', *Tales of Belkin*, 'Snow-storm', and – most important – *Yevgeny Onegin*.

When later I come to read those books myself, I been starting to understand something about my mother, namely that the world she been living in is not always looking like the world everyone else been living in.

Their world got cockroaches, bed bugs and bureaucrats.

Hers got noble emotions, mystical destinies and love.

And that is what start me thinking maybe this all got something to do with such unusual place we been living in –

namely town of Vitebsk – which been making us behave in somewhat strange fashion, namely not quite in the ordinary real world.

Why this should be?

Maybe it got to do something with old Marc Chagall whom I been mentioning you. Please think: when you see Vitebsk in Chagall paintings, pretty strange things always happening, such as couple of peoples in wedding dress floating in the sky, or Jewish men in clouds playing violins and so forth.

So I been thinking, maybe that strange other life really is existing, all round us. Maybe not everyone is noticing it, being so busy living in the ordinary world. But maybe some people – old Chagall for sure and also, it seems, my mother – *can* see this other reality, and some of them actually preferring to live in it.

I guess that why Chagall been striding off to Paris.

And I suspect my mother been wanting to do the same . . .

I remember from my childhood my mother got some special books which she always keep locked away and never show to no one. When she is reading these in an evening, I can see they all written in strange letters and some of them got little pictures of a penguin on orange or green front covers. Sometimes my mother is telling me what happening in these books, and quite often it concern tragic events such as vital letters going stray, women separated from a man they love, or noble families forbidding heroine daughter to see hero son from another clan. Lots of them are happening in London, concerning very rich aristocrat peoples.

But my mother never tell me where these books come from, or how she got them in her possession. It seem that having them is dangerous, but also great pride to her. On one occasion she just make a casual mention to me that they are gift from a very special person, and that our piano with golden foreign lettering which Mr Abel so admiring is also the gift from that same source.

But coming back to my six weeks of broken leg and artistic enlightening, what I can conclude?

In firsts, it is very marvellous time in my childhood's life. That is for sure. In seconds, I am learning many new things, get good at piano, painting, poetry, chess; and also start to understand my mother – maybe also myself – better than before. But in thirds – and this is bad thing – these weeks are also beginning a very great curse on rest of my life.

You surprised of this?

Well, it is true. Because from that time onward, art and poetry and music all start to open dangerous doors for me.

You asking what doors?

Well, I tell you.

Doors to other reality, outside of real life Soviet realism reality. And this very endangerous indeed . . .

Now I tell you what happen to me in respect of football – which I am not playing of course on account of my leg broken up by Vova – and also in respect of forementioning Vova his self.

While I am lying in bed, many visits been taking place to me by schoolfriends who are telling about football games and what matches being played and who beating who and so forth.

Vova never coming to see me – not big surprise, because he must be pretty shameful of what he done to me – but for sure he been playing football, and guess what? this is moment when selections being held for Vitebsk region junior league team, when best players from all school teams, kolkhoz teams and so forth getting a chance to make audition for playing in the big league.

And yes, I think you understanding now: Vova makes the audition, Vova Pa speak to selector panel and Vova get selected.

So how his future is looking?

His future looking beautiful like roses.

Because playing in Vitebsk junior league mean first step up the staircase to senior youth team, then oblast division, then republic level competing, and then glorious future with Dinamo, Spartak, Torpedo, CSKA, Zenit and starhood for USSR national team . . .

OK, maybe this all somewhat hypotheticated at this stage. But still real annoying for me. Because I know I am better player than Vova, and coach always telling that *I* got the best prospect for audition to big league, and here I am lying in the bed while Vova – Vova Smirnov, aargh! – get the prospect instead of me.

I am getting madder and madder, and even my dreams now start changing. Previously I alway dream about me playing centre attack for Moscow Dinamo and then winning World Cup for Soviet Union; but now what comes dreaming to me instead?

Ha! Full colour nightmare of Vova! Vova dribbling the ball in vanguard of USSR national team and me trying to run after him, but with my leg all broke up so I am running on crutches and everyone in whole stadium is laughing at me, especially Vova and his Pa.

Aaarrrggghhh!

Back in reality life, my leg is finally getting mended and I know I soon got to go back to school.

My mother is pretty sad, part because she not going to have

me at home no more and also – pretty big part – because Dr Astrov no longer be coming to see us.

And while we talking about Astrov fellow, I tell you something I discover at that time: my mother write him a letter.

How come I know?

Because I find the sheet of paper with her writing on it in drawer of a cloths chest while I been rummaging around for some socks or pair of shorts.

OK, I tell myself rightaway: Zhenya, this is you mother secret stuff and you better not be reading it or even look at it!

But obviously I am very curious or maybe very bad person. Because I do read it.

And guess what? it look like the rough draft of a letter, but all written in poetry, with lot of crossings out and writing again, such as:

> *I write to you . . . no more to say*
> *It's in your power to make me pay.*
> *But pity me in my sad state*
> *And accept my offer of a date And do not leave me to my fate.*
> *When I used to see you once a week,*
> *Saw your face and heard you speak,*
> *I'd wait all day to hear your greeting*
> *Then think of you till our next meeting.*
> *My son was sick — you came to right him*
> *And in our house you brought the light in.*
> *You nursed my son and charmed his mother.*
> *I cannot think of any other*
> *Man on earth who'll make me smile:*
> *Searching's just not worth my while.*
> *Why did you come into my life,*
> *You fount of joy but source of strife?*

Before you came my soul was tranquil,
But now I toss and turn at night.
For your sweet presence I am thankful,
But cannot bear to leave your sight.
So tell me, will you hear my prayer,
Or must I drown in deep despair?

Signed,
Your sad but very loving Tatiana.

Well, this stuff all sound pretty strange to me. I always know my mother been writing poetry, but actually *sending* it to Dr Astrov! That seems real crazy idea.

And one other thing: this poetry remind me of something else – something I previous been reading somewhere but can't remember where. Maybe at school.

Anyway, if poetry of my mother seem crazy, guess what else I find in that drawer? On other piece of writing paper – answer from Dr Astrov! Also complete with many correctings and also writing in poetry! These grown-ups, they all completely mad!

My dear, your letter I have read;
I keep it with me ~~by my bed~~ in my head.
Your poems touch me to the heart,
Your words are pure, devoid of art.
They show how fine a love can be
But sadly, love is not for me.
My life is empty; none can save me.
Passion's embers all have died.
And now I mourn alone and gravely
For tears that once in streams I cried.
For me, the only solace now
Is graft and toil by sweat of brow.

So, maiden, do not cry for me,
Your love deserves better. Tenderly,
Your Astrov (Dr. med., U. Moscoviensis).

Well, what you can say? It seem my mother been living in her own world, world that been created by Pushkin and Byron and other such fellows. I am real surprised, though, by Dr Astrov also inhabiting in such a world, judging by how he been writing and playing his part in this literary romance.

But soon I get starting with some doubts. For several reasons, which I explain to you.

In the firsts, my mother never been referring to this exchange of billets-doux when she been talking to me, or ever saying anything bad about Dr Astrov for turning down her ardourous-ness.

And in the seconds, all the handwriting on Dr Astrov's letter looking pretty much the same like handwriting on Tatiana's letter.

So what we are supposing?

That maybe they both been writing by the same person? Hmm . . .

Finally I am concluding that same person got to be my mother.

Oh, boy!

Some strange reality she been living in.

And one thing worrying me more than any other thing: what happen if my mother's reality get mixed up with other people's idea of reality? What if them two realities starting clashing into each other? Seems a pretty worrisome idea.

Anyway, for me, infortunately, real Soviet reality soon start reasserting itself and I got to go back to school.

*

When I get there, I find some things been changing.

For a starting, old Olga Borisovna, teacher with dirty nails and fat legs, is gone and young new teacher with very slim and very nice ankles now taken her place. This new teacher called Zoya and she is wearing the tight skirt and high heels shoe, and also wearing perfumes that producing real pleasant effect on me, although not conducing very strongly toward much learning of school lessons.

And other thing happened while I been off sick: new teacher Zoya start to lead our class into glorious Young Pioneer Movement, which pretty much resemble your Boy Guide Scouts, only we all wearing white shirts and blouses with very bright red neckerchief round our necks. (Also, we all swearing eternal loyalty to Soviet Union and fierce determination to destroy your capitalist system, but do not worry about that – we not really meaning it.)

Well, this Young Pioneers affair look pretty good fun, what with parading and singing songs to glory of motherland and Communist party and Great Leader and Glorious Lenin and so forth, especially on the May Day or October Revolution Day, which takes place in November (something you all finding pretty confusing but nothing more natural for us Russians).

Then at weekends, unless we all having to help our parents with working a *subbotnik* and sweeping up some streets or shovelling away leaves or snow or so forth for benefit of great Soviet people, we often getting dressed up in Pioneer uniforms and going off to a colony. But not capitalist colony like you thinking, maybe enslaving some black peoples in Africa: no, this one is more camp-like colony where we all go to the countrysides and play educative games and find out more about our socialist inheritance from learned people including my very favourite learned person, namely new teacher Zoya.

I am pretty happy with being in Young Pioneers.

Only thing bothering me – Vova also in the YPs, always being number one in all departments, especially including with Zoya who always giving him *chetviorka* or *pyatiorka* (meaning number four or number five, being top marks what you can get) while rest of us still getting the old *opyat' dvoika* (you can guess this).

And all this time, Vova boasting about himself being the top footballer and getting try-outs with junior oblast league, but never mentioning that he is even tiny bit sorry for breaking up my leg, which is now keeping me completely out from the big time!

One day, Zoya tell us all to gather in the big circle and sit on the floor round her chair, which I am doing pretty fast in order for being in front row where you get good perspective of her ankles and high heels extruding from her skirt, and Vova is doing likewise and coming to sit next to me.

Zoya is bidding us all be quiet and she going to recount us very important story about very important person in our socialist history, who just happen to be a young child like all of us sitting there in that very room.

And name of this young child?

Pavlik Morozov, of course.

OK, I explain you. Everyone in Soviet Union know about Pavlik Morozov. He is real famous just like you got maybe Huckleberry Finns or Brady Bunches or some such. But Pavlik Morozov much more important because he is real-life hero, really existing, and everyone who want be the good socialist got to emulate his example.

In fact, Zoya tell us that Pavlik is official patron saint of Young Pioneers (except Soviet Union is firmly atheistic state, therefore not having any saints in a way you understand it, but you know what I am saying here).

For me, that day when Zoya introduce us to Pavlik is real important event in my socialistic development and soon going to have pretty direct consequences for me, as you now going to learn.

In order for you understand all my feelings of that day, I better recount you the history of Pavlik Morozov exactly how Zoya recount it to us.

You see, Pavlik is young boy and living many years ago in 1930s in place called Gerasimovka in Siberia. Now, Zoya tell us Gerasimovka is pretty much like Vitebsk, only little bit smaller, with agriculture and collective farms and so forth, and Pavlik go to school just like us, joining Young Pioneers just like us, and got some brothers just like some of us got, but not me.

Pavlik always been top boy at his studies and very good socialist and learning all his lessons and being good at sport and very handsome and all the girls falling in love with him and teachers love him too.

But trouble begin for Pavlik because his father, name of Trofim, is chairman of local council and start getting ideas too big for his shoes. For one thing, Trofim move out of Pavlik mother's house and get living together with a woman called his mistress, which is not making me like Trofim too much and I guess Pavlik feeling pretty much the same way.

Other problem with old Trofim, he start acting against interests of socialist propriety, helping out some kulaks in exchange for dirty moneys and briberies. In fact, Trofim refusing to respect interests of Soviet people and thinking only about his capitalistic self. He start getting in contact with kulaks who been exiled from Gerasimovka on account of they rapacious behavings and selfish hoardings of grain and other vital food-stuffs at time of people's national need.

And he say to them, Look, I want help you guys: if you just give me some of those large money riches you all accumulated, then I write you pretty good official pardon and give you permit for coming back to Gerasimovka where I protect you as chairman of council.

Wow! What a bad guy, abusing his socialist responsibilities!

Pavlik is pretty saddened by his Pa's behaviour and he know he got to do something. From the one side, this guy is his father of course; but from the other side, Pavlik know for sure that his duty got to be for stopping such abuses.

So he makes himself pretty darn brave and decide he better tell the competent organs what been going on. And Pavlik is sure making the right decision there, because competent organs tell him he is hero of socialist propriety and promise they going to arrest his Pa pretty damn quick before he do any more damage to the Soviet state.

And that is exactly what happen. Old Trofim Morozov gets brought to the speedy justice before a people's court and correctly sentenced to deportation to prison camp where he later meet a traitor's end (meaning he die there).

Pavlik and Young Pioneer comrades now working closely with some Communist Party plenipotentiaries who been sent to Gerasimovka for unmasking and rooting out any further nests of kulaks to hasten socialist road to happiness and radiant future.

So everything looking hunky and dory. But wait!

Those damn traitors are much more dangerous than anybody think.

Soon afterward, little Pavlik is gathering apples in the Bezhin

Meadow near his mother house when four felons, looking very like Trotskyist hyenas and enemies of the people, descend on his defenceless neck and kill that poor young hero. Pavlik is age just fourteen, so he sure meeting the very tragic untimely death.

Fortunately, socialist justice come to the forefront once again: those felons get swiftly arrested and, guess what? they all turn out as relatives of aforementioned convicted traitor Trofim Morozov.

As we are often saying in old USSR, the apple don't roll very far from the apple tree, meaning you can be darn sure that relatives of wreckers and Menshevik lickspittles always turn out wreckers and lickspittles themselves, and usually in need of decisive, firm eradication.

Anyway, indignation of the people is getting pretty enflamed by revanchist cruelty of these class enemies, so everyone is rejoicing when whole bunch of them, including Pavlik grandpa, godfather and uncles, are coming to appear at public show trial and getting sentenced to death and promptly given well-deserved 9 grammes by competent organs of OGPU-NKVD (maybe you not understanding: 9 grammes equal to weight of lead in a standard Soviet bullet, which all traitors getting to earn in back of they heads on account of they degenerate social-fascism).

Well, me and young comrades are pretty indignant by the way Pavlik been treated, and Zoya tell us that his example is pretty darn good one for all Young Pioneers to follow: getting to fall as victim sacrifice in struggle for triumph of socialism is pretty noble cause for us all, especially as Pavlik now so highly evaluated all over the USSR, what with him picture in every classroom, books and movies about him – even by famous director Eisenstein – and statues of him holding up flag of the Communist Party in our parks and squares.

So after Zoya's lesson, we are all walking home and talking about Pavlik Morozov and all agreeing he sure was a top hero. Some of us start saying we want be brave like Pavlik; and when we arrive at that big apple orchard near the river, Vova start asking me to re-tell our famous story about three boys discussing the building of socialism, which I been declaiming in school when Olga Borisovna was still our teacher.

So, just to show I got the good memory and maybe also show Vova I am still top dog at the declaiming, I say OK and start declaiming very heroic, such as: 'A schoolteacher tells his pupils about the new Five Year Plan and all the wonderful things it going to produce, and three boys discussing this. First one say, "I would like to go to sleep and wake up in five years so I can see everything all built at once." Second one say, "No, I would like to see great Soviet nation building all these marvels." But third one say, "I would like do all that with my own hands."'

And so soon as I finish this tale, all those around me start clapping and cheering, so you see the hearts of everyone now pretty fired up with socialist enthusiasm.

And this socialist ardour is still burning at our Young Pioneer group next meeting, because so soon as teacher Zoya begin the lesson, Vova put up his hand and ask permission of speaking.

Since Zoya is always indulging Vova, she say, 'Yes of course', and Vova come to stand at front of the class.

And guess what? Vova say he been thinking about the noble example set by Pavlik Morozov and decided he also got to do his duty just like Pavlik, so he is coming here now . . . to denounce old Finkelstein!

Well, a little murmur goes round the class and Vova says, 'I tell you something about old Jew Finkelstein: he been hoarding up the grain just like an unprincipled kulak!'

Now everyone in class start tittering a little bit, because everyone know this is actually completely *pravda* (or completely *kosher*, ha, ha, ha!), but no one is ever taking much notice of it or even caring about it, because Finkelstein never really been doing any harm.

But Vova hears this tittering and start getting mad.

'You think I am joking?' he ask, mostly rhetorical and little bit threatening. 'Well, I tell you something else about Finkelstein. He been putting sugar in the tractor fuel and sabotaging all the tractors at the MTS' (I explain for you: MTS mean the Motor Tractor Station, where all the machinery and so forth that we use in our joyful communal labour is being kept).

'And why he is doing this?' Vova now asks, still in the rhetorical way. 'He is doing this to undermine our socialist labour and prevent our kolkhoz from over-fulfilling it Five Year Plan. He is doing this thing to get my father in a trouble with the Raikom and allow class enemies to reassert themselves.'

Well, all Young Pioneers are pretty silent now, because they realize things starting to get serious.

So Vova decide time is come for clinching the stroke of evidence: 'And I tell you something else that no one can dispute: Finkelstein been using his Jewish sorcery, Kabala, for make our kolkhoz horses go lame. This is proved fact, comrades, because when that bay mare been going lame last month, my father seen Jewish symbols stamped on her backside! So this is reason – only reason – why our kolkhoz been failing to fulfil it production quotas. As usual, those cosmopolitans and their black magic is to blame, not anybody else!'

Now, Vova been judging things pretty well because any mention of Jewish treachery in those days is almost certain to get people shouting and demanding just retribution.

So, right on cue, everyone start exploding in the rightful indignation against old Finkelstein, and Zoya come running up to congratulate Vova on such noble act of unmasking a traitor. She says she going to pass on Vova information to the competent organs and leave them to take necessary actions.

So it seem pretty clear old Finkelstein is heading for a high jump.

And that exactly how things been turning out.

Few days later, competent organs send round a people's militia for arrest Mr F and take him away where he can't do no further harm. And when those people's militia start digging at his house, they find lots of interesting evidence, including buried grain – which we all know about – as well as foreign money, bomb equipment and documents proving he is secret agent of some imperialist intelligence agencies, which we sure *didn't* know about.

Anyway, old Finkelstein disappear out of Vitebsk.

But somehow he is not disappearing out of my thoughts. Pretty soon I get to thinking about what been happening to that old man and feeling darn sorry for him. OK, so maybe he hoard a bit of grain; and sure he come a-lusting after my mother on Sundays and other public holidays; but what harm he really doing to anybody?

Not so much, in so far as I can see.

All those angulations about him putting sugar in a tractor fuel and hex on our horses seem highness of nonsensical to me, and pretty clear that Vova only been saying them to help out his Pa who got in the spot of trouble through lack of over-fulfilling the kolkhoz Five Year Plan.

And more I am pondering about Finkelstein, more I am getting mad with Vova and his Pa.

I tell you what happen next.

About two week after Finkelstein disappear, Zoya ask all our class to gather in a Young Pioneer study hour for special session to evaluate events of his unmasking. Now, what Zoya really mean is she want us all to highly evaluate Vova and very lowly evaluate old Finkelstein.

So I am sitting there and listen to all those classmates heaping great praises on Vova Smirnov and socialist abuse on Samuil Finkelstein. And I am feeling anger bubbling up in me like it does sometimes, I confess it, with – I also confess it – sometimes very negative and dangerous consequences.

In this case, I am unsure what is major causing of my anger – is it hearing all that *govno* (I too ashamed to tell what that Russian word means) heaped on poor Mr Finkelstein, or is it hearing all that high evaluations of Vova Smirnov, when everybody know he is actually just the little creep?

Anyway, that is remaining theoretical question.

But when Zoya turn to me and ask for my evaluations, I am standing up in front of our whole class and start making some remarks.

And, first big mistake, I am not very clear thinking where these remarks going to lead to. I begin by saying maybe old Finkelstein is not really such the bad guy, and how he help my mother with her garden and odd jobbings and so forth.

I can see Zoya looking little surprised by this.

And this lead to my second mistake, namely realizing that I am not really liking this Zoya, even despite of slim ankles and high heels and skirts, and I am starting to feel increasing argumentable at the sight of her sitting there and looking disapproval at me. So I say maybe someone made the big misjudgements about old Finkelstein; maybe he is not any kulak or saboteur, and maybe he now sitting in some gulag eating rotten cabbage and so forth when in fact he not really deserve this whatsoever.

And when he hear this, Vova gets standing up and say: 'So you being the class traitor too, Zhenya? You supporting that old kulak? Well, maybe you also enemy of the people. One fisherman always recognize other fisherman, as wise people say!'

Well, now come my really big mistake, because this straw been breaking my back and I start heaping some serious *govno* on Vova and saying how he broke up my leg on purpose because he so mad about me getting declaiming duties at the school festival and how he only been unmasking old Finkelstein to help out his Pa following him not overfulfilling kolkhoz quotas and how it is pretty darn stupid to blame Jews for everything and anyway they are sure not having any special black magic hexes at all and that just plain superstitiousness.

Uh-oh!

Things starting to get to right out of the hands now, because whole class is making like the breathing-in sound *phhwoot!*, and Zoya starting to say something, but I am not letting her because I got lots more to say such as telling everybody how Vova's Pa been pretty unrespectful of glorious Soviet state and telling jokes like 'What is difference in between capitalism and Communism?' with answer being that under capitalism . . .

But I never get to tell them the punching line because Vova is running up and give *me* real good punching line right smack on the nose, which immediate start with the fountain of blood big as Bakhchisarai, and Zoya also coming up and telling me I better be quiet and get out of here pretty darn fast.

And now I know for sure that great *byeda* is swiftly on its way to me and my mother (I explain you about *byeda*, which is something as bad as anyone possibly imagine, bringing trouble, unfortune and despair to all unlucky receivers, and nothing whatsoever you can do to get out of it way).

And when I get home to our house on edge of the forest, I am not telling my mother anything about what been happening and just say my nose got busted in some little accident.

But that night I start dreaming my old crow dreams again, with nightmare of birds scratching on my window and trying to get in. And in the morning just as sun arising, I am sure I hear a sound of that real darn crow banging himself on our window downstairs . . . and it is scary sound, but somehow familiar one too.

Well, no point in trying to hide things from my mother for long, because pretty soon those dramatic events of Young Pioneer meeting are talking of the whole town. So I tell my mother everything and she just give me the little smile with lips sort of pressed together, which probably mean 'You been acting honest, Zhenya, but you been acting according to rules of a different reality, not Soviet reality; and that is pretty bad mistake . . .'

She is right, of course.

Don't forget that in those days unmasking is going on everywhere. Everybody unmasking everybody else. Newspapers all full of small ads saying 'I, Ivan Ivanovich, do announce my wife is enemy of the people. Therefore I am breaking off with her' or 'My father is traitor to his country, therefore I not having any more to do with him' and so on. And this unmasking get so common that these small ads no longer seem shocking and becoming just as ordinary like 'Carpet for sale' or 'Tuition available in maths and Hegelian dialectics'.

That is just how Soviet reality is in those days.

I guess my big error is not having proper understanding of this Soviet reality and not knowing there is no sense unmasking those damn Smirnovs, because they are the ones controlling it. They are the people in charge of the reality rules, and nothing bad ever going to happen to them, however true the stuff I been saying about them.

And even worse!

Old man Smirnov now feeling pretty damn sore. I can see he is looking pretty hard in my direction. And outcome of this looking is following just as inevitable as historical determinism.

Next week, some special delegation from the kolkhoz is coming round to our front door with information that the farm committee been re-evaluating all manpower requirements for agriculture in Vitebsk region and this been leading to big changes, including one change being that my mother no longer required for work on Mr Smirnov's collective farm.

And, consequent on such new reality, there going to be implications for kolkhoz accommodation structures, one being that since housing is now available only for active farm workers, we got to move out of our existing accommodation by end of the week! Well, my mother just start crying and kolkhoz delegation looking a little bit embarrassed, but soon start shrugging off their shoulders and say they got to go now.

And before they go, they hand my mother official letter with all regulations properly quoted and formal note of new abode we shortly got to be occupying, which is turning out as one room of ten square metres in filthy *kommunalka* right on other side of town. OK, I explain what is *kommunalka*, because actually it is great Soviet invention and not existing in many other places. *Kommunalka* idea been starting after glorious October revolution when Bolshevik party is bringing just retribution to former aristocrats and despotic repressers of the people, who been living until then in luxury and palaces (or at least in very nice apartment). And Great Lenin been wanting everybody, including even humblest peasant and worker, to have these same luxuries including a palace of their own.

Infortunately, even great Great Lenin cannot make palaces grow from the ground, so instead he make several decrees such as: all former aristocrats, merchants and generally anyone who owns a nice apartment got to be promptly thrown out and hand over all property to the people. And this is very wise and just decree, but infortunately we got many peasants and workers and not many former aristocrats, with result that handed over property is not actually capable of fitting everyone in.

So Great Lenin decide that, seeing how all property is theft, buildings, apartments and other accommodations henceforward got to be divided up according to Soviet norms, meaning everyone gets fitted in, but no one gets much room for swinging any cats. And in particular, those apartments where just one family of parasites and exploiters been living now got to become home of eight worthy and deserving families of peasants and workers and be called *kommunalka*.

This is great socialist idea and Soviet people all very grateful to immortal Lenin. But problems also starting pretty soon, such as everybody sharing the same kitchen and lavatory and sleeping in corridors and this often leading to conflicts over who stole Miss Petrovna's pickled cucumber or Mr Stansky's tobacco or Mrs Knipper's husband, and why can't that stinking Khlebnikov ever come home sober and not slam the front door and then lie down snoring in the hall like some armoured train speeding to confront the white armies and keeping the whole house awake until 6 a.m. when we all got to get up anyway and go to work, so it is hardly surprising Mr Voloshin took the wood axe and split that scoundrel's skull open last December.

Anyway, I think you getting a picture and maybe understand why my mother and me are feeling pretty unhappy in our new abode. Now we are mingling with many stark unbending elements of Soviet reality and everybody knowing we been expelled from former rural paradise of the kolkhoz, so some odour of culpability must be attaching to us.

And I tell you, at that time I am feeling pretty sad and low down. My mother is crying the whole time because our room so small that our piano and wooden chest take up the whole floor space and our *kommunalka* neighbours always wanting to use our books for heating materials in the fire stove, and I am feeling real guilty because it is my Pavlik Morozov initiative over old Smirnov that been the major causing of all this.

And strange to say, I start having dreams. Not bad dreams at first – not like some crazy old crow or anything – but dreams about various things and places, and all involving one particular person. Like, for example, I am riding my bicycle along a deserted track through fields and see an unknown man standing at a crossroads and waving me to stop. And when I reach him, I think I recognize him but somehow not remembering exactly who is he.

So I stop and ask him. He tries to speak and open and closes his mouth, but seems unable of making a sound, so instead he just make a little sad smile and point at my bicycle. I know he is saying he want to come with me and his eyes look very pleading. I am not very sure about this, but he is insisting and seems very anxious to go wherever I am going, and also seem pretty friendly despite that scary factor of not being able to speak.

So I say OK for him to climb on board and start off going toward Vitebsk. But he is clearly not wanting to go this way, because he keep pulling and tapping on my shoulder and trying to speak, but only making a sad little crying sound. This man want me to take the other road of the crossroads, but I never been that way before and my mother previously been saying this is very dangerous road with brigands. He keep insisting and pointing, though, and seems quite affectionate – although also quite desperate – so I agree for taking his requested path and start going down a track which turns out very rough and full of pots hole, and my bike is shaking and rattling and that man is holding me very tight.

And then . . . that is all.

I wake up.

That evening, I tell my mother about my dream and describe what the man is looking like.

She gaze at me rather strange for a few minutes, but not saying anything.

And several days later, the same man is in my dreams again. This time, I am climbing up some old stone stairs in some old building like the castle and arrive in front of a big wooden door with black iron hinges and handle. I know I must go in this room, so I turn the handle and start pushing. But the door is locked.

I bend down and look through a big old keyhole and inside that room I see the same man again. He is standing with his back to me dressed in the old-fashioned white night dress. He is very tall, and now I see he got no hair on the top of his head, but round the sides and back it is whispery and white. At first I think the man cannot see me, but actually he is holding a small hand mirror with very beautiful silver frame, and by looking into it he can see behind himself and I am pretty sure he can see me peering through the keyhole. This time, he is not waving or trying to speak, but his eyes in the mirror keep staring straight in my eyes and they look full of tears and *toska* (which you remember from earlier, meaning real desperate sadness or yearning). When he sees me watching him, the man give a little smile and his lips move for saying my name, silent but very clear, *Zhenya, Zhenya* . . .

Then someone behind me make a polite coughing sound and I stand up. It is a young woman dressed in black and white maid's uniform from old capitalist times, and I say to her, Who that man is in there?

She says, He been waiting for you for a very long time, sir.

And I say, Can I go in to see him?

But she says, No sir; I am very sorry but that is not possible.

Then I wake up.

I feel pretty puzzled by all this and wanting to know who is this man and why is he intruding in my dreams.

So again I talk to my mother and describe what the man look like.

And my mother sit there all quiet again, but I see she been doing a lot of thinking and turning things over in her mind. She ask me to describe the mirror which the man been holding.

So I tell her about the silver frame and long handle and how the glass looks little bit blurry and so forth.

And my mother seem quite scared. She get up and goes to our Great Chest, which is place where Russian folk keep their real important stuff (like for example rich peasants keep money, or young maiden keep love letters and so forth, so it always locked out and no one ever get to see inside it), and she open up that chest and take out some little package all wrapped in old brown paper and covered by strings and tapes.

And so soon as my mother start unwrapping that package, I know what will be inside it. It is that very same mirror which I seen in my dream, with very same handle and very same silver frame and even same blurriness in certain part of it glass.

Now *I* am feeling scared, because for sure I never seen this mirror before in real-life reality. But just last night I been dreaming about some man looking at me through it and whispering my name.

I ask my mother, 'What is going on?'

And she look at me and smile. But her eyes look sad.

I think she know exactly who is this man and for sure she know where that silver mirror come from. But she not replying much except to say, 'Maybe you seen this mirror in our house one time long ago, little son, and now you just been remembering it in your dreams.'

I tell her this not possible because she never ever open up that Great Chest and never ever take things out except one or two special, secret books writing in the foreign language.

And I can see she knows this is true, but she is not willing to tell me any more.

So our conversation is over and I go to bed feeling worried.

And guess what?

That night, I am dreaming once again about that same mysterious man. Only this time, something real strange. This time, I am dreaming myself coming home from school, only not going to the *kommunalka* where we now really living, but instead going to the kolkhoz where we been living before. House is looking just as same as previously, same furniture, same pictures, even same piano and same old books, but everything now is complete still and silent, as if human life been suspended here. I am looking round our old living room, but not feeling like I belong here any more, as if time moved forward and things changed, but my mother and me got left behind and we are not realizing this.

So I try coughing to see if anyone is there.

But no sound is coming from my throat and even when I try calling out 'Mama! Mama!', everything stay real quiet as if that house has been frozen to silence and refusing to accept I am standing there or even acknowledge I exist at all.

And that is when the real sudden terrible explosion happens.

So much noise it makes me shudder. So much noise as if all those words which people been saying in that house for hundreds of years are being said all at once and making frightening hellish din. And just as that loudness comes bursting in, the black crow comes smashing through the glass window, only this time the same size as a human person and all covered in blood and broken glass, but still alive and squawking and flying at me and pecking me.

I am so terrified of this crow with the burning red eyes and the noise and the breaking glass that I start running upstair to my old bedroom to get in my bed.

But I see somebody is already lying in my bed with a white sheet pulled over his face. And I know what awaits me under that sheet, but still my dream is making me go and lift it up.

And there is that same man again. Only this time he is completely white except for some bruises or cuts on the front and side of his bald head and maybe some little green colour appearing in his neck.

I take his hand, but it is cold. His skin is thin like paper that cracked and wrinkled and has little blue bruises under it.

The man seem much smaller than when I saw him last. As if he has shrivelled to just a bone skelet.

But I know he is alive and want to talk to me. Despite of everything, he still got a smile on his face and his blue eyes open and look at me.

For very first time I can hear the words he is speaking. 'I'm glad it is you who came, Zhenya. I've been waiting.'

He tries to stand up and get out of bed. But a nurse rushes in and say, 'No, you must stay there. You know the rules.'

So he lie down again and for some reason I say to him, 'Are you all right? Are they looking after you?'

And he say, 'Oh, yes. The food is very good in here' – which make me laugh a little bit, and he laughs quietly too – 'only, you know, Zhenya, I want to go home and they won't let me go.'

And in my dream, I understand I must help him get out of there and go home, so very carefully I lift him from his bed – he is very light – and put him in some wheelchair that has deep padded cushions so not to damage his thin body and fragile skin and also straps to put round his feet so they don't slip off and get tangled up, and I start to wheel him out of that room into a long corridor.

But halfway down this corridor, another nurse rushes out and say: 'No, no, you can't do that. He got to stay.'

So I start running with the wheelchair and the man is saying 'Be careful' and making little sounds of fear.

And now we are going downstairs and the wheelchair bumping on stone steps of the castle, but they change back into stairs of our old house and we are back in our old living room and I feel safe again, but then that crow – who has grown to height of over three metres – suddenly appears and I leap back in terror and forget to keep holding the wheelchair, which goes racing off down a steep slope, and I am yelling, 'Help me, please, help me!' . . . And then my mother is shaking my arm and saying, 'It's all right, Zhenya, it's just a nightmare. Don't worry, little son . . .'

And I wake up.

And while my mother is cradling me in her arms, I say to her that now she must tell me what all these dreams are portending, and she says OK, soon I am telling you, but first I got to go see somebody in order for seeking advice.

Next day she goes off and not returning until darkness. I am already in bed, but when I hear her coming in, I feel pleased of knowing she is back home and with me.

Next morning, my mother say, 'Zhenya, I need to ask you one question. I need to know if you are feared of that man you see in all these dreams, or rather you feel he is wishing you well?'

So I think about this and decide I am not feared of him, but sort of recognizing him and knowing he is not wishing any harm to me.

So my mother say, 'Good. Now I go straight back and tell this to Mavra, and then I think she probably want to see you also.'

Now, I hope you excuse me just for one moment, because first we better take the little diversion in order I tell you about Mavra.

Probably you unawares that Mavra is Vitebsk wisewoman. Wisewoman is special Russian thing and occupying very important place. First, they knowing many facts, especially facts ordinary folk unable to comprehend, such as who young girl later be marrying, or when death will come for us, or which unholy spirits abounding in our houses. Wisewoman certainly got the gift for seeing in the future, usually by throwing candle-waxes in jug of water and other such methods, then telling us what our dreams all meaning, what life and fate bringing for each of us, or helping destroy our enemies and so forth.

They are mysterious people. Maybe you be calling them witches or such like, but this is not really correct describing. In Russia, wisewomen enjoy respect as well as fear, and all people are needing their help from times to times.

And that is why my mother go right now to see Mavra.

This is end of diversion.

When she come back, my mother say: 'Zhenya, I have spoke to Mavra and give her roasted chicken and such necessary things. Now she requesting to see you for hearing what you been dreaming and determine what this all meaning.'

Next morning, my mother give me butter-bread in large linen bag with pumpkin seeds and slicing of watermelon and tell me go down to main highway, where kolkhoz delivering truck will take me into Vitebsk and place me on bus to Chimki village outside town; then I must follow certain paths to heart of the forest and make turns at special places where indications attached to birch and lime tree, until reaching Mavra hut.

I am pretty worried from all this, so I tell my mother maybe she better come with me.

But she say, 'No, little son. Mavra want to see you by your own; you got to be brave. You go find out about those dreams and come back here to me, and then I tell you certain very important factors regarding your life and my life.'

So I travel in that kolkhoz truck and chauffeur ask who I intending visit; and when I tell him, he is frowning and say, 'No way I ever be visiting that old witch Mavra. You must be pretty brave young *molodets* if you going there', which is making me feel even less brave and even more worried than I been before.

But finally I arrive at Mavra hut and knock on her door.

That wisewoman is sure appearing pretty old and scary, with long white hair and black eyeballs staring right in my eyes.

But she smile and says, 'Come in, sweet one. Come in and sit by my warm fire, while I get you hot drink.'

And despite of me saying no thank you to any drink, she bring it out and insist me to drink it, and it turn out to have the very strange taste, not like tea and not like *kvas*, but very sweet and also very salty.

I can see Mavra watching me real close while I drinking from her cup.

And so soon I finish, I start feeling tired and Mavra point to where some fresh hay is lying, and looking real comfortable and inviting.

Then she smile and go out the door and locks it behind her, and I am left alone in that room and my eyes close into very deep sleep.

But strange to relate, no sooner my eyes have closed and Mavra gone out the room than I see her right next to me again, leaning over me with bony hands stretched out. I try to tell her to leave me alone, but no sound is coming from my voice. And now her hands are holding my shoulders and her grip not like an old woman's but very strong and frightening. I am scared and try to run away, but Mavra looks at me with eyes that have the strange flashing sparkle and I cannot move. And all the time, I am thinking I got the fore-knowledge of these events, like somewhere I been reading this story concerning witches and their tricks, for now I am sure Mavra must be one. And just as I reach this conclusion, I feel Mavra take my hand

and pull it down to her long black skirt and I feel her putting my palm on something inside it. And suddenly I am holding the thick, meaty thing and I know this is Mavra witch's tail! I try to pull my away hand, but my arms and legs are turned to stones. In one single movement, much too nimble for an old woman, Mavra swivels up her hips and jumps on my back. Her nails are cutting my shoulder and she is beating me with her broom.

Then, *ookhty, bookhty!* we both fly out the window and up in the sky, no longer clear and blue like before, but night-time sky with a green moon throwing sickly light on the white clouds. We are rising higher. The hut is small behind us and disappearing in the forest. In lakes far below I see reflections of myself like a ghostly horse being ridden by the witch.

We are travelling along a border between two worlds: above us, the dark sky and green moon, but below us the reality world in bright sunlight and peasants all sleeping where they stand, not moving or talking but frozen with mouths and eyes wide open.

And how I am feeling as we go rushing through the sky above Soviet Union?

Well, to tell a truth, not too badly now I got used to feeling the air all round me and overcoming the fear and motion sickliness.

Mavra has stopped beating me and her body feeling warm and soft. Instead of flying, we seem like swimming through warm, green water, making steady rhythmic movements together as we surge forward. My soul is seized by sweet sensations of falling.

Yet I never fall.

My heart is tired but elated. My head starting to droop and

eyes closing, but Mavra senses this and beats me again to stop me sleeping.

I turn to face her, but in place of an old witch is a beautiful maiden smiling and kissing me. I am filled with excitement and throw my arms around her. But this unbalances us as we fly and we are falling down through rushing air to the earth. My beautiful maiden shrieks and cling to me, but we hit the ground with a terrible sound of breaking bones and air squeezed out of our lungs. My vision goes dark and when it returns, my head is full of pain. I have fallen to earth on top of my beautiful bride. She has saved me, but I have crushed her to death.

People are gathering, all dressed in black. Family of the dead maiden looking at me with suspicion in their eyes. Her father approaches and says I must to mourn his daughter and keep her vigil.

Things happening so fast I feel out of control. I am scared of this vigil.

But somewhere in that crowd I glimpse Mavra looking at me and seem to be saying, 'Yes, you must do it', and I hear myself say, 'Of course I keep her vigil. Where it will be?' And her father says, 'In church with her coffin.'

I am in a small country church with the coffin and the corpse.

The story is happening very fast now. Time hurrying forward. But always I sense this all happened before and I read about it in a book or remember it from somewhere. The church is dark and cold. I want to leave, but the doors are locked. I light some candles. Behind me, noise is coming from the coffin.

The lid has opened and she is lying there in her wedding dress. I know I must not look at her face. But I cannot resist. She is so beautiful. I glance and turn away.

The feeling comes again and I have to look at her. Her face is in shadow. A tear seeping from her eyelid. Her beauty is pulling me in. I wipe her tear with my thumb, but it is blood. As I pull my hand away it is red and, oh horror, her eyes flutter and open. She is staring at me.

And on her lips . . . a smile. Not happy . . . a kind of sad, sad smile.

I turn and run to the altar. Trying to remember the right prayers for warding off the evil ones, but I hear myself declaiming that fable of the farmer and the wolf and the story of three boys building socialism. This will not keep me safe! I am seized with panic.

When I turn round, the corpse is lifting its head. Trying to get out the coffin.

I am becoming part of an old story. I must draw the circle round me and round the altar. Keep away the visitors from the other world. But the corpse has escaped from the coffin and walking toward me. In her outstretched hand is that same mirror from my dream. Her eyes are shut but staring in the mirror. It is helping her see something I cannot see. Something in the other world. It is me she is seeking.

The real world and the other world coming together now.

Danger.

Her arms and neck no longer white like before. Her body covered in soil; pulled from the grave. Her lips moving, pronouncing her own incantation. Calling forth terrible visitors.

They are outside, scratching the windows, flapping their wings, trying to burst in. The empty coffin flying through the air.

Glass shattering.

Icons falling off the walls.

Loud wing beats.

An explosion of voices.

The visitors have broken in.

Sleek, black, shiny creatures flying through the church. Filling it with cackling.

I know where this story is leading. Tomorrow peasants will find my body, hair turned white, horror on my face.

But now something unexpected. The story lurches to a different ending.

The man from my previous dreams appears. He smiles and smoothes my hair. Walks up to the corpse without fear. Puts his arm around her shoulders. Leads her gently to her coffin. She also seems to smile, and climbs inside. The man closes the lid. Turns the bolts to keep it down. Then he waves me to the sacristy.

I follow him.

The noise dies away. I am back in Mavra's hut.

I lie down again on my bed of hay. A hand is shaking my shoulder. I think it is the man from the dream. But it is Mavra. Calling me to wake up.

Is this more dreaming or reality?

Mavra says to me, 'Quick. You must tell everything you seen in your sleep, which has lasted ten hours. And you must tell it at once, before your vision fades.'

So I tell her everything and she is sitting there and nodding.

And when I finish she says, 'Well done, my little one. Now drink this tea and soon I come back to reveal you important things.'

After all that been happening, you probably guess I am pretty doubtful of drinking anything from hands of Mavra! So this time, when I see her not watching, I pour it out the window.

After half an hour, when I am feeling restored, Mavra say to me: 'All right, my dear. Now you must listen while I give you some knowledge you need for living in the reality world. First thing, you must very beware those *kosomoltsy*' (well, Mavra is wisewoman, but she not too smart with socialist terminology, because she is saying *kosomoltsy*, which mean someone who pray to sickles – and maybe she think also to hammers! – instead of saying *komsomoltsy*, which of course mean Communist Youth. But I understanding what she saying). 'Those people misleading you, Zhenya. They all very proud of their Communist reality and socialism realism and such. They telling everyone this is only reality which exist. But that is untrue. All those Communists, they think reality is simple and they can control it with their quotas and plans and such. They think they got everything figured out, but they are wrong. Wise people know our world is real deep, little son, and got many different layers underneath it.'

I kind of understand what Mavra is saying, but the idea of all those different layers under our world got me pretty worried, so I ask what kind of different realities she is referring to.

And Mavra says, 'Take your mother, for an example. She know about different realities. She know about that ordinary, usual reality which is full of sour milk, dirty dishes, rotten meat and angry peoples in crowded *kommunalkas*. But she also know about other reality such as poetry and books world, and sometimes she prefer living in that reality. Now, is her life better because she know this? And because she does not refuse to believe in it? Of course it is better.'

I am immediate recalling that Pushkin-style poetry my mother been writing and all that romance of her and the doctor which probably never been happening except in her head. So I say to Mavra maybe she is right, but what about the consequences this can be having for people involved in it? And most of all, I tell her I want to know what reality all my nightmares been coming from, since they are not popping up only out of paintings and books (although maybe some of them are).

'Yes,' say Mavra. 'I think you better consider it this way: some realities we can accept or not accept according to our own choice. As for example, your mother can refuse her special world and just try to be happy with sour milk and Five Year Plan stuff. But she don't do that. She choose to go barging into Pushkin world and pretty much living there. Well, in same way, people from other realities sometimes come barging into our world. And these people maybe friendly or maybe not so friendly to us. Some of them come for evil purposes. Some of them are lonely and pining in their world and want to take you back with them. Like that beautiful maiden you been telling me about. That maiden is your death, Zhenya. She want you to go with her into world of the dead.'

'But, Mavra', I say, 'she is so beautiful.'

And she say: 'Death can be beautiful, little son. You are not knowing this yet, although one day you will. But good things also come to us from the other side, and I think that man you see so often in your dreams maybe one of them: he love you and he want to help you. He want you to know this, Zhenya, and that silver mirror you see him holding is his only way of coming to you right now. That is meaning of your dreams.'

Well, this is all pretty strange for me. And pretty scary.

Mavra will not tell who is that man, even though I am sure she knows. She just keep saying, 'You mother know who he is. Maybe she tell you. Remember to ask her about the mirror. I think it time you go back now.'

Well, of course I got no choice in this affair, since old Mavra is the wisewoman and I just the little boy who got to do what he is telled. So I say thank you – even though I am not sure what for – and off I go back through the forest, to village of Chimki where I am waiting about three hours for kolkhoz truck to come and pick up milk, and also pick up me.

When I get home, my mother runs out to meet me like I been away two years, not two days.

First she is showering me with kisses and also with *tvorog* and plum jam. Then she give me bottle of Narzan to drink for restoring my strength and start telling how she been worrying about me and asking all about travelling experiences and so forth. And finally she ask me what Mavra wisdom been revealing me.

So I tell her whole story, exactly like Mavra been saying it, and I see my mother eyes start to fill up and she give the little *vskhlip* (meaning of which I previously explained you, so I not doing it again, sorry).

I can see this whole dreaming thing is highly affecting my mother, but I am still no further informed of what is going on, so I decide to follow old Mavra suggestings and I ask my mother: 'Mama, you got to tell me about that mirror and what it is portending. It is true I never seen that mirror before it been appearing in my dreams?' And my mother say, 'Yes, Zhenya, it is true indeed. And very strange thing how such an object can be appearing to you, without you ever knowing of it or ever seeing it. Mavra says that mirror must be existing in both realities – both here and in the other world – so it is very special magical link for taking us backwards and forwards between them. And Mavra say this only ever happen when our dreams are holding very powerful meaning and maybe bringing important message from the other shore.'

I am pretty curious of course for knowing where that real

mirror – one in my mother's secret chest – actually come from, and this time she agree to tell me.

'Zhenya,' she say, 'that mirror is not coming from Soviet Union. It is coming from faraway land, from England, from London, and it is wrought by finest silversmiths in all realms, colonies and dominions of His Gracious Majesty empire.'

Well, this is pretty surprising stuff. Not just facts about England and London. But also my mother's way of expressing, like something I never heard her speaking before, especially back then in old Soviet Union where nobody having much truck with gracious majesties and colonies and dominions and such like.

So I say to her, 'Mama, how come that we got this precious object in our family?'

And she just take the deep breath and say, 'Because, Zhenya, that mirror and all those books and also our piano royale are objects of your father. And that man you been seeing in your dreams, who been looking through that very mirror and trying to talk to you . . . he is your father.'

And my mother make a little sniff and say very quiet, 'So there, now I told you, and now you know everything!'

Well, it certainly don't feel like I know everything, because about one million questions are popping in my head and more of them occurring before I can even ask the first ones.

Only thing I can manage to say, 'Mama, how can he be my father? This is old man appearing in my dreams, with grey hair and so forth, but you always telling me my father been just the young boy when he is falling victim sacrifice to evil fascist forces at great tank battle of Kursk salient. How this can be, Mama?'

'Well, Zhenya,' she say, 'I got to make you apology and also explain you this mystery. For many years I not been telling you whole truth about certain things. But this is not intended for hurting you, little son. It was necessary deceiving. And now I will tell you the reason of it. Your father was not soldier in our Red Army, and not dying at Kursk. This story I been telling because I must conceal the truth. It is easy story and everyone believe it because it happen to so many mothers, and many children not having any living father in these years, like you know. But you and me are not like other people, little son. We got the very special history and also very special destiny. But it is hard destiny and something we must not expose to other people here.'

And my mother look in my eyes and say, 'So now I tell you, Zhenya. Your father is not any Russian boy at all. He is very special man. Your father is high and noble lord of great kingdom of England and plenipotentiary of His Gracious Majesty.'

Well, please to imagine what effect this news is causing me!

One minute I been thinking I am just little Zhenya, war orphan like many others and therefore destined to exist only in reality of Soviet Union, where mankind all very free and noble etc., but also with no hopes of anything except working on kolkhoz and living in *kommunalka*; and next minute I am turning out as son of a noble lord and therefore destined to be lofty aristocrat and maybe even future duke of England!

And my mother is crying and hugging me and I am hugging her and crying, but also thinking of many new questions to ask, such as, How come you got to marry this noble lord and where he is now and when he is coming back to his bride and his son?

But my mother says she cannot answer any questions until she drink some Georgian tea with extra sugar in it, so she go off to kitchen where I hear her shuffling around and blowing her nose, and I am sitting waiting for her and reflecting on such amazing developments.

But pretty soon some doubtfulness start creeping in. Like, for an example, since my mother never been out of Soviet Union and not too many English noble lords come visiting in Vitebsk, as far as I am knowing, exactly how come she been meeting this fellow? And when she did meet him, what been happening to him afterward? Is he just disappearing? Walking out and abandoning us? Even with my own very small, Soviet knowledge of noble chivalry tradition, I know for sure this is not something any English lord would ever do! And how come my mother never been trying to find him in all those years since I been in this world? OK, I understand why she been keeping this lord secret, of course: in old Soviet Union, it is not such great idea to tell everybody you got the class enemy and paragon of repressive capitalism in your family.

But how come she never even tell me about it?

When my mother come back from kitchen and after she drunk five cups of Georgian tea with extra sugar and also made me drink the same, I am asking these questions.

And my mother just graze at me with her sweet eyes smiling, and she say she going to tell me all the whole story.

And this is my mother's story, exactly as she recount it to me all those years ago in Vitebsk, and which is leading to so many extraordinary events happening later in my life as direct result of what she been telling me that day . . .

Her story begin several years before Great Patriotic War, at the time when my mother is still the young girl and very beautiful and slim but also real smart in her studies at Vitebsk Gymnasium and always coming out top in the literature and art and music. This is middle of 1930s and extreme dangerous time, when many foreign enemies of Soviet Union been preparing the violent aggression, and Soviet leadership in Moscow is hesitating what to do and not even knowing who is our worst enemy and which side we better make alliance with, maybe opting with capitalist England, France and USA, or maybe with Hitler Germany, which we not yet been calling bloody fascist clique.

So what Stalin is actually doing at this time? First, he is preparing mass mobilization plan in case of war bursting out, and he also sending special commissars to all schools throughout Soviet Union on important secret mission.

Pretty soon one commissar coming to Vitebsk Gymnasium and my mother recount me how she and some comrades been observing him talking to school principal, and wondering what this all portending.

That afternoon my mother and friend Valya get called to principal's study and told they are top students of whole Gymnasium and therefore been selected for very great honour, namely Valya going to get taken away and given special instruction in the German language and culture and my mother be receiving same in the English.

And that exactly what is happening.

Two weeks later, these young girls get taken to special army barrack outside of Moscow, get joining together with many other top students from all over Russia and Byelorussia, sleeping in the dormitories, eating in canteen with Red Army men and political commissars, and having lessons from eight in a morning till seven at night for learning about Soviet Union's future allies or enemies – who knows which will turn out as which? And this is important time in my mother life, because she is being made full member of Communist Party, not just Young Pioneer or *komsomolets*, and also starting to learn many things which ordinary *narod* (this being just regular people like peasants and workers) never allowed to learn.

For instance, to help with learning English language, those

students get watching certain capitalistic movies such as *Great Expectation*, *Man Who Work Miracles*, *Pygmalion*, *Lady Vanish*, *39 Steps* and *Star is Born*, which they strictly instructed not to be enjoying whatsoever, due to unsuitable ideological content, and only to watch in order for improving English grammar and accent and so forth.

After two years of such studying, my mother is speaking English pretty good, although still with the big Russian accent because they can be no real English or American people teaching there, on account of them all maybe being future enemies of Soviet Union, who knows?

Politcommissars always instructing young students not to be imbibing any decadent Western values along with Western languages, but my mother is young girl and what you can do? She start to like what she is seeing and hearing about these faraway places, and even start yearning for maybe one day going to London or New York and see for herself. So she is very happy – by now this is end of March 1939 – when her instructor come and tell that she and Valya again being identified as star students, always getting *pyatiorkas*, and both been selected for special government duties involving translating and interpreting.

That night, my mother and Valya say farewell to comrades and get taken to brand-new *obshchezhitiye* (being special residence place where bureaucrats and functionaries and interpreters all living together) and told they been attached to Soviet Foreign Ministry so right now they got to just sit there and wait for orders.

And next morning all young people in that *obshchezhitiye* get talking to each other and nobody can figure out what is going on. All they know is they all been doing the crashing course in new languages, mainly English, French and German, all of them been specially investigated for reliability and loyalty and not having no kulaks in their families etc., and all been summoned here for the very special purposes.

One week later they get the visit by extreme top man, namely Comrade Vladimir Pavlov, chief interpreter for Great and Wise Leader and therefore in charge of everything. Now this Pavlov is pretty tough guy and also pretty jealous of anyone threatening his own job, because it seem his English speaking actually not too great, according to some rumours going round those students. So Pavlov tell them they all be remaining pretty junior ranks, maybe just typing or filing documents etc., and only reason they all been brought here to Foreign Ministry is because lots of extra language work coming round the corner owing to impending international developments.

When one student ask him what these developments can be, Pavlov – who always wanting to seem pretty important to everyone – say that actually he just been speaking to top Commissar of Foreign Affairs, Maksim Litvinov, who been telling him confidentially that big delegations of Germans and English and French all coming to Moscow soon for seeking a help of our Great and Wise Leader in making international alliances, so we all going to have lots of work to do.

And my mother get real excited at hearing this, and thinking she soon going to meet real foreign people from capitalist West.

But she is in for big disappointing. Because those delegations that everyone been expecting are just not arriving. At least, no English and no French. Maybe couple of Germans coming but everything remaining very quiet and secret.

So all these young people just waiting around in Moscow and spending happy hours visiting Park of Culture and Leisure in Name of Gorky, or eating the ice creams in Old Arbat Street or going to Bolshoi ballets, and only Valya getting couple of little documents for translating or type out in German, being mainly letters from certain Mr Von Schulenburg asking real politely if great Soviet Union and great Stalin maybe interested in signing some non-aggressing pact with Third Reich or something.

Anyway, Valya say she is pretty bored stiff by all these affairs and my mother say she even more bored stiff waiting around with no work at all and no Englishmen coming to Moscow whatsoever.

But later, in summer, things are changing, because Adolf Hitler start getting everyone pretty scared and saying he still needing more *Lebensraum* and therefore maybe Poland be just right for him and all his comrades to live in.

Suddenly this development making everyone get more urgent, and by June my mother start seeing some documents arriving from His Britannic Majesty, get translated by Pavlov's big wigs and then handed to my mother department for typing and filing. These letters all about how England and France really want to be friends with us, despite of calling Soviet Communism instrument of a devil and biggest threat to world peace and non-stop insulting us for last twenty years.

So things is hotting up on an Anglo-Saxon front, and my mother department soon getting lots of correspondence, including one letter in which great Stalin is showing his usual wisdom by cordial inviting those English and French to come to Moscow and talk things over, and biting his lip about all those bad names they been calling us in previous times.

But, uh-oh, Valya is also busy with her Germans and one day in July she tell my mother that very important face, namely Herr von Ribbentrop, is now cabling and writing to Kremlin like maybe twice every day and trying to be even nicer friend to us than Britannic Majesty and French fellows.

Soon the competition gets going in between my mother and

Valya, and both of them wagering whose country – England or Germany – going to win the race for a summer marriage with Comrade Stalin.

My mother think she got a cat in the bag on 23 July when she get a letter to type from Comrade Molotov to Britannic Majesty, agreeing for talks with England and France and suggesting that if a high delegation from London and Paris get to Moscow pretty sharpish, then maybe they get rewarded with treaty agreement of mutual assistance in between us.

That same evening, she gets instructed to hold in readiness for additional duties, which turn out to be attending a meeting between Comrade Litvinov, Comrade Molotov and His Britannic Majesty Ambassador, Sir William Seeds.

When she arrive, my mother is told to observe and take note on interpreting which is going on, because it seem some misunderstandings been happening at meetings where Pavlov been the official interpreter, and those British been complaining about his poor English.

My mother is pretty scared for doing this duty, of course, especially as Pavlov is looking with the daggers at her and saying with his eyes that she better not be criticizing his interpreting, or else *she* might be needing interpreter in basement of Lubyanka!

In fact he don't need to worry, because my mother say old Sir William turn out to be from place called Belfast, where no one actually speak English anyway, so there is no way she can understand any word he is saying and therefore she just write a report saying Pavlov get everything right and nobody got to worry about nothing.

That evening she is in the *obshchezhitiye* drinking tea with Valya and telling her that Great Leader soon going to sign up with the Allies because Sir William say an English delegation coming right away. But Valya just laugh and say, 'Maybe that cat not quite in your bag, Tatiana, because – guess what – my Germans coming too!' and maybe now it going to be the real race and everything actually depending who arrive here first.

And after few more days my mother is getting in real big despair because those British just so darn slow, maybe having to drink some tea and play the game of bowls before starting out for Moscow, which they don't do till 5 August and then not even on an aeroplane but actually on some real slow passenger-cargo boat called *City of Exeter* which is taking five days to sail to Leningrad and all the time my mother's department waiting impatient for them to arrive in Moscow, because Valya keep telling about new letters from nice Mr Ribbentrop and how friendly Comrade Molotov starting to behave with the Germans and so forth.

And when British do finally arrive in Leningrad, guess what! they decide to take off a day for sightseeing: my God, don't these people know there is a war going on, or at least about to be going on if they don't hurry up and start making friends with Uncle Joe? So it is actually 11 August before those English and French get to Moscow, and by this time my mother say everyone got into pretty bad moods and the weather so hot and everyone getting warm under a collars and pretty much suspecting now that Gracious Majesty actually been fooling us around pretty bad and maybe we better sign up with those nice Nazi fellows instead.

But that day, something is happening to make my mother forget all about international diplomacy and Poland and races to war and such like. When English delegation arrive in Moscow, they all get transported to large evening banquet at Soviet Foreign Ministry residence on Spiridonov Street and my mother instructed for attend also, in order to repeat observing and reporting duties on the interpreting affairs. When she get there, she discover she got to report on old Mr Pavlov again, but this time another junior interpreter been instructed to attend and report on my mother! Well, that just the way things get done in those days and my mother not turning too much attention to this.

But she is turning attention to those Englishmen! Because they all so tall and slim and handsome and looking gorgeous, just like Robert Donat in *39 Steps*, and wearing so beautiful suits and so dashing moustaches that my mother immediately falling into love with all of them.

Lord Strang is leader of delegation, and he kiss my mother hand when Pavlov introducing her, and she is nearly fainting from being so close to real Englishman, because these English are so different from Soviet *muzhiks* she been having to put up with all her life, owing to them being polite and considerate and speaking nice to women and even sometimes ask their opinion about things, which no Soviet man ever thinking of doing because he is such uneducated peasant.

Also present at banqueting is top military man, named of Admiral Reggie Drax, somewhat old and greyish, but wearing very attractive uniform, and also Marshal Charles Burnett and Major-General Heywood, both being height of charming.

For my mother, all these people look like visitors from another world, so to say, from magical world of elegance and beauty and tender consideration for human feelings. But most charming of all is one Englishman who is keeping always in a background, just observing what going on, exactly like my mother is observing from her side, and never saying anything except 'good evening' and 'thank you' and 'please to pass the port' etc. At first, my mother is thinking this man – young and tall with the brown moustache – is maybe junior interpreter similar like herself, so she is smiling at him with shyness, and he is smiling right back and looking very handsome, with large brown eyes and straight white teeth and no gold fillings at all.

But she is pretty mistaken about him being junior official, because Pavlov see her smiling and pass her the note saying, 'Attention, comrade. Immediately desist from flirting with distinguished visitor', and when she open Pavlov note, my mother blush very red and look straight in distinguished visitor eyes, who seem quite amused by all this going on and also happy for see her looking at him and blushing red.

Well, most of banqueting is taken up with vodka and toasts and long speeches, and then more vodka and even longer speeches.

Admiral Drax especially turning out to be the expert at long speaking. First he tell all about British Navy and its long history and how it respected and feared by whole world, which actually relevant to impending talks about military alliances etc., and then about recent regatta of sea-going yachts at Portsmouth and bridge evening with his wife and trout fishing and writing some letter complaining to *Times* and other such stuff, which is definitely not relevant.

By end of Admiral Drax's long speaking, old Pavlov is getting pretty hoarse and out of voice, so he tap my mother on a shoulder and tell her she got to do some interpreting now, which coming as the big shock but she say all right and start relaying very long interventions from Comrade Voroshilov, People's Commissar of War, and Comrade Shaposhnikov, Chief of General Staff.

And her interpreting seem to go pretty good because

Admiral Drax is smiling and so also Marshal Burnett and Major-General Heywood, and so especially that mysterious young Englishman with large brown eyes.

It is after midnight when all this banqueting is over and my mother preparing for return to *obshchezhitiye*, but Voroshilov make the signal to her and say she and Pavlov got to accompany him back to Kremlin while he compile official report on the Englishmen. She is pretty nervous about this but not having much choice in a matter.

And just as they exiting off the premises, she feels the light touch on her arm and turning round she see that very beautiful unknown Englishman smiling at her and secretly placing something in her hand while Pavlov and Voroshilov getting their coats and therefore not observing what is going on.

And very beautiful Englishman just put a finger up to him lips for tell my mother to keep silent, and she blushes and hurry out to follow her Russian *muzhik* bosses into large black Chaika that is driving them off to Kremlin.

This is greatest adventure of my mother's life. She is driving into mighty Kremlin with Soviet Union Commissar of War, and guards are saluting them and they are sitting in Voroshilov office and he starts asking her and Pavlov what the foreigners been saying in their English language so he can compile his report and take it in to Great and Wise Leader whose office is just down a few corridors, *and she is not even taking notice of any of this!*

She is thinking only about that small piece of card she got in her left pocket, all squashed up and squeezed by her fingers and containing vital message from most beautiful man in whole wild world and she not even been able to read it yet and terrified that *they* going to discover it and take it away from her and her happiness will be dashed to pieces and she never be happy ever in this world even if she live to one hundred and ten like those wisewomen who know secrets of the everlasting life.

And she is thinking all this and her head so spinning she can hardly notice when Voroshilov is answering a special red telephone on his desk then talking with quite loud voice but she not really understanding what he is saying her, so he got to repeat it, 'Tatiana Aleksandrovna, please come now. Comrade Stalin wish to see us all in his office!'

Then they are walking down long corridors with soldiers guarding several doors and saluting and strong smell of cabbage and Georgian tobacco, but my mother cannot even think of Great and Wise Leader because she has secretly taken that small card out of her pocket and it says, 'With compliments of Lord Edenby-Gore, KCMG, Foreign Office Liaison Staff', and on back written with mauve ink and very beautiful handwriting: 'Gorky Park, main gate, tomorrow 8 a.m. Melvyn' . . .

OK, stop straight away please!

Here is Zhenya intervening to suspend this storytelling right now!

How come?

For reason you sure all knowing, and please do not pretend to contrary. Namely you all additioning twos and twos for making up the fives.

Please do not deny it. I know you all been thinking, 'Oh! . . . English Lord . . . in Moscow . . . Tatiana getting fallen in love . . . maybe Zhenya father really is . . .' etc.

That what you been thinking?

Well, maybe you right and maybe you wrong. But things is not so simple as you all supposing, OK?

First, I got to point out few important factors to you. Such as, these events all happening in August 1939. And do not forget I am not being born till outbreaking of Great Patriotic War, so

June 1941. Please pardon gynaecology details, but how this is physically possible?

And also, you all pretty naive if you thinking some young interpreter in Moscow can just go out from *obshchezhitiye* for meeting some foreign visitor at secret rendezvous of Gorky Park without maybe two dozens of NKVD people following her, not even mentioning all those NKVDs which also following that distinguished foreign visitor his self!

OK. Now you understanding little bit better?

I hope you also understanding what I Zhenya am thinking when I hear this story from Tatiana, my mother. I am thinking lots of things, all at simultaneous times. And then asking many questions.

First I am asking her if it is true that she really been meeting mighty Comrade Stalin, and she say, Yes but she cannot remember too much about it, except that Great and Wise Leader is very short and ugly with strong personal body odour and keep breaking cigarettes open for stuffing tobacco in his pipe with yellow fingers, thereby being complete utter opposite of Lord Melvyn who is beautiful and God-like in comparing.

And when I ask her what is happening next, she recount how Voroshilov been taking her and Pavlov back to his office, about three in a morning now, and some flunky is showing them late night secret cable that been intercepted from Sir Strang and Admiral Drax back to Sir Halifax and Sir Chamberlain in London.

Since this cable is in English, she and Pavlov get instructed for translate it, and it turn out as highly secretive cable revealing how those sneaky English are actually determined to delay and sabotage all negotiations with us, according to categoric instructions from Sir Chamberlain himself. It seems they trying to avoid signing any treaty so that England's enemies, Nazi and

Communists, get every opportunity for fighting a war exclusive between themselves, consequently letting English and French stay safe and off a hook while Germany and Russia fight each other into the soils.

Talk about a perfidious Albion!

And what a shock to my mother. She is so upset of learning about this English schemingfulness that she start thinking maybe she better not go Gorky Park next morning after all. Or perhaps she better even inform People's Commissar all about her secret invitation to romantic rendezvous with Lord Melvyn Edenby-Gore.

But here is problem: she got to choose between patriotic duty and emerging love for Lord Melvyn. This is not easy choice because Lord Melvyn is beginning to seem to her like answer of all her prayings, namely she believe fate been sending him to love her and marry her and take her out of such terrible world which is Soviet Union, where everyone afraid and worrying and living in dirty, ugly lives, into magic new world which is beautiful place where people all happy and kind and caring about each other in gleaming white city with clean parks and friendly policemen.

But when I ask her which path she been choosing – denouncing or not denouncing – my mother start avoiding the question and not telling any answer whatsoever, except for saying, 'I went to see him, Zhenya. How can I not do this when I love him?'

And when I ask about her patriotic duty, she say, 'What is difference, Zhenya? Comrade Stalin was already knowing those English are negotiating sham with us and to trying trick us for fighting Hitler on our own, so he took historically correct decision to sign non-aggressing pact with Germans instead. How can this matter what decision I been taking on denouncing Lord Melvyn or not denouncing?'

She simply will not tell me any answer, but my mother is my mother and I am trusting her in all things, including the affairs of patriotic duty.

What she does tell is that this Lord turn out to be most charming man ever seen in Moscow and very much in love with my mother as she in love with him.

So when they are talking and walking in the Gorky Park, he tells her all about his ancient family history which go right back to William of Conquering, and about his great love for Russia, which he been studying in British Foreign Office, and he tell her she is very beautiful Russian girl, which make her blush, and he buys the *bublichki* for breakfast and then . . . he kiss her.

And afterwards he is asking her all the usual things that lovers do, like where she come from and how she been learning English and what she know about Voroshilov and other Soviet cadres and can she please describe layout of corridors and offices inside Kremlin, and how many Red Army units she has seen in Moscow and what is state of their morale and what equipment they are having and so forth.

So this is very romantic meeting and they agree to meet again, which they are doing many times during ten following days, both inside negotiating chamber where my mother is making more and more interpreting due to Pavlov being pretty useless, and outside in Moscow most mornings and also nights, which they are spending secretly together deep in the love.

Sadly, though, soon come 21 August when Stalin patience with subterfuging British is finally running out . . .

That afternoon, Voroshilov is reading out a statement of the Soviet leadership to British delegation, complaining how they been deliberate delaying and sabotaging negotiations right from very beginning, and sternly concluding, 'In view of above, all responsibility for suspension of talks must rest with British and French sides.'

So negotiations are over and done to, solely due to English's perfidy, and couple of days later Valya says that she been summoned to Kremlin to interpret for special high meeting with Herr von Ribbentrop who just arrived in Moscow from Berlin.

Well, guess what? those Germans sure must be better at talking than the Englishes were, because that same evening, 23 August, famous Molotov–Ribbentrop non-aggressing pact gets signed, with Valya interpreting, and England's has been well and truly settled. Lord Strang, Lord Drax, Sir Burnett, Sir Heywood, and – most sad of all – Lord Edenby-Gore now got to depart from Moscow with tails held down low.

And this is completely natural, of course, because what any Englishman can be doing in USSR any more? Now our Great Leader got allied with Great Führer, so how those English can ever be coming back here?

How Lord Melvyn can ever be coming back?

Answer: they can't and he can't.

These are big geo-political realities resulting from unstoppable march of history.

And history been marching pretty rough over my mother too.

When Lord Melvyn got to depart, her heart is broke and weeping, but just before he is leaving she tell him she always love him and they must be together for ever.

Hmm.

Nine days later come fateful events of 1 September 1939, and whole world is moving into whole new era.

My mother and comrades get called to central assembly

hall to hear special radio address by Marshal Stalin and he is telling how Germany is now our ally, and England and France is not.

After couple of weeks, our glorious troops are invading Poland and meeting up there with glorious German comrades.

What you can do?

Things all looking different now. Looking pretty bad for Poland naturally, and not too great for my mother neither, because her idea of someday going to promised land of England is suddenly seeming extreme far-fetched due to aforementioned geo-political realities. And this is only making her even more yearning to get there and causing some real bad *toska*.

But you can imagine what I actually want to know from my mother is upshot concerning Lord Melvyn.

So I ask her vital question, Is this noble Lord fellow really my father? And how he can be coming back to Moscow during following two years of 1939 to 1941 when we are allies with England's enemy Germany? And if he is not coming in that time before I am born, then how he can be my father?

My mother look at me kind of sad and say she cannot reveal me answer of these questions, except that strange things happen in this world and sometimes, when people very deep in love, then even impossible things happen.

And that is all.

My mother will not tell me more. She just grazes on me and smile and say how I am extremely resembling to beautiful Lord Melvyn and also that I am bearing his name, by the way, which is something I never thought of up till then.

To understand this, please be casting back to that naming affair I been mentioning on very first time of talking to you, namely that my name and my mother name is Gorevich.

OK, Gorevich is pretty ordinary Russian name, this is true.

In our case, though, maybe it really is coming from Lord Gore and my mother really is adopting it for show that she is his bride, like she been telling me.

This is possible.

And one more thing to note, please, somewhat worrisome. *Gore* in Russian language actually meaning grief or woe. Maybe this is simple chance. Maybe not signifying. But in my story, strangely, like in my dreaming, it seem most things are turning out to have a meaning.

When my mother finish recounting me her life history, it is late of night and we both pretty tired. So I tell how much I love her and she tell how much she love me and gives me the large hugging, and both go to bed.

But I am not sleeping too good, because I am pondering everything I been hearing that evening, and from times to times I hear my mother getting up also, maybe because she is reliving all those drama events of 1939, seventeen years ago, or maybe because she drunk too much Georgian tea with sugar and therefore having to go to lavatory pretty frequent. And next day, just as I am departing to school, my mother tell me that Mavra wisewoman (you remember her) soon be coming to our *kommunalka* in order for divining any presences of spirit world in our atmosphere and consequently exposing significance of those dream visions for my future, so we got to make the real big effort to clean and tidy up this apartment, which is not very easy matter owing to it being pretty dirty, smelly and cramped place where everything cracked and broken, therefore being very in contrast to our nice cosy kolkhozy house where we been living before.

Oh well. Life is such.

*

At school, my brain is feeling under siege and I spend that whole day thinking of those strange magical things I been learning from my mother. As the result, I am not turning much if any attention to learning my school lessons, which is highly annoying teacher Zoya and consequently giving her renewed opportunity for rebuking me, just like she been doing pretty much constantly ever since infortunate episode of me counter-denouncing Vova Smirnov after him denouncing old Finkel-stein, who by the way is now returned from that camp he been sent to.

You surprised by this?

Surprised to be hearing about old Finkelstein again after him previously being sent to gulag and therefore clean out of this story?

Well, me too.

I was sure not expecting him back either, but suddenly there he was, and here he is, right here on this page.

I better explain you reason for this, namely: the big politics of Soviet state life. Please do not forget that year I am talking about is when I am turning to fifteen, so actually working out at 1956. And by 1956, USSR got the new management, namely Ukrainian peasant fellow called Nikita Khrushchev.

How come we got this new management?

Because couple of years previously, Great and Wise Leader been suffering heart attacks and strokes and sadly dying. This is tragedy for USSR and also for whole of humankind. Millions of people been mourning throughout Soviet territory and territory of fraternal countries, excepting for just one place.

And where this place is?

Inside of all prison camps, of course. When they hear news of Comrade Stalin death, those prisoners are pretty darn glad and many of them cheering and throwing up their *shapkas* in the air, for which they all getting punished with reducing rations or solitary confining.

But after some elapse of time, when dust is settling down and they all getting back out of the solitary, things is turning out pretty good for those guys, especially if they been convicted of political articles in Soviet penal code, such as propaganda or slandering against Great and Wise Leader or – specially lucky for Mr Finkelstein – being kulak. Because soon all those prisoners start getting amnesties from new Ukrainian fellow, who got his own, unusual ideas of Soviet justice and also wanting new dawn in our country, so thousands of people getting out of a gulag and coming home to former abodes, including home to Vitebsk.

So that explain how Mr F come popping back up in our story again, OK?

Actually, I better inform you something: Mr F not going to play any big role in our future events now, so no need of you worrying about him or looking back in previous pages for checking out who he is (he is that kulak and crow killer with very big gun, remember, but this not important now so please just forget it), because I guess he just went off home to him old dwelling place and picked up same old life again, namely being rich peasant and hoarding grain, although not doing any espionage, which he pretty sure wasn't doing before anyway, just being framed for this by some enthusiastic NKVD fellows.

Now, why I am telling you about Mr Finkelstein?

Oh yes. It is because I been recounting about teacher Zoya and reason why she been constantly directing rebukes to me.

Well, that day at school she sure been doing plenty of rebuking, some of it fair rebuking and some of it not fair, but actually I am not getting too upset at all by this.

Why not?

For two reasons.

First, I am feeling pretty excited and pleased of myself because of everything I just been learning from my mother's story. So more Zoya is rebuking me, more I am thinking, Why can I be caring about this stuff? If I am transpiring to be English Lord, then all this Soviet pettiness is not mattering to me any single jots. Being English Lord means I can be washing my hands about this life here; can be escaping from all rebukes and denouncings and counter-denouncings; can leave behind unpleasant smelling *kommunalkas* and dirty streets and false comrades like Vova and old Smirnov who are having the power to make me unhappy.

And, you know what? more I start pondering what my mother been telling me, more I am liking her story and – also – more I am getting convinced it got to be true. OK, there maybe some problems (I told you about them), but now I am feeling less worried about these things and much more enthusiastic about being son of Lord Melvyn. Because with Lord Melvyn as my father, all problems of this Soviet life starting to look pretty insignificant, that is for sure.

And second reason for my happiness growing?

This one got to do with Ukrainian fellow I mention you earlier. Because Nikita Khrushchev not only been letting gulag people go home, he also starting the new policy of liberalization called *ottepel'*, meaning getting all thawed out. As for example, he now allowing some people to write new novels and stories which actually concerning other stuff than just heroism of Soviet nation and glory of Communist Party (like books always used to be), and maybe even allowing some criticizing of things (although not too much criticizing, and usually just criticizing of stuff that been going on at time of Great and Wise Leader, not at time of General Secretary Nikita).

One guy even been writing some supposed diary of a fellow called Denisovich who been living in a gulag and having general hard time of things, and old Nikita personally directing that this book got to get published.

In art world too, thaw is also beginning, although pretty confusing one in this connection. For one thing, that *Third Course Book for Young Artists* I been using with my mother (remember? with big introduction by Comrade Stalin?) is getting thrown out real quick, and some people start thinking maybe socialist realism now been consigned to a trash can of history so they start painting pictures without any red banners or happy peasants and workers and such.

And at first everything seem hunky and dory, what with exhibitions of this stuff going on in Moscow and even being reported in newspapers and no one really knowing if it is OK to be doing it or not, so they just carry on doing it anyway. But then some artists getting little bit large for their shoes and just going too far, such as making paintings where you can't even tell what subject is.

And General Secretary starts getting pretty mad about this, him being fiery Ukrainian peasant type, so he goes to one exhibition at famous Manezh Gallery near the Red Square and he starts shouting and tearing these pictures down because they are a *bezobraziye*, meaning he thinks they all pretty ugly.

And next day, official state bulldozers arrive for consigning all those paintings into some real trash cans.

And then people are the getting message that you can be free and liberal and so forth, but not too much, please. In fact, just around that time of me being fifteen, in 1956, General Secretary Nikita been making the pretty important secret speech to Communist Party Congress, but no one been getting to know about it because it is secret.

And in that secret speech he been secretly revealing that Great and Wise Leader actually been a total disaster, not being Great and certainly not being Wise, owing to the fact that he been shooting several million people and sending some millions others to a gulag and also starving some other millions to death in Ukraine (where Nikita coming from) by introducing forced collectivizing and shooting all successful peasants who been keeping the agriculture going, on account of them being evil kulaks.

Oh boy! It seems you can't get nothing right in this country.

Funny thing is that Nikita himself actually been working as pretty close helper of Great and Wise Leader for whole time while these new discovered bad things been going on, but nobody seem to remember about this or pointing it out, mainly because he the boss now, I suppose (or maybe because that well-known secret speech really is so secret that nobody know anything about it and these questions are just not arising. It sure is strange time round about then!).

Also, rumours about this speech been causing some problems in fraternal countries such as Hungary, where population been erroneous thinking this mean the end to fraternal socialist repressing and therefore forcing Nikita into spot of friendly invading for showing them they got this one wrong for sure.

But sorry for diversion.

Getting back to me that day at school again and what I been thinking when Zoya been rebuking me: I am saying to myself this new guy Khrushchev and his *ottepel'* maybe pretty good news for me. Because his approach to politics sure seem more helpful for sons of an English Lord than the previous guy's. For instance, belonging to foreign capitalist aristocracy under Comrade Stalin is *really* bad idea, whereas under this new guy, who knows? Maybe things become bit easier for us English Lords.

And also, that former Great and Wise Leader been real set against any Soviet peoples ever getting out of bounds of mighty USSR, so for sure he would be vetoing one big idea which recently been appearing in my mind, namely going off to London to reintegrate into bosoms of my family, Lords Edenby-Gores. Comrade Stalin been sending people to gulag even for thinking such idea; but this new guy, well who knows . . . ?

That evening, I am sitting home with my mother, talking about all this, and she seem real pleased when I tell her I am getting used to idea of Lord Melvyn being my father and even starting to like such concept.

My mother say to me, 'Oh, you are just like me, little son. We both the same, both having same ideas and same feelings. And maybe now you understand why you never been happy here in Soviet Union, just like I am not happy too.'

And when I ask her why exactly we both unhappy, she say, 'Because we don't belong in Soviet reality, Zhenya. We belong in another world, in a world where things are good and noble, just like we are. You only got to think about it, little son. You are not just some little Soviet boy and therefore feeling at home here: you are offspring of noble English Lord, of such beautiful man filled by elegance and culture, so of course you can never be happy here or anywhere, except in high circles of fine, sensitive noble people . . . over there in London.'

Well, now things starting to make sense.

Now I am starting to understand how come I always been feeling pretty blue here in Soviet Union reality and therefore yearning for another reality existing somewhere on far side of the mirror or the glass window, so to say, just like that old crow I been telling you about.

So when Mavra arrive at our apartment following day, we are expecting the pretty good news, namely I am destined to rediscover Lord Melvyn and reclaim my noble heritage and bring my mother to the emotional reunion with her true love and my father. And things start well because old Mavra is arriving in very good mood, which is improving even more after my mother hand over necessary payment of two rabbits and one capon.

She take off her coat and begin divining process, which involve walking round our apartment with eyes closed and very deep concentrating.

But first problem – Mavra can't divine nothing at all, because signals from other world not coming through too good at this moment. So she ask my mother if she got any special object connecting with the individual who been trying to contact us in my dreams.

I see my mother hesitating, because she not wanting to tell too much about legacy of Lord Melvyn, but I am real eager now to find out about him so I say, 'Mama, you got that mirror and also special books and our English piano royale.'

So my mother sigh and say all right, and she open up the chest where all secret stuffs is stored and fetches that mirror and books with little penguin on the covers. Mavra takes these objects and go to sit on our piano stool, closing her eyes and frowning so she can see into other worlds.

She is sitting there for twenty minutes, swaying little bit from sides to sides and also muttering things under the breath which we cannot understand, but actually being very powerful incantations revealing her to access in special realms of perception.

And when she finished all this divining, she look real serious and say, 'I got the good news and also the bad news. First the good news. I seen that man you both been describing, who been appearing in Zhenya dreams and who been you true love in old Moscow days, Tatiana Aleksandrovna. For sure this is great Mr Lord Gore from London. I see him in my vision looking exactly like you both been telling. I also see his house, which is very large and got the white front with many window situated on some beautiful square with garden in the middle of it, locating behind black railings. Mr Lord Gore got many servants and large green car resembling to extra special Chaika limousine. But now bad news. Mr Lord Gore got the wife, looking beautiful and dressed in elegant balls gown, greatly enjoying dancing and ride the white horse . . .'

When Mavra mention Lord Gore wife, I am secret glancing at my mother. She look just like someone hit in her face and she is trying not to cry, but still the little tear appearing in her eyes.

'One thing about Mrs Lord Gore, though,' say Mavra continuing, 'she is not having any children. And this is making Mr Lord Gore pretty sad. So it seem in my vision that they been adopting the foundling child, young girl, maybe about ten or twelve year, from state collective orphanage or somewhere. They both loving this child and she becoming Princess Gore, I think. But Mr Lord Gore he still seem pretty sad. How come? Maybe because this is not his real child. Maybe because it is little girl and not noble son. And maybe for other reason I am coming to in the one moment.'

And when she say this last thing, Mavra look right at me, so I kind of guessing what is coming next.

'Yes,' say Mavra, like she been reading in my thoughts (which actually she probably is doing, seeing that she is wisewoman).

'Yes, Zhenya, I think you right. I think Mr Lord Gore is sad because he remember his love with your mother and now pining about her. And somehow he sensing of you existing also and being his real physical son, not just adopted from some found-ling place.'

Well, this news is making me pretty excited so I ask Mavra what else can she see in the divining, but Mavra look real stern and say, 'Wait some moments. I tell you I got the bad news and here is it: I see Mr Lord Gore very ill and even think he soon be dying, which in fact he may be, as I can sense from the spirits.'

I am not looking at my mother this time, but I hear her give a little *vskhlip* and then she blow her nose and go real quiet.

Meanwhile Mavra is saying, 'Because Mr Lord Gore seem so ill and maybe think he going to die, he start feeling regrets for the past, like we all do when we contemplate our own grave. For him, these regrets revolving around you, Tatiana Aleksan-drovna and around you Zhenya, and when restless spirits are approaching the other world, often they are calling out to those people they once wronged and to those they are yearning for. And I think this is what been happening in Zhenya dreams: Mr Lord Gore is so yearning to see his bride and his son that he come appearing in the night-time visions and wishing to be reconciled before he die.'

Well, this divining from Mavra is producing pretty strong effect on me and my mother. It is making the many things clear. But at the same time many other big questions now arising.

And when Mavra gone and we alone again, we both feel-ing something been disturbed in our existence and finding it pretty hard for settle down how we been before these things got revealed to us.

From the one sides, my mother is happy because now I am sharing in that story she been carrying inside her for so long. She has drawn me into her world of hope and yearning and imagining, where she used to inhabit all by her own.

But from another sides, knowing about such other world is pretty unsettling, because you can't help comparing it to the reality life you got to live in every day here and now. OK, when you lying awake in middle of the night, you can comfort yourself by thinking of beautiful world just beyond a horizon; but then it is even more tormenting because you know it will remain beyond and complete out your reach.

I am not feeling much like amusing at this situation, of course. But it is reminding me of one joke very popular at this time (and also safer to be telling since new guy Nikita arrive in Kremlin).

Here is joke.

At national conference of Soviet geographers, Communist Party ideologue is explaining how march of history is always bringing closer that Socialist paradise promised by Lenin, and he tell how Communist ideal is already on horizon. But one geographer is standing up and say, 'Comrade, as geographers we are interested in definition of horizon, which we collectively agree is imaginary line where sky come together with earth and which moves off into distance when you try to get closer.'

OK, maybe this not so funny, but I hope you getting a point of the joke.

And life at this time is getting tough for my mother and me, so any bit of laughing really is pretty important.

*

Ever since we been thrown out of kolkhoz and having to live in a *kommunalka*, we been getting more and more problems and lot of these got to do with old Mrs Deneikin.

Who is Mrs Deneikin?

Mrs Deneikin is babushka who been living in that *kommunalka* ever since Great October Revolution, so nearly for forty years. Now maybe you not knowing, but these babushkas are pretty tough old birds, always wearing thick padded jackets and long fat skirts, with *valenki* on their feet (being like felt boot things) and flowery scarf on the head. And for sure they are the boss of all things, like who got to clean the lavatory and who decide the rota for using oven in the kitchen and who can have visitors coming in apartment and who cannot.

This last point is particular problem for me. I tell you why.

Because of babushkas, there is special rule existing that no boyfriends and girlfriends is allowed inside any apartment in *kommunalka* until they are married and officially registered in people's palace of matrimony.

Actually, there is not any rationality in such rule, because those apartments all so small and young people in them so squashed together with sisters and mothers and aunts that no possibility existing of any immoral enjoyable behaviour anyway.

But you don't go arguing with the babushkas. This is simple law of existence. So Masha and me are doing like everyone else: meeting in the courtyard outside *kommunalka* and sitting on a bench by the wooden fence.

Oh, you wanting to know about Masha?

OK, I tell you.

Masha is girlfriend.

Now, maybe you all saying, 'This pretty strange: no Masha ever being mentioned previous', and so forth.

Maybe you even taking quick look back to list of friends

appearing in Young Pioneer brigades and not seeing any Masha there.

Well, don't go looking for Masha in YPs or in any location connecting to glorious Communist Party of Soviet Union, that is for sure!

Why not?

Because Masha is pretty independent girl and not being slave of any party or anything or anybody, like she tell me straightaway when I first been meeting her.

And where that first time been taking place?

Strange to say, in a haystack actually.

Yes, haystack.

How come? Because this is story occurring during harvesting time when, maybe you recall from our earlier conversing, Young Pioneers all get drafted in to help farmer and peasants collect up wheats and throw them on kolkhoz truck for going to get winnowed.

We young folk all pretty much enjoy this time of year because we all working outside in golden fields and usually got fine Soviet sun shining on us so consequently imparting mood of joviality and comradeship. And concerning my age group (namely the teenager) it is tradition for such joviality sometimes developing little bit further than comradeship.

OK, you all thinking sex not existing in Soviet Union? You thinking sex only been invented in swingeing sixties of London, Paris New York?

Well, please get thinking again.

It is not sex that not existing in Soviet Union; it is just people talking about sex that not existing.

And what is reason for this?

It is because great Soviet leaders all got real old and also got real ugly wives, so they are pretty much forgetting about sex and decide they don't want no one else enjoying something they are not enjoying, and for sure don't want other people talking about sex because that just make them feel even unhappier about not enjoying any for their selves. So when these Great and Old leaders deciding what the guidelines got to be for everyone writing books or painting pictures or making sculptures or composing songs and so forth, number one rule always: No sex.

(Rule number two: Lots of Communist heroes and full complement of evil capitalist villains, but this not relevant just now because we talking about sex here.)

Anyway, direct result of rule number one is pretty boring books and pictures and also big effort by everyone to have as much sex as possible in order for making secret protest against boring old Communist rules and boring old men in Kremlin.

OK, this is background to haystack incident.

Now I explain you what actually leading up to it and also resulting from it.

On last day of school year, all we Young Pioneers come to class with bundle of cloths for lasting four weeks and also butter-bread long enough for a journey, and municipal trucks carry us off to bosoms of *Rodina Mat'*, great Mother Russia (meaning about twenty kilometre outside Vitebsk actually, along main Minsk highway).

We all singing the joyful songs and generally looking forward to month in the country (and I not meaning Turgenev book here, just in case anyone already been spotting too many literary referrings in this story).

When we arrive, we all get welcomed by committee of local peasants who show us to our sleeping quarters, namely some barns in a field.

That night, secret vodka bottles that been smuggled in student knapsacks get produced and we all singing and laughing and dancing till the cock crowing, so next morning when peasants wake us up, we all feeling incapacitated and not much use for gathering wheats or anything else for that matter.

But, as is known, Soviet youth is famed for its resilience and hardiness, so within couple of days we are combining drinking, singing, dancing and also gathering wheats all at a same time. Fortunately for fate of Soviet agriculture, though, golden youth is not being left to its own devices in this.

We Young Pioneers all get a tutelage of experienced practitioners in the wheats gathering, namely sons and daughters of peasants from Sovkhoz where we are working. These sons and daughters not much older than us – maybe eighteen or twenty something – but they sure know plenty about country things and picking up the wheats without breaking your back or getting blisters all over your hands, and also – especially – how to make cruel mockery of us students when we trying to do the same.

And that is how I got to meet Masha.

One afternoon, soon after we arriving, I am gathering up stray wheats that been scattered around and dragging them to very large pile in centre of a field.

Now, this is hot afternoon and also following long drinking and singing session previous evening, so I am sweating and struggling with some heavy wheats on the end of my pitching fork when I start hearing some voices laughing and seeming like they calling out to me.

I am looking all around for sourcing of these voices, but no one to be seen anywhere and I begin to feel the little bit uneasy.

First I am thinking, OK, this is very strong sun beating

down on you neck, Zhenya, and also you feeling pretty unto-wards from effects of last night very strong vodka, so maybe you being somewhat tired and hallucinatory.

Consequently, I drop off that pitching fork and sit down to re-gather up my thoughts and drink few mouthfuls of water. But even with such precautions I am still hearing mystery voices coming from the thin air and really starting to get worried.

I am recalling up scary tales of Ukrainian peasant Nikolai Gogol (sorry for sudden blossoming of Ukrainian peasants in this story: our world is deep and full of strange events) and these tales all involving voices from the evil spirit realm sum-moning us to our death in midst of the life and bright sunshine of the hot summer afternoon. For making things worse, I am also recalling certain words of old Mavra who been telling about that spooky dead girl in my dream coming to call me into the kingdom of darkness.

And all the time, these voices keep calling and laughing and I cannot understand what they are saying except I know they must be directed at me.

And then I see that pile of wheats in middle of the field start to move and I am convinced this is end of my earthly existence because some Gogol monster of Vyi is coming to drag me into the dank and darkened chambers of the underworld.

But guess what? emerging from that haystack is not any evil creature whatsoever, but actually two pairs of very beautiful girl legs, not wearing any shoes or stockings, looking very brown from country sunshine and waving around in extreme pleasing manner. And those voices I been hearing are suddenly bursting into great pealings of laughing and start shouting, 'Over here, you townie bumpkin fellow! Don't you see us in here? Don't you know we been watching you all this time?' and then more great pealings of laughing coming in my direction.

And so I am relieved for being spared from the Vyi monster that I can't think of anything nonchalant and sophisticated for saying, except, 'Thanks God. You been scaring me!' and those two girls start laughing even louder and shouting me to come right into that haystack with them.

So I do.

And I never been in a more lovely place in whole of my life. Inside that haystack everything is so warm and soft and scented with the fragrance of fresh cut wheats and hot brown skins and little specks of chaff floating in the sunlight coming directly from heaven that it seem to me like I arrived in paradise.

And when they finally stop laughing, those girls say to me, 'What age you are?' and I am thinking fast and reply, 'Eighteen.'

Now maybe you spotted I am not telling a complete truth here. Maybe you also understanding why I am not revealing of being only fifteen years. And maybe you thinking, OK, this is not such a big dealing.

But actually I want you to know that I Zhenya am honest fellow. So consequently I am pointing out this small untruth. And also I am making you a confession: in some places of my story, which I been telling you up to now, I also been telling some untruths.

Am I going to tell you what are these untruths?

Well, answer is no.

For several reason. Including I cannot remember exactly where are these untruths in my story. But in future from this point onward, I am going to make big efforts for not telling you any further untruths whatsoever. OK?

Other than when it is real necessary to do so.

Right, now you know.

Let us go back to me and Masha and Tanya (which is what those girls turning out to be called) all together in that haystack, which is pretty happy memory for me, for sure. And also a memory I often been conjuring up in later times, especially when I am lying lonely in my bed at night and can't get to sleep. Or at times when I get consumed by the *toska* pretty bad. At those times, I think to myself at least I got one or two good things in my head and nobody can take them away from me even when they taken everything else away, which is situation I am later finding myself in, as you soon be seeing if you come with me to end of this journey.

Anyway, those girls with sun brown legs must be feeling pretty darn bad about scaring me because when I get into that haystack with them, they suddenly treating me extremely nice and friendly. And even though they still teasing me somewhat and giggling, they are also pulling their arms around me and making me warm from their bodies which are radiating all that sunshine they been drinking in all their life.

And that is not all.

Pretty soon Masha and Tanya are both laughing and asking each other who is going to be first to kiss me and I say I sure don't mind one little bit and if they both want to kiss me then they both extremely welcome. But these are Russian peasant girls, don't forget, and peasant girls are pretty strong-willed and independent and always wanting to show they cannot be bossed around by any man, including by me. So they do some more laughing at my expenses and decide to draw straws for who will kiss me and it is Masha who get the winning straw and I am pretty happy by this (although for being honest I guess I would be pretty happy if it been Tanya too).

I am feeling two warm soft lips on my lips and closing up my eyes and falling into sweet reveries which I am still remembering even now as I sit here so many years later. And while I am in these reveries with my eyes closed, I am feeling hands around my waist which I guess must be Tanya hands and they starting to unfasten my leather belt and also my pants buttons, and I am thinking *Ookhty, bookhty!* this must be my lucky day!

Those hands are pulling down my pants to round my knees and I am getting the strong feeling that love is going be mine for first time in my life, and very pleasant feeling it is, which I am highly savouring in my mind and my body. But suddenly, at same time of this pleasant feeling, I also start to get very *un*pleasant one involving series of sharp pains in the buttock region and I am not sure what this all about and, since I never been experiencing love before, I am wondering is this maybe some necessary part of the whole process?

But then I hear those girls start laughing so loud at top of their voices that I know something is wrong here and maybe this is not actually part of the love experience at all.

And I am right!

When I open up my eyes from the sweet reveries, I see the only reason those girls been taking down my pants is for pushing my bottom in a wasps' nest that is hidden right there in that haystack.

What a cruel tricking!

Masha and Tanya are both roaring with laughing and hugging themself and pointing at me.

I am pretty angry with those girls, of course, and pretty disappointed of not getting to know love after all, but now, many years later, I am often thinking of that time and often it is making me smile.

Because now I understand those girls and their desire for always laughing in life, for always blocking out the bad stuff. And also because of what been happening later between Masha and me, most of which been proving she is actually the good person and not cruel and uncaring at all, and even for some time I think she is really loving me with all her soul.

But we come to that in a moment.

And we also come to bad things which later been happening in between us.

And if sometimes I do tell the untruths about my past, like I been warning you just now, it is only because my present is not so much fun, what with being sixty-five years old and being kept in here where they don't treat you too good, and no one really loves you or feels much about you at all.

So many hours now I spend in recalling days gone by.

In my memory, I see me tearing off those daily pages of the *bloknot* calendar in our Vitebsk homes, first with my mother then later without her, and in my mind I see every day a page fly off in the air and these pages are all swirling round my face and turning into little wasps becoming angry and stinging me till tears come to my eyes and here am I now at age of sixty-five and I am crying, and they are coming to me and give me medicine to make me calm. But there is no medicine that can make me calm. Probably nothing can do. Because I see the days all have flown like wasps in the air and first they stung me and then they flew away and never will return.

And sometimes when I am so sad I can no longer keep my pain inside me, I shout out loud and they come to me and I cannot move. And sometimes . . . they pour cold water on my head.

Excuse me.

This is not the tone.

I am telling you about Masha and me.

About that day in the haystack and that sunny afternoon in

bosoms of *Rodina Mat'*, our great Homeland Mother, which burn so bright in my memory for ever.

And about that evening also. That country-summer evening when Masha and Tanya both came with me to the Young Pioneer camp and each of them holding my hand in secret in the darkness while friends and comrades are singing together such revolutionary songs and the *garmoshka* is playing its sweet melody of hope and faith for our future lives.

And then Tanya smiles and bids us goodnight and Masha come with me to sleep in our fragrant straw bed under the noble Russian sky where the stars speak of eternal justice and all Soviet people here and everywhere are happy and at one.

How lovely was that dwelling place.

And how lovely was Masha and her love for me.

The Soviet sky blessed our union that night. In the morning, we swore to love each other for ever.

And for a while it seem like we spoke the truth.

Because after the harvest season, Masha is coming to Vitebsk to find work on the local kolkhoz in order for being close by her lover, namely me.

I am returning to my mother and to my studies, but every evening I am meeting Masha and our love is growing always stronger and sweeter.

Only hitch, as I been telling earlier, this love now got to be an open air one, on account of old Mrs Deneikin and the babushkas not permitting any young lover inside *kommunalka* apartments for committing the unseemly acts.

So we are meeting in the courtyard and sitting on a wooden bench near the wooden fence, same as everyone, and just holding hands and sometimes slightly embracing when those babushkas not looking.

But just one problem.

Masha is the proud and fiery girl, as you probably already notice. And she is not liking to be bossed around by any babushkas, or by anyone for that matter. So every evening she is putting up her thumb in the nose to Mrs Deneikin by making loud derogating remarks and also telling lots of very riskable jokes just when she know Mrs Deneikin and babushka friends sure to be listening.

And this actually getting me pretty worried because these Masha jokes are real dangerous to be telling, even despite of new guy in the Kremlin, such as:

'One secret policeman ask another secret policeman, "What you think about the government?" Other fellow look around and say, "Same as you, comrade," and first policeman say, "In that case, it is my duty for arrest you."'

Or, 'Man go to post office and complain, "These new stamps with Khrushchev is not sticking any good", and clerk just reply, "Comrade, you been spitting on the wrong side."'

Or, 'How many times you can tell the political joke in USSR? Answer three: once to friend, once to investigator and once to cellmate.'

Sorry for long list of jokes but they all been pretty funny in those strange old 1950s.

Of course, I know the real reason why Masha telling them is not solely for humour. It is so the babushkas can hear them and understand pretty clear that Masha and me don't care too much for them being boss of everything and we are the young generation and we do daring things in despite of what you old folks say, and so there.

And this got me real worried.

Because I know those babushkas are pretty cunning.

For sure they all go to church, this is true. And for sure they not actually being Communists or even liking Communist reality too much.

But they also pretty darn smart. And everyone know they always hoarding up useful information to use against people in future, pretty much like old Finkelstein always hoarding up the grain. But for now, they are just listening, time is going by and many more daily pages are getting torn off the *bloknot* calendars in our *kommunalka*.

I am continuing my studies; Masha still working on the collective farm. But now she is taking the educational painting course during her spare times. I can see she is becoming top class artist, much better than me or my mother, making beautiful canvases of wheats fields where she is working, and of friends and comrades in labour, but always refusing to paint any red banners or Great Lenin and suchlike textbook subjects.

Masha and me keep seeing each other every day, still in love so it seems, and pretty soon we are sharing all our secrets between us. Like, for instance, she is telling how her brother recently been spending some time in prison for speculation, this being traditional Soviet crime of buying some article and then selling it again (maybe seem strange to you, but Soviet 1950s is pretty strange place). Article in her brother's case turn out to be some old Moskvich car which he been acquiring from his mechanic friend who repair it after a road crash incident. And all seem hunky and dory, except Masha brother is actually selling that car to leading party member and local councillor of Vitebsk Soviet who later been having the subsequent complaint over faulty headlights and therefore revenging himself by reporting Masha brother as economic criminal.

When he is appearing in court, things looking not too bad, since this is his first transgression and anyway justice situation is looking more relaxed since Nikita fellow been in the Kremlin.

But trouble is that Masha brother is pretty big joker, just like Masha herself (as you know), and when judge ask him please to explain why he been doing such automobile speculating business, he say he been doing it to help solve the plumber problem.

Judge is pretty puzzled by this and also intrigued, so he ask him, 'Please explain what is the plumber problem?' And Masha brother start telling some long story about what is happening to people when they trying to order new Moskvich car from state monopole dealer.

According to this story, lucky purchaser of new Moskvich go to the salesman, pay up his money and ask when his car going to be delivered. Salesman tell him in two years' time. So purchaser say thank you and start leaving, but then he turn back and say, 'You know which week, two year from now, new car is arriving?'

Salesman checks up and tell him it is two year to exact week from now.

So purchaser say thank you, start off again but turn back: 'Is it possible you tell me what day of a week, two year from now, car going to arrive?'

Salesman check again and say it is exactly two year from this week, on Thursday.

Purchaser say thank you and once again starting to leave. Halfway through the door, he hesitate, turn back and walk up to salesman. 'Sorry for being very much troubling, but you know if that is two year from now on Thursday, in morning or in afternoon?'

Salesman look through his papers yet one more time and say it will be in afternoon, two year from now, on Thursday.

'That is a relief!' say the purchaser. 'Because the plumber is coming in the morning.'

Well, this joke is pretty funny and pretty accurate too and some people in court start laughing, which is real annoying that judge, because instead of letting Masha brother go free, he condemn him to one year in the labour camp with hard regime.

This is harsh punishment!

But Masha brother later say it is worth it just for satisfaction of scandalizing judge and Soviet court, which I am finding pretty strange, although Masha seem to agree with her brother opinion.

I am only finding out later why these two are acting and thinking in this way, namely they both pretty disgusted with the whole Soviet system owing to one previous event in family history, connecting with they father.

Before Great Patriotic War, it seem this father been a peasant on some Soviet collective farm and not causing trouble to no one. But then, in year of 1937, which – maybe you not knowing – is most terrible year of purging in our country's history, his family is getting woke in middle of the night by loud knocking on the door. In USSR, loud knocking in middle of the night mean only one thing, namely visit from NKVD, which in fact it is. Masha father is bit sleepy, of course, but when he look out his window and see large black truck with engine running, he know for sure this is the *black raven* come for him (in case you don't know, black ravens is those special prison wagons used by competent organs when they going around their business arresting enemies of the people).

So those NKVD guys produce the arresting warrant for Stepun Karlovich Shlyapnik, listing pretty serious charge of anti-Soviet slander and treason, and they asking which person here answering to that name.

Well, Masha father just start laughing when he hear this, because that Shlyapnik fellow been dead for maybe three years, maybe four, ever since he been falling head first into the mechanized threshing machine, and since then his hut been taken over by Masha family.

So Masha father explain all this to NKVD and they looking pretty perplexed by such unexpected developing. Problem is that time is now nearly 4 a.m. and these guys are coming to end of their shift with only two criminal elements been arrested and sitting in back of the black raven, which mean they still at least one criminal element short of necessary quota. So NKVD boss man start thinking and, infortunate for Masha father, reaches pretty ingenious solution to this irking bureaucracy problem, namely they just going to arrest him anyway.

Hmm.

Masha father is not laughing any more by now, but despite his strong protesting and also protesting of his wife (Masha and her brother age only one and three at this time, so they not really protesting but just crying a lot because they got woke up in middle of the night), he got to gather up the small bundle of cloths and possessions and jump into NKVD black raven along with other criminal elements.

Ookhty, bookhty! This is real bad outcome for Masha family, and especially infortunate because it all happening in 1937.

How come?

Because 1937 is when NKVD Order 00447 start operating.

You not knowing what is Order 00447? Order 00447 is good news for all NKVD guys.

But real bad news for criminals, former kulaks and other anti-Soviet elements, because from now on there is no need of bringing these fellows to trial any more and it is OK for them to get judged by special new NKVD troika system, meaning just three guys from competent organs having a chat and deciding what to do with them. And actually these NKVD guys are all pretty busy so they are making up the special simplified system to speed things along and get home to family hearth quick as possible, namely they just picking which category each prisoner going into: category one meaning death by shooting, or category two meaning gulag. NKVD sure don't have time for all that stuff like hearing evidence and arguments and so forth.

Which is real infortunate for Masha father, because two month later, when he meet his troika guys in Vitebsk, he start off saying that Stepun Karlovich Shlyapnik been dead three years and I am certainly not this fellow or engaging in any anti-Soviet slandering but just being a peasant and working in the fields.

But these NKVD fellows are pretty smart and they heard all this stuff hundred of times before, so they adjourn for consultation – meaning some vodka glasses – and come back to announce the good news, namely Masha father fortunately got put in category two, meaning he just got to do ten years in a gulag.

Infortunately, Masha father is not so very happy with this and not realizing his bread actually buttered pretty well, so he start complaining and calling those competent organs whole lot of slanderous names, which is having real negative consequences for him and also for Masha mother.

Masha mother?

Oh yes!

Because those NKVD guys are getting so annoyed by this ungrateful behaving that they suddenly remember one other NKVD Order, number 00486.

You want to know about Order 00486?

Order 00486 say that in cases of particular gravity, which clearly being the case here, not only criminal element himself got to be repressed, but also family of criminal got to suffer same repressing too.

So net result is not only Masha father get sent to a gulag, but Masha mother also making the trip with him.

And, sad for relating, neither of them ever coming back again to Vitebsk; maybe they settling down happy in Siberia after sentences all finished, or maybe for some other reason, I don't know.

But whatever is causing of this, Masha and her brother both growing up orphans and I guess this is explanation why they both feeling pretty bad about Soviet system in general.

Well, now that I understand Masha views on Soviet reality, I am resolving to tell her my secrets too, namely I am also unhappy in this reality owing to my father being Lord Edenby-Gore and consequently I got to get out of here at any costs and go to England where my only happiness is.

Masha is looking pretty surprised when she find out her boyfriend is an English Lord and asking me lots of questions about my mother and so forth. In addition, she look pretty sad when I recount her my plans for leaving USSR, and I think this is because she is fond of me and not wanting me to go away from her. But since this is 1950s, however, and there not seeming very much chance for anyone going anywhere, I guess she figure this is only hypotheticated possibility anyway and not too much problem in a near future, so she is cheering up somewhat.

Well, many pages are now being torn off the *bloknot* calendars and whole piles of pages – meaning whole calendars and therefore whole years – disappearing pretty fast. *Bloknot* for 1956 been finished long ago; also for 1957, 1958 and nearly 1959 as well. And in all those years, ever since I learn about my

English Lord father, I am always pining for going to London, but not really seeing any way to do this, which is highly increasing my *toska* and also *toska* of my mother.

For all these years, she been teaching me English in preparing for my triumphant arriving in England, and by now my speaking and writing the language of my ancestors is getting extremely pretty good.

For one thing, I been reading all those secret books with little penguins out of my mother trunk, which are turning out such as Jane Austen and Anthony Trollope and Charles Kingsley and Dorothy L. Sayers *Unpleasantness at Bellona Club* and Agatha Christie *Mysterious Affair at Styles* and so forth, and they been giving me the pretty accurate picture of life in London, with highly cultured and handsome aristocrats always attending great balls in carriages and horse-racing and wearing top hat and jewels and beautiful cloths and discussing beauty of music and art and not really noticing when underclasses are sending little children up their dirty chimneys.

And this seem so marvellous life to me that I am constant dreaming of going there, but all the same time, infortunately, living in real miserable life of Soviet *kommunalkas* and kolkhozes, suffering from bossy babushkas and dirty quarrelling drunken *muzhik* neighbours and such like, making my dream of happiness in England seem even more beautiful, but even more impossible.

Year of 1959 is drawing towards closing time and unusual things are start happening in Soviet Union and also happening in my life. As for concerning Soviet Union, main event generating the big excitement is launch of first ever Sputnik to travel round the moon, to great pride and joy of General Secretary Nikita.

Like all Soviet peoples, I am sitting with my mother in front of wireless set listening to Radio Moscow, and what we are hearing? Electronical music of celebrated Soviet composer Vyacheslav Mescherin, sounding like blip-blippity-blip but actually making the stirring tune of workers' anthem, 'Internationale', beaming direct from Sputnik to all peoples of earth, moon and elsewhere in whole universe, urging immediate arising up in final struggle for freedom and 'a better world's in birth, you slaves no more in thrall, the earth shall rise on new foundation: we have been naught, we shall be all'.

Hmm.

Meanwhile down here on earth I am turning to eighteen at last, Masha is twenty-three and I am still in love with her.

Time is come for moving out from my mother apartment.

I am sad to go, of course; mother also sad. But I tell that I will be coming often to see her even though I am moving into kolkhoz hut with Masha and now becoming that girl's life partner for henceforward.

And it turn out that Masha and me is pretty happy there in that hut. She still working on the collective farm, still being very beautiful girl with golden brown skin and Russian blondeness, but also developing her painting talent which I been mentioning to you. Now her pictures often getting selected for hanging in dining and recreation halls of kolkhoz and one picture even get hanged in local Raikom council headquarter, which is high socialist compliment, although Masha is pretty much laughing about Raikom people and all their stupid party affairs.

As for concerning me, I am now studying for entry exams into Vitebsk Polytechnical Institute for being the engineering student. Main reason is that this is safest way of prolonging my English learning, seeing as engineers get allowed the language studying for assimilating capitalistic knowledge of technology areas where USSR is not yet leading the world (even though not any such areas existing whatsoever) and also for postponing call up for compulsory conscripting to army, since students in national importance subjects get the reprieve of all this militarism which is not appealing to me very much in a slightest.

By the way, this remind me that Vova (in case you forgot him, he is that boy which been breaking up my leg and denouncing me and also having his Pa, old Mr Smirnov, boss of local kolkhoz, where Masha now working, and candidate member of Vitebsk Region Raikom), Vova also managing to avoid a military conscripting due to becoming the good footballer.

How this can be?

I explain.

In Soviet Union those days, sport is real big deal of national prestige, so best players in regional leagues all getting recruited and offered chance of playing for army instead of fighting for them.

In 1959 Vova is now age eighteen, like me, and been recruited by CSKA Moscow (which, in case you forgot, is initials standing for Central Sporting Club of Red Army). So he been moving house to Soviet capital where he become pretty famous as right-winger (footballing, not political of course) and get highly evaluated by manager, football fans and many pretty *devushkas* in Moscow and whole of USSR.

Aargh!

This is real upsetting story.

In my viewpoint, it should be me doing all this footballing success, not Vova. Because of him, I been losing my chance of training to become international footballing genius.

So while Vova been hitting big times in Moscow, I been hitting low points in Vitebsk.

But I tell you one thing, whenever I get the real bad *toska* about all this, I am always reminding me that I am the English Lord and Vova is not. So whatever he been achieving, like playing for the team I should be playing for and getting high adulation from everybody especially including pretty *devushkas*, this is nothing in comparing to what I one day will be.

In meantimes, I am living the obscure life in obscure hut on Vitebsk kolkhoz and waiting and planning for final struggle of a better world in birth (we have been naught, we shall be all etc.). And all this time, I am loving Masha, Masha loving me, and also teaching me to paint. Maybe you remember I been learning some artistic stuff before, but comparing to Masha I am actually looking pretty hopeless and she is looking like extreme great painter of the future.

All her teachers say she got the top talent and better keep practising, because one day she is sure becoming Artist Laureate of Soviet Union and winning Lenin Prizes and so forth (Stalin Prizes been ditched by new Kremlin fellow, by the way, and we not having any Nikita prizes yet, although maybe we going to soon, who knows).

But something I notice, Masha paintings are pretty unusual and individualistic, just like herself. For a starting, they all resembling to avant-garde, no red banners, sometimes looking pretty abstract and even little bit Formalist (uh-oh) and often depicting sex, which is completely banned in USSR, like you know. But, one thing for sure, she is real expert painter and very smart with drafting and drawing.

And soon this going to be important in my own story.

How come?

Because, strange to say, it turn out that Masha is holding key to reclaiming my noble birthright.

Soon I tell you about this.

But first, I must relate very unpleasant episode concerning my mother and old babushka, Mrs Deneikin.

Ever since my mother got fired from working on kolkhoz back three year ago and got sent to *kommunalka* apartment, she been having the pretty tough time. She got no regular employing any more so she got to take any available jobs, such as washing cloths, doing ironing, cleaning apartments and such.

Most annoying is how other *kommunalka* people all treating her, namely calling her social parasite who been thrown out of kolkhoz, and also bourgeois remnant on account of having piano and books and speaking English (even though she been keeping this pretty secret) and therefore maybe also enemy of the people and so forth.

And who are ringing leaders for this campaign?

Old babushkas, of course, and especially Mrs Deneikin.

And why they are doing this?

Maybe because they feel jealous to my mother and me; maybe because that is just how they like to live life; or maybe because Masha and me got them angry from all that disrespecting and joke telling I been mentioning. Who knows? Whatever is a reason, they are constant slandering over my mother and eventually old Deneikin is finding golden chance for do her down. This golden chance is resulting from disappearing piece of meat out of *kommunalka* kitchen.

For understanding this, you got to know some things, including that kitchen in such buildings is always communal shared place where different families all leave their own foods and everyone supposed of trusting each others, so stealing any such food is actually the pretty big crime.

One evening my mother is coming to me and Masha hut on kolkhoz looking real worried and upset. When I ask what is a matter, she is telling that those babushkas all accusing her of stealing this meat and there going to be *kommunalka* people's court session on following Sunday, with all tenants gathering for hearing accusations and pronounce the people's righteous judgment.

This is pretty hard thing for any son to see his mother in such state of sorriness.

First, it is sad for her. But for son, it is revelation of things all changing in life, namely in the past it been a parent looking after a child and appear infallible to him, but now things are reversing themselves and that parent is becoming the little infant depending on his help and protection. Life don't look too certain any more.

Anyway, I am comforting my mother and promise to come to *kommunalka* trial on Sunday, which actually transpiring to be big mistake . . .

When I arrive there, Mrs Deneikin already giving her evidence, which is turning out mainly olfactory observations of her own nose, namely that she been smelling very strong odour of roast beefs coming out my mother's room just after that meat been stolen, whereas it is established fact that Tatiana Gorevich is bankrupt social parasite not ever affording meat, therefore she must be the thief.

Some neighbours are questioning this, but Mrs Deneikin is staring them so fierce in the face that they soon shut up and it look like the judgement going badly for my mother. So I conclude I better step in pretty quick and therefore stand up at the kitchen table and explain why it cannot be my mother who is thief, for reason that she is woman of top noble character with highest values and principles and never stooping to take other people's foods even if she is starving to death.

But Mrs Deneikin is looking at me real calm while I saying all this, and I am sensing she got something in ready waiting to take out her sleeve.

I am right.

So soon I stop talking, this old babushka is smirking and smiling and say, 'If Tatiana Gorevich really is such great paragon, how come she always getting fired from places, such as from kolkhoz and before that from fancy translating job in Moscow?'

Well, this last thing is big surprise for me because I been thinking nobody know anything about my mother working in Moscow. But old Deneikin obviously been doing her house-work, namely she been prying into my mother's past and seem like she found out some stuff which is better unfound out.

When I look at my mother, I see she is melting of shame and also signalling me to stop defending her because she don't want no more revelations coming out from that sly babushka.

But old Deneikin not finished yet, because next she is telling how she know that Tatiana Gorevich been personally fired by Comrade Stalin for incompetent translating during Great Patriotic War and got to come home and work on Vitebsk kolkhoz with the black mark under her name and then she even got fired out of that job too, and all this been reliably informed by boss of the kolkhoz and candidate member of Vitebsk Regional Raikom, Comrade Smirnov, so how anybody can think this woman is innocent, comrades? and for sure she must be thief of that meat, no doubting whatsoever.

I am getting pretty confused now, because so much stuff is news to me and I start saying something to that old babushka, but quick as the flash she start revenging on me and Masha too, telling how we been overheard circulating anti-Soviet propaganda in form of slanderous joking and storytelling in public places and maybe everyone better go right away and report this to KGB (which now been replacing those NKVD fellows we previous been hearing about) and I can see my mother signalling me to sit down and be quiet and I am getting pretty alarmed because things all in a spiral out of control, but also getting real angry now, so I am just about to start some vigorous polemicizing when my mother gets up on her feet and says very calm and clear, but real quiet: 'All right. Please cease arguing, everybody. I wish to acknowledge I am a person who been taking that meat and therefore prepared to accept a judgement and punishing by this court. Sorry.' And suddenly there is silence in that room and everybody looking at my mother and – fortunate for me and Masha – forgetting all about reporting us two to KGB.

And then old babushka Deneikin get on her feet and make a triumphant announcing of guilty verdict and proposing people's punishment consisting of Tatiana Gorevich got to clean whole *kommunalka* on voluntary unpaid basis for next twelve months and also carry out trash from all apartments to communal dumpster for same period of time. And even though this is crazy severe punishment out of all proportioning with offences and even though it mean my mother going to lose main source of her revenue income, she just say 'I accept' and run out from that kitchen looking humiliated and sad and into her room, where she lock the door and refuse to open it even though I keep knocking and pleading her.

It is three days before my mother agree to talk, and she is looking so disconsolated I cannot bear to ask if she really did steal that meat or if she just been confessing in order for protect me and Masha.

From now, of course, life in that *kommunalka* going to be like hellishness on earth for my mother, because everybody for sure be shunning her and making existence miserable. And she is suffering so much and so ashamed and hurt that I am in despair of ever seeing her happy again. She just keep repeating that no happiness is available for her in this place and in this Soviet reality, and only chance now is for escape from here and regain our true position in that better world we all been hearing about for some time now.

And I am feeling pretty similar, partly because I am suffering for my mother behalf and partly because these latest incidents been making me see how cursed from cruelty and injustice is this life we all living in this world.

One problem, though, all this is starting to be real weightful burden for me, because it pretty clear I am the person expected to make all things come right and avenge all injustices by forging the triumphant path out of Soviet reality and into that other beautiful world, because this is now the only way to rescue my mother, rescue me and put right all those wrongs we been suffering at hand of capricious fates.

And for being frank, I just can't see no way of doing this.

So this is period when my mother and me start getting that very bad *toska* I been mentioning.

We are talking and talking but not actually getting anywhere.

For changing over subjects I enquire her about those Moscow incidents mentioned by old Mrs Deneikin and if it true that she been fired off from the Kremlin and she say, 'Yes, that is true little son, but it not like that old babushka been suggesting.'

And my mother tell me the whole tale of this episode which is pretty strange and involve the new English ambassador, name of Archibald Clark-Kerr, who been replacing that inunderstandable Belfast fellow back when my mother been translating and interpreting during Patriotic War.

It seem this new fellow is also somewhat difficult for understanding, not this time in regard of his accent, but mainly because he is pretty darn clever and always writing things in peculiar ways nobody can figure out, not exactly in code but using many strange unusual expressions to give our translators the big headache when they intercept cables from Sir Clark-Kerr back to Sir Churchill in London.

One particular cable been causing everybody problems and my mother say she still can't figure it out. She go to her secret trunk and hand me out one sheet of paper, with top secret following text on it, which I am still keeping here in my pocket even now so many years later:

From Sir Archibald Clark-Kerr, HM Ambassador,
HM Embassy, Moscow.
To Lord Pembroke, The Foreign Office, London.
My dear Reggie,

In these dark days man tends to look for little shafts of light that spill from heaven. My days are probably darker than yours and I need, my God I do, all the light I can get. But I am a decent fellow and I do not want to be mean and selfish about what little brightness is shed upon me from time to time. So I propose to share with you a tiny flash that has illuminated my sombre life and tell you that God has given me a new Turkish colleague whose card tells me that his name is Mustapha Kunt.

We all feel like that, Reggie, now and then, especially when spring is upon us, but few of us would dare to put it on our cards. It takes a Turk to do that.

Sir Archibald Clark-Kerr,
HM Ambassador.

Well, I keep reading this cable and even though my English pretty darn good, like you already been witnessing, I am complete at the losses for understanding what it is talking about.

So I ask my mother what it all mean and she say she got no idea either, and basically that is whole problem.

Back in old Kremlin days, these sort of clever messages been going backwards and forthwards whole time in between English embassy and London Foreign Office, and soon Comrade Stalin gets convinced that some kind of secret plotting is going on with hidden meanings we are not figuring out whatsoever.

In consequence, Great Leader becoming pretty angry with Pavlov, chief interpreter fellow, who keep telling that he cannot translate anything or explain what such messages are about. So when this latest cable get intercepted, Pavlov figures he better protect his own interests and cleverly decide on passing over to my mother to do the translating and presenting to Comrade Stalin.

Uh-oh!

My mother feeling pretty anxious about this whole affair which is not foreboding her anything good. And when Great Leader summon her for translate and explain, she is so nervous she cannot answer even a simplest question and consequently he start drawing some conclusions on his own about what this cable is meaning, such as it must be containing personal slur on himself and on Soviet Union and maybe even portending some plot of assassination or such.

By now, of course, my mother is so terrified she cannot make any sensible remark whatsoever, and she got no idea what Great Leader is talking about, except suddenly he is picking up special red telephone and shouting, 'Lavrenty Pavlovich, I am ordering immediate arrest of Mr Kunt!'

Later that evening, my mother is talking to boss Pavlov and he ask her what been transpiring. Pavlov seem pretty merry that he evaded himself from wrath of Great Leader and also drinking several vodka glasses, so when my mother tell about Comrade

Stalin telephone call, he is laughing out loud and not caring at all about the fate of that poor Kunt. He even start recalling some jokes about similar Stalin episodes, such as time when Great Leader been receiving delegation of Armenian Communists in his office and, after they all leaving, he is unable for locate his pipe so he call Comrade Beria to find out if anyone from that delegation been taking it. After half hour, Stalin is finding his pipe under the table and call Beria to let delegation go, but Beria tell him: 'I am sorry, Comrade Leader: one half of them already admit they took your pipe and other half died during questioning.'

Well, Pavlov is laughing out very loud at this own joke, but my mother remaining pretty glum and also highly fearing some bad consequences of that day events.

And she is right to do so, because it soon transpiring that after intensive interrogation – meaning he got beaten up and some fingers broke – Mr Kunt been declared innocent of any crime and Kremlin having to make him official apologies, also telling him that his arrest been a result of administrative error for which one junior interpreter already been disciplined and dismissed from her job.

So there you are.

This is true story of my mother career in Moscow and how it been ending with infortunate return to Vitebsk and local kolkhoz, where you remember we been starting this whole thing some time ago by appearance of big black crow and old kulak Finkelstein with the very big gun.

Anyway, now you are learning about these strange events, I guess you maybe saying to yourselves they are all highly peculiar and highly improbable.

Well, I got to agree with you.

Real extraordinary things sure are happening in this world. Not very often, maybe, but for certain they do happen.

By now I am starting to feel like old Russian *bohatyr* hero Ilya Muromets at outset of his famous *podvig* adventures when he know he got to slay several hundred enemies, giants, lions, ogres, monsters and suchlike in order for attaining a glory and maybe some fair hand of *prekrasnaya dama* (meaning very beautiful, but also very unattainable lady).

In alternative words, I am feeling under the big pressure.

I am remembering vision of Mavra wisewoman, who been telling how Lord Gore is pretty sick and maybe even dying. This thought is buzzing in my head every day and every hour and making a strong urgency of finding my father before he die. I got to find some way out of Vitebsk and into London pretty darn quick.

To London! To London!

But how I can do it?

You remember I been telling that Masha is holding a key to this? Soon you going to see it turning out.

But first you got to know something about news events of these years we are talking of, namely ending of 1950s and starting 1960s.

First, the sportive news.

1960 is real big year for Soviet football.

Why?

Because ours are winning first ever organized Championship of Europe, being held in France, so proving that ours is top fellows and USSR is greatest country in whole continent.

Molodtsy! Molodtsy! Molodtsy!

Just one problem arising during this tournament, though,

connected with well-knowed fascist dictator, Franco of Spain, who is refusing his team to play against USSR and withdrawing them in protest at us being workers' state, people's democracy and home of world revolution.

And just one mystery also, being strange absence of Soviet Union top centre-forward, Eduard Streltsov, who is sudden disappearing from football field and also from public life altogether. No one know what been happening to this poor fellow, but I promise if you come with me to very end of this story, you be learning truth behind this mystery.

Now, the space news.

I been telling you already about famous Soviet Sputnik going round the moon back at end of 1959. Well, plenty more of these been following on behind, and next year new fellow in a Washington white house, name of John Kennedy, is asking our fellow Nikita if he like to have a space racing, and Nikita say OK.

And this is part of loving and hating relations in between these two, involving good stuff and real bad stuff over next few years. Such as when Nikita last been in New York he been borrowing somebody shoe for banging on a desk (due to him not ever taking off his own shoe in public owing to strong foot odours). And now he been visiting US cornfields and say how we Russians going to show you Americans Kuzma's mother (don't worry too much about this), and also telling how Soviet Union going to bury you, which is somewhat of misunderstanding actually, due to Sukhodrev (new translator fellow coming in after Pavlov gone) making the bad interpreting, but which sure got you Yankis pretty darn worried nonetheless.

Then in 1961, USSR is scoring big space racing victory because Hero of Soviet Union and very handsome fellow, Yuri Gagarin, is blasting off into orbits before any American can do it, and him and Nikita both riding through Moscow in the big black ZiL and appearing in the Red Square, looking very pleased by themselves.

Back down here on earth again, I am turning to twenty, still studying those engineering and English faculties in order for keep postponing military serving, still worrying about my mother, and still getting real desperate of finding the way to England and escape from all this reality before it is too late.

Well, guess what?

One night Masha coming home from the artistic class and say me, 'By the way, Zhenya, big new art competition being announced by CPSU and going to start up pretty soon.'

What this competition is?

Turns out it is some new attempt by Nikita for showing Mr JFK and other capitalistic fellows that Soviet people all darn happy with their socialist lots and you Westerners better get used to this because you grandchildren going to be living under Communism, not ours living under capitalism and so forth.

So Nikita big plan is for getting hundreds of ordinary Soviet folks, mainly youngsters and workers and *komsomoltsy*, painting the beautiful happy scenes of their lives and then these all going to get judged and top efforts hanging in Soviet embassies and cultural centres round the world so bourgeois classes can see what they all been missing by never instituting socialism in they own countries.

This is great idea, I suppose.

But when Masha tell me she going to be entering that competition, I am somewhat laughing, because her paintings not precisely conforming to required rosy tinting vision of shining future, but actually looking somewhat strange and abstract and bilious.

But she is determined lady, like you know, and for several

weeks she is attending special lecture and demonstrations where they explain what theme these paintings got to illustrate in order for entering in first round of judging, namely regional competition for Vitebsk Oblast area.

And it turn out this theme going to be 'Great Lenin and glorious fraternal countries', meaning places like People Republic of Poland, German Democratical Republic and so forth.

Well, Masha is painting away and I am not turning much if any attention to this because I got the other things in my mind. But I can see she is making the real big effort because her painting is not in usual abstracting style with colours all splashed and mixed up together, but actually look just like that kind of stuff they actually wanting, being real recognizable picture of Vladimir Ilyich meeting German revolutionary Rosa Luxemburg in Berlin and preparing for world revolution.

One evening when painting is nearly finished, I ask how come she been expending such big Stakhanovite effort and she say because of prize being offered by CPSU, namely top young painters get taken on the special trip to Soviet embassy where their picture going to be hanged.

Well, now my interest starting to arouse.

I ask Masha where this embassy can be and is it confining only to fraternal countries in forementioned painting theme, but she say No, fraternal theme is just for first round and winners then required for producing further painting on choice of themes such as Lenin in Zurich, Lenin in Paris, Lenin in Munich, Lenin in London . . .

Ookh!

At mention of London my heart is leaping all its beats and vision of the future happiness surging up before me.

London! Here is my chance! Destiny come knocking at my door and everything now coming clear.

Much for Masha surprise, I am straightaway seeking out my own painting equipments and erecting up my easel next by hers.

That evening I cannot sleep. I am not even going to bed, but continue with painting right through night-time hours in the marvellous creating frenzy, seizing the moment of high inspiration and completing the beautiful painting of immortal Vladimir in Warsaw with Nadezhda Krupskaya, his beloved wife and companion, meeting the Polish social-revolutionaries and pointing out a path of socialistic future for all Polish lands.

This masterpiece going to take me to London and my father!

Next morning, my cloths all covered in paints and I am exhausted by artistic exerting, but so happy of producing this work of art to send me to fulfil my destination in England. Such is the moment of swellful emotion and dreams finally coming true that I awake Masha to show off my masterpiece.

And when I do, she open up her beautiful eyes and I embrace her with the tender kiss of triumph.

And show her my painting. And ask her for assessment.

And already I am tasting sweet fruits of the vindication when she look at my painting and say, 'This is rubbish, Zhenya.'

Oh.

With such cruel stroke all my dreams are crashing away and descending from peak of Parnass Mount to furrow of despair.

How this can be?

Here was the golden chance for going London, presented me direct by hands of fate. This was preordained thing. Yet now it is snatching away from me as result of hopeless incompetence with a painting brush.

I see Masha is right: this effort is not winning any artistic tournament whatsoever, even if judges all been selected from Vitebsk Institute for Blindness.

What a disappointing is here.

For several next days, I am sinking into the gloom. Masha is trying to cheer me up, but I keep reflecting how I missed my unique opportunity to make sense in my life, my one and only chance of redeeming wrong things which been blighting my existence. I cannot smile or find any cheer up at all.

And when she see this, Masha is making the bold resolution, very secret from me but destined for come to my aid. For three days, she is spending whole time working on her own painting of Lenin and Rosa Luxemburg, which really is full of genius and artistic meriting.

And on fourth day she take my hand and ask me to approach and see a completed article.

She tell me to close my eyes, and when I open them up, she show me the magnificent painting of Lenin and wife Krupskaya with German Marxist revolutionaries in Berlin . . . very beautiful socialist masterpiece.

And on this painting, is not Masha signature . . . but mine, Zhenya Gorevich!

Masha been loving me so much that she agree to give me her own painting to enter that competition and withdraw her own self out of it.

I am kissing her and hug her and thank her with deepness of gratitude.

Now my hopes all flying again. And with correct cause.

Because at ceremonial judging in main hall of Vitebsk Raikom party headquarter, my painting (well, you know) is getting highly evaluated and I am triumphantly selected for entry in Republic-wide finals of whole Byelorussia, being held next month in Minsk. The judges are highly praising my artistic skill, although pointing out that Lenin and Krupskaya never actually been meeting with Rosa Luxemburg in Berlin, but this is OK because of socialist ideological veracity of such artistic concept (message is that you allowed to use your imagination for socialistic purposes, but not for any other ones of course).

So next step now is to prepare new painting for grand final round of competition in Minsk. And, just like Masha been recounting, specified themes for this are including Lenin in London, which I tell her she now got to get painting.

As you understand, I am very exciting. I am visiting Vitebsk library and historical museum to find out what stuff Great Lenin been doing in London in 1902, and it seem he largely been visiting reading room of a British Museum, travelling on top of London double-deckers (being special type of horse-power bus they been having in those days) and also stirring up world revolution. So I decide best thing is for Masha to get painting immortal Vladimir on top storey of bus to Bloomsbury with large hammer and sickle on the knee.

And Masha is beginning this task.

One evening, though, when we are talking together, she ask what is my intention if I actually win trip to England and I get very excited explaining how I will be finding my father and reintegrating into bosoms of the Edenby-Gores and becoming pretty important English Lord myself, with own house in London and Rolls Royce car and servants and so forth.

Masha is grazing on me quietly for some minutes.

Then she look very serious and say, 'Well, I better get back to painting for you, Zhenya. And for improve the concentrating, I am taking my easel into privacy of hay barn.'

And that is exactly what she does.

*

For next three weeks, Masha spend every evening after kolkhoz labours in seclusion of our hay barn and never let me see what masterpiece she is creating for me.

And even when picture is finished and day of judgement arrive and we are travelling on *elektrichka* train to Minsk, she always keeping it secret wrapped in the large piece of sacking cloth.

When we get to Minsk, we got to hand over my picture together with twelve other finalist painters and they all get taken to Great Hall of Soviets.

At three o'clock when judgement is scheduled for commencing, all thirteen art works get put on the easels in that great hall, but all covered up with the special red velvet drapings in order they can be spectacular unveiled one after one.

And we all got to stand by our paintings and await for judges coming around, which mean I never actually seen my own painting and only going to glimpse it for very first time when it get unveiled. But I know Masha is high artistic talent and I am waiting with big exciting as judges start progressing round that room.

First paintings unveiled are all pretty good and showing things like Great Lenin in London meeting English revolutionary workers, or Vladimir Ilyich in London writing home to wife Krupskaya in Moscow, or immortal Lenin in London visit Karl Marx grave in the High Gate and so forth.

And then, with great flourishing, judges come arriving at my canvas and throw off the velvet cover to reveal large oil painting of . . . a haystack! And not just ordinary haystack, but haystack with two pair of naked legs extruding out of it, one pair very hairy and belonging to a man, and other pair wearing black silk stocking and belonging to a lady!

And – *Oozhas! Oozhas!* – these pair of legs are intertwining each others and making the very passionate sex!

I am covering with embarrassment. All those judges are shaking off their fists and shouting very loud, 'What for a *bezobraziye* is this!' (meaning very ugly and shameful thing, like you remember).

And I cannot answer them because it not me been painting that picture, like you know.

And judges all shouting, 'Who legs these are?'

But I cannot say.

In fact, Masha is only one remaining calm in that whole room, and I hear she answer them with the little smirk: 'These are Trotsky legs.'

So judges ask, 'And who legs these are?'

And Masha is smirking bit more and say, 'These are Lenin wife Krupskaya legs.'

And when they hear this, those judges all whipping into righteous fury of socialist indignation and all yelling together: 'And where is Great Lenin?'

And Masha burst into the very loud laughing and reply them, 'Lenin in London of course!'

Well, you imagine this is complete nightmare, and pretty soon violence is breaking up in that hall and Masha and me got to flee from enraged mob of indignant socialists, and only stop for breathing when we already jumped onto *elektrichka* out of Minsk station and back to Vitebsk.

And I ask Masha why in name of a devil she been doing such thing to me and ensuring that I never win art competition and never go to London to fulfil my destination?

And Masha just reply she figured that if I win and go to England, I will never come back to Vitebsk and she never see me ever again.

And whole way back home on that train, we don't say one single word more to each others.

Now time is reaching turnabout point in my life. On the one hands, I understand that Masha been doing such terrible thing because she love me and not want me to leave her and go off to London. But on the others, she also certainly knowing that getting to London is most important aim of my whole life, so sabotaging this is real cruellest thing she can ever do to me.

For couple of days after returning from Minsk debacle, we are continuing life together in that kolkhoz hut as seemingly things all normal and no one ever mention what we both reflecting over in our minds or even talking about any important stuffs at all except maybe like weather or harvest and such.

But after one week, I am packing up my baggage and departing. Because I just cannot stay there.

And when I knock on my mother door in that horrible *kommunalka*, I know I am making the real big decision for future of my life. For the one thing, if I been opting to stay with Masha, this will mean end to whole dream of escaping from Soviet reality, whole dream of attaining other, better world. It will mean just resigning to material world right here, maybe marry Masha, have few childrens and get some job earning money to buy bread and vodka and herrings.

Yes, herrings.

But going departing will mean farewell to such easy life of simple Soviet fellow forever, and hello to future of seeking, quest and tribulatings, all in hope of uncertain better reward.

So moving back with my mother is pretty tough decision.

She been growing real upset and also little bit strange while I been away, what with losing her job and friends, and with babushkas making her the constant misery. Moving in with this little bit flaky mother and her constant expecting me to set out on some heroic *podvig* to win redeeming in London is no picnicking.

After couple of weeks, I hear from the mutual friend that Masha want me to return, and I am very tempting to do so and give up any idea of *bohatyr* type quest.

I tell this mutual friend that if Masha come and ask me direct to return home, then I will do so straightaways.

But Masha is not coming, which is no great surprising to me due to her being so fiery and proud, as you already understand.

In fact, when I reflect about it, that girl is real odd mixture of joyfulness, sorrowful and craziness of laughing, like as if she always hating Soviet reality but also wanting someone to come and tell her that life is such, so she better just accept things and get on with it.

And I guess I am not the right guy for doing this. So both of us sit in our little corners, waiting for other one to call out.

But no one is calling out.

And that is last time I ever see Masha in my life.

PART TWO

Maybe you think I am crazy. Maybe I am crazy. But some-times when you get a summons to *podvig* quest in life, you just got to answer it. And in 1961, at age of twenty, that is my big problem: how in name of a devil I am going to answer this summons?

You can guess how that disaster *byeda* of art competition been leaving me the shell shock, and for some long while I am just lying in bed and convincing that my only chances now gone forever.

But soon I starting think again and making new plans.

And, strange to say, these plans all revolving round big world politics, which in some respect been looking little bit grim at this time, like for instance JFK been trying to invade island Cuba just because it got socialistic fellow in charge who is friendly with our Nikita, and also invading Vietnam and other places; while we been making some trouble for those Yankis and English in Berlin and so forth.

But one thing I been noticing about old Nikita, namely that even though he always attacking those capitalist fellows, often with pretty rude words and bumpy sayings (like showing them Kuzma's mother as you remember), he is also looking kind of envious at what they been achieving such as washing machine and television set and even dishwasher in every householding.

And later in that year of 1961 something real interesting is happening. *Pravda* and *Izvestiya* front pages are reporting triumphing visit of Soviet hero Marshal Yuri Gagarin to Manchester England where he been meeting some boilermakers (this is kind of strange but true) and getting mobbed by young girls outside of Old Trafford footballing ground.

And in his speech, which for sure been written for him not by him, Yuri is telling those Manchester people about Soviet desire for some cooperating with the West, like maybe one day our Soviet spaceship can be landing on the moon and disembark scientists from GB and USA. And he also telling how his own spacecraft been containing just one cosmonaut (namely his self), but actually 7,000 Soviet scientists, workers and engineers 'just like you' been decorated for working on it, which is provoking the stormy applause from that crowd of boilermakers.

In a result of this Sputnik and Gagarin fevers, many Soviet firms are exhibiting at famous Earl Court exposing centre in London and finding all their ordering books filled up just inside a few days.

Well, this is good news for Soviet Union, good news for East and West cooperating, and also giving me idea of good news for me, Zhenya Gorevich, namely brand-new strategy emerging in my brain and this time not relying on any Masha help for fulfilling it.

What is new strategy?

Very first thing when studies start up again after summer vacation of 1961, I am going to my Vitebsk engineering faculty and make the complete list of all courses having to do with aeronautical engineering, and especially with supersonic flying technology.

You want to know why I been doing this?

Aha!

It is because I been making real clever deduction about

international developings, namely that English fellows, and also French, just been announcing they going to produce world first ever supersonic passenger jet craft, which is called by a name of Concord.

Like most young fellows, I been thinking this is pretty cool thing and sure to be path to a future. And then I am thinking, hmm, that future also got to include Soviet Union, right?

Old Nikita already been pretty fed up about all those dish-washers and TV sets, so he sure don't want supersonic jet craft being added to list of USSR being second best.

And, guess what? I am right.

Soviet scientists straightaways getting interested in copying those Western fellows' ideas.

And also guess what? how exactly they going to be copying British and French?

Answer: only by someone going over there and observing.

So why that someone will not be me, Zhenya?

Oh yes!

If Nikita is hoping for catch up and overtake the West, he going to need some young Soviet engineers learning about Western inventings and secret developings and so forth.

So in following months, I am making sure to enrol for all supersonic options of Polytechnical Institute, also being real good student, constant raising up the hand with answer of lecturer question, hanging round after class for further expose my knowledge of supersonic vessels, writing extra theory paper for impress professors, and mentioning how good I am speaking English, so if ever Nikita is looking for supersonic engineering student to send on *komandirovka* to England university, he absolutely not got to look any much further.

And it turn out this is pretty good strategy, because in spring of 1962 Soviet engineering cadres are starting secret work on socialist response to capitalist Concord vessel, later being given not too original name of Konkordski.

After all that racing in space, it seem we going to have a racing in passenger jets, too. And this look like big chance for Zhenya Gorevich, who been getting pretty specialized in knowledge of Mach One, Mach Two and so on.

Already I am plotting for future *komandirovka* to England in connections with such flight technology (*komandirovka* by the way being pretty much only way Soviet citizens are allowed to travel to West in those days and meaning official state business posting decided about by Party and government), and at end of 1962 Technology Research Directorate of Aeronautical Engineering Division of Soviet Academy of Science is circulating information form to all final year student of flight engineering having the good knowledge of supersonic flight technology to apply for special research programme in Moscow.

Quick as supersonic jetliner, I am applying for one place on this programme and all my professors are real happy to apprehend recommendation endorsement.

And things look like they working out in correct direction because pretty soon I get the notification that student Yevgeny Gorevich been selected for supersonic flight technology programme and just got to forward attestation of academic record, Party affiliation and certificate of good Communist morals from local Raikom council.

Things looking pretty hunky and dory!

Next stop London!

Or so I been thinking.

Except that once again, things is about to get undone by unforeseen stumbling stone, this time taking shape of Vitebsk Party Raikom and one particular fellow you probably remember from previous episodes in this tale (or maybe you not remember him if you all belonging to those sort of readers who always skipping over large chunkings of story in order for faster terminating and getting more time down in village tavern drinking vodka and eating herrings for disguising alcohol fragrances so that wife and mother-in-law cannot notice anything when you come returning home real late at night with no verisimilitudinous explanation of prior movements and little bit unsteady on you legs, but don't delude yourself because those wives and mother-in-law know for sure what you been doing despite of eating every single herring in whole of Baltic Sea and Sea of Azov combined, OK?).

Right.

So for benefiting you guys, name of this stumbling stone is old man Smirnov.

You remembering now?

He is that kolkhoz chairman fellow, candidate member of Vitebsk Raikom and Pa of Vova Smirnov, sneaky guy who been doing me down and breaking up my leg.

Well, it seem this Pa Smirnov been continuing the good work because now he become chairman and boss of whole Raikom and very influencing man in this town, and guess what? it is old Pa Smirnov I got to go and see in order for receiving aforementioned certificate of Communist morality.

What a bad luck this is! Because if I don't get no good behaviour certificate, then I can't get internal passport, which everyone needing in those days if they want to travel in between Soviet cities and regions, and especially necessary if they want go to Moscow.

And, no surprise at all, my interview with Comrade Smirnov going real badly.

When I arrive, he is making out all friendly and joshing to me and even start repeating that fatal joke which been causing big denouncing scandal so many year ago, namely 'What is difference in between capitalism and Communism?' but then he smirking at me and say, 'But of course, I not need tell you the answer of this, do I, Comrade Yevgeny, since I guess you remembering this joke real well all on yourself', and he make the little smile like he saying 'This is great pleasure for me having a chance to revenge myself on you, little Zhenya.'

First he is taking opportunity to ask how my mother and me enjoying life in a *kommunalka* and expressing hope that rat infesting problem not been causing us too much trouble. Then he is speaking at substantial length about many achievements of son Vova, who now playing regular games as right-winger for top football team CSKA, which currently occupying leading position in All-Union Soviet league, and how Vova so much enjoying life in capital city, which is very beautiful place and full of shops supplying luxury goods such as sausage of first category that is always unfindable here in Vitebsk and very rare even in Minsk.

And old Smirnov is telling how Vova often inviting him and Mrs Smirnov for visit to Moscow and how much they both enjoying this and maybe it be nice if I Zhenya go see old schoolfriend Vova in his luxury apartment there, but oh! I just been forgetting, you not having any internal passport are you, comrade? So let me see, you come here asking me to sign a certificate of good Communist morality ... OK, let me have little look at you file, comrade ... ah, but what is these remarks I seeing in here? Some report from KGB fellows in Minsk regarding art competition and, what this? – haystack ... pairs of legs ... and Krupskaya ...! Well, comrade, you got to excuse me, but this don't look much like any good morality behaving, does it? So, regretfully I got to refuse this request for certifying and you better just get used to living here in old

Vitebsk and get some job like janitor or trash collector or road mender maybe. Good luck to you, young Zhenya. Please close door in departing.

Aaargh!

This is not the outcome I been desiring, but it sure is one I been fearing.

That evening when I am sitting at home with my mother in our *kommunalka* and drinking some Georgian tea with extra sugar for nerve calming purposes, I am beginning to conclude this is complete end of my any hopes for getting out this place.

And if this is true, I am real worried for my mother, who been getting pretty strange recently and behaving real gloomy. What will be her fate if we never getting reunited with lost Lord Gore, her true love and my father?

Answer is unclear and extreme alarming.

And just then, out of corner of my ear, I seem to hear the big black crow making noisy pecking at our very dirty windows pane, which my mother never bothering to wash nowaday. But when I look up, it turn out as being those big black rats that Smirnov been referring to, clattering across our very dirty wooden floorboards.

And that night all my nightmares are dreaming back to me again, including hoardings of black rats and black crows and black ravens, and Lord Gore in black tuxedo and tails with black shirt and collar and sharp black beak in a place of his nose and also swarmings of wasps attacking and stinging me.

So when I awake in the morning, it is clear to me that now is time for resolute unprecedented actions if ever I am going to carry out the great *podvig* quest. Otherwise I will remain here forever, my mother will enter depths of hopelessness and I sink under gloom of responsibility for so many unfulfilled dreams.

I am asking myself, what would great folk hero Ilya Muromets do at such a time before setting off on his *podvig* quest with Prince Vladimir Red Sun to combat Solovey-Razboynik, monster living deep in Chornye Gryazi forests of Kiev and possessing a scream more piercing than a wolf's howl, more fearful than a bear's roar, more blood-chilling than a snake's hiss and so terrible that leaves wither on the trees, sandstorms blow like a hurricane and anyone hearing it dies from the instant and horrible death?

But answer to this question is not actually all that helpful really, because Ilya Muromets is superhuman *bohatyr*, living in ancient *byliny* folk tales and got the supernatural powers at his disposal which I do not got. Infortunately.

What I do got, though, is *blat*.

You not knowing what is *blat*?

Well, this show you are not inhabitant of Soviet reality, because all inhabitants of Soviet reality got to know what is *blat*.

Blat is ancient Soviet tradition of corrupting, bribery and influencing very central to whole way of doing things in a glorious socialist state. *Blat* mean if you got enough smartness, money or friends in useful location, you can usually get most things that been seeming complete impossible only very short time previous, like for instance I been telling you about those old-time kulaks who been expelled from Gerasimovka village but later getting completely forged pardons for returning out of exile from corrupt father of young martyr boy Pavlik Morozov (if you don't remembering this, then I know for sure you all belonging to those vodka and herring types who been skipping big chunkings of reading and therefore I not going to help you with any further remindings whatsoever in future: you all on you own now, so too bad).

What is point of this recounting?

Point is that if those kulaks can get *blat* permissions for escaping out of exile, then for sure I Zhenya can get some little internal passport which I need and which old Pa Smirnov been treacherous denying me!

Answer is I just got to use some *blat*.

Problem is I don't got too much influence or money or high located friends.

But where there is willingness there is also wayfulness, like they say. And by now I am becoming pretty determined fellow and also pretty desperate, by the way.

So that morning I am directing myself toward offices of local Party printing works, which is located on far side of Vitebsk near to that apartment house where Mr Abel been living (I not even going to ask if you remembering Mr Abel: I already told you – you all on you own now).

And I am on my own too, because when I arrive at those printing works, I not got the single idea of what I going to do.

So I go round to back entrance (you know that one where big Kamaz trucks always getting loaded up with piles of Party edicts and agitprop leaflets), and go inside of loading yard acting all sort of nonchalance.

Sitting by gas pump where it say No Smoking, two young lads are having the cigarette.

I walk up and say *Privyet rebyata!* How things are?' and they just look to me and say '*Normalno. Ty otkuda?*' which is roughly meaning 'Who hell you are?'

Hmm. Not very promiseful start.

So I am rapid thinking on the toes and begin looking very frowning and pointing at that No Smoking sign like I am someone pretty important and they better watch out if they not wanting any serious consequences to be flowing.

And such is psychology of fear back in those days that this is doing the tricks. Those lads are sharply extinguishing the

smoking materials and become more respectful by calling me
'*Vy*' instead of unpolite '*Ty*', and I am quickly pressing on
advantage by giving firm instruction to take me at once to chief
printer.

Well, this chief printer fellow turn out to be mousey little
guy, maybe forty year, with thin white face, thin mouth, thin
moustache and very thick glasses like as if too much of doing
something been making him go blind.

And clue to what exactly this something can be is hanging
right there behind his desk in shape of smudgingly printed
pictures of some *traktoristka* girls lying in a wheats field with
nicely shaped and very naked bosom.

Now this kind of thing is pretty rare in those old days, since
page three of *Pravda* and *Izvestiya* usually devoted to minutes of
Central Committee and Politburo or such like, so I am quick as
a flash drawing conclusions about this fellow's life interests, and
making tactical opening remark such as, 'Those pictures you
got there looking real nice, comrade. Pity they all printed so
smudging.' And this fellow look at me and start weighing me
up and down and probably concluding I am also printer too
and got similar interests like him, so he say, 'That is true.
Problem is no one got any right inks nowsaday and these Soviet
machinery all pretty crap and only any good for printing little
marriage certificate or residence permit and such . . .'

Whoa!

When I hear this, I am thinking I sure come to a right place
here, so I say him, 'What if maybe I get you some real high
class pornography material, comrade? That be interesting to
you?'

And I see it sure is interesting him, but he is not wanting to
admit this in case of me being some professional speculator
fellow looking for the big money payment, so he say, 'Maybe.

But I am just simple printer, comrade, and unable of paying for fancy pictures that coming from Finland or any stuff like that.'

But I say, 'Do not worry. I am not wanting any money for this material. Just some little favour from you . . .'

And within couple of minutes we been concluding the real typical Soviet *blat* affair, namely I bring him that aforemention pornography material following day at 6 p.m., while printing plant taking the break in between shifts and all Party supervisors gone out eating borsch and pelmeny, and he provide me with one internal passport certification, printed on official blank, completed with name of Yevgeny Gorevich and signed by his printer fellow brother who is actually pretty experienced in forging signature of Raikom chairman, Comrade Yu. A. Smirnov.

Well, this is real satisfactory deal for all parties, but maybe you thinking 'Where in a devil Zhenya going to get this high class pornography material in order for fulfilling his part of a bargain?'

Do not worry!

Next day I am arriving at that factory with large object tied up in the piece of sacking cloth, collecting my new internal passport and then unwrapping that parcel to reveal extreme beautiful oil painting of haystack with two pair of naked legs making the very passionate sex!

My printer friend is real happy; likewise me too. I am putting my precious passport document in the inside pocket and running very excited all a way home to *kommunalka* on other side of Vitebsk.

At last, my strategy is working out and next stop look like Moscow, even if not yet London!

That evening, when I am sitting with my mother and telling that I am soon departing for capital city, she look pretty sad.

But when I explain her that only reason I am going to Moscow is to embark on a quest for her lost love and my lost father, she is cheering up little bit and telling how she will always be waiting here in this *kommunalka* and always hoping I am coming back to collect her one day and take her with me to beautiful new life in other, better world.

And I say, 'OK, Ma, do not worry, that sure is what I am doing.' But actually I am secret thinking this is pretty tough task she been setting me and perhaps it never be coming true at all.

After celebrating Christmas of 1962 – maybe final Christmas at home, who knows? – I am packing up my baggage one more time and preparing for walk to Vitebsk rail station and catching early morning *elektrichka* to Smolensk.

My mother been saying she going to come with me to rail station, but at last minute she say, 'Actually, you better go by your own, little son, and I just stay sitting here by my own at home.'

And during all months and years which are coming afterward, I am always recalling this last picture of my mother telling how she going to stay sitting at home, and I am constant imagining her always there on that broken chair on those dirty floorboards under that dirty windows pane and crying every night when she is thinking about her son and her lost husband many hundreds of versts away from her and who knows what they becoming or what they became?

Life is such, of course; I know this is true. But still I am thinking this is all pretty cruel, and getting the *toska* real bad every time I reflect about it.

That day I been walking to the rail station all by my own

and feeling pretty sad that this is last time I will see Vitebsk for long long time. And even though for sure it is dirty boring provincial hole, still I know I am going to miss it.

When I get to ticket office, I am showing my new internal passport, all filled in with official approved journey itinerary to Smolensk and then Moscow, and clerk is looking at it and smiling somewhat, like maybe he been seeing such similar printing before and maybe even recognizing who exactly been signing old man Smirnov's signature for him, but still he accept to take it, and stamp it up with official stamp of Soviet railway and issue me with the hard class category seat (meaning cheap and incomfortable) all the way to great capital city of Soviet empire.

Well, it is big swellful emotional moment for me when I get on that train and pretty soon I am seeing my future opening up before me like some vision of the very large map with little locomotive train chuggling along a line of railway tracks through vast wheat fields, across broad rivers and big cities until arriving at a final destination looking like the Waterloo Station of London and I am seeing Englishmen all with top and bowler hattings and I am filled up with excitement . . . but then I wake up and hear some old train guard shouting, 'Smolensk! Smolensk! Everybody change here for next Moscow train!'

Oh well.

It not before 2 a.m. on a following morning that I arrive in Moscow. And in case any of you not knowing this, arriving in Moscow in middle of a very snowing, slushing and winding winter night with not any place to go to is pretty difficult experience for a young fellow who hardly ever been outside Vitebsk in the whole life.

By that time, Byelorusski Station is full up with Moscow

night people, meaning mainly drunk fellows trying to sleep somewhere dry, but pretty soon militias are coming and throw everybody, including me, Zhenya, into street.

If you ever been at Byelorusski Station, you sure to remember that big square outside it with garden containing statue of some Byelorussian poet fellow and OK for sleeping in, but only when no snowing and winding is going on. When things is wet and cold, only place to go is that underpassing which you know, where Butyrski Val Road is going beneath Gorky Street. Down there is out of rain and snow, although not much space, so everybody huddling together on narrow sidewalk and try to get little bit of sleeping done.

But, uh-oh, soon coming to the dawn time. And also beginning of morning traffic going through that underpassing, which is real infortunate because roadway now full of the dirty slushy puddles and so soon as a first Kamaz truck go rumbling past, we all get soaked by the heavy shower of water. Some experienced night peoples got the technique of sleeping through all this, but not me.

So I decide I better get out of there, which is causing grumbling and swearing from fellow sleepers being disturbed by me.

And when I pick up my suitcase, which is usual Soviet manufacture and therefore made of cardboard, so much water been splashing on it during the night that whole one side and also bottom been disintegrating and all socks and undercloths are falling out in the large puddle where they get immediate runned over by next passing Kamaz.

Aargh!

This is not the introducing to Moscow I been dreaming about.

And, sad to recount, it is by far not the worst blow befalling me that day.

When I gathered up my cloths, I am setting off for Leninsky Prospekt No. 14 which, like you know, is headquarter of renowned Soviet Academy of Science.

But when I get there and ring on a bell of those famous old gates, I guess my appearance is looking pretty bedragged, because two uniform militiamans are coming out and strongly suggest me to get lost and go back to vodka drinking and stop bothering their professors and learned folk.

But I am pointing out they error and also showing official invitation from academy aeronautical department (pretty wet and dirty but still readable), and they both grunting and grumbling little bit, but agreeing to telephone main reception people who indicate for let me in.

At main reception there is usual Soviet pantomime about 'You come at wrong time' or 'Professor NN who dealing with this affair gone out of town and not returning for three months' and so forth.

But do not worry. This not so dramatic like it maybe seeming; because all Soviet people used to such approach and therefore knowing how to deal with it.

So I am just sitting there and say, 'OK, I wait here for whatever long is necessary, three month, four month or maybe even seven.' And guess what? just half hour later, necessary person is entering, asking for inspect my documents and telling me to wait while he check things out.

Then I am sitting there for one other hour, which is only pair of nothingness in Soviet waiting scales, and not too worrying.

But after two hours I am still hearing no information and

therefore becoming somewhat anxious and asking secretary girl who sitting there what is going on, but she just shrug off her shoulders and carry on eating sunflower seeds and splitting out the shells in a trash can.

After three hours, I am getting pretty alarming and also hear some worrying conversation going on behind a closed door of neighbouring office. Actually, this only one end of a conversation because person is speaking on telephone, but I am hearing real distinct words such as 'Yevgeny Gorevich', 'internal passport', 'Vitebsk Raikom chairman', 'forgery document' and . . . uh-oh, looking like time for me to get exiting! So I am standing up and smiling to secretary girl, who still not desisting from eating sunflowers, when in burst that necessary person I been meeting three hours ago, followed by same two militiamans from guard post at front gate.

Whoa!

This is tricky moment and demanding some rapid thinking, which is leading me to three concludings: one, it is not propitious moment for waiting and explain affairs; two, it is not time for gathering up that cardboard suitcase with sock and undercloths; and three, get running out of there, Zhenya, right now and fast like a devil taking your hindmosts! And that exactly what I am doing.

And not stopping till I reach that scruffy little park you probably know, halfway down Leninsky Prospekt, where I throw myself onto first wooden bench which is coming to hand and panting and sweating and holding on the head by the hands and then hear some voice coming from under the bench and it say, '*Ekh, ty!* You in pretty bad state. Have some vodka,' and I say, 'For sure. Give me bottle.'

And, you know what? six hours later that park is looking real beautiful like the green tropical oasis, I am feeling happy again and night is starting to fall. And lucky for me, I got a new comrade, who is turning out to have name of Igor Ivanovich, and he show me very best way for making real comfortable tent, namely take several leafy branch off neighbouring trees, drape over seat of the park bench and crawl underneath.

At midnight, this is seeming to me like some romantic fragrant palace.

At 6 a.m. it all wet and freezing and full of dogshit.

And strangely I cannot move and cannot feel any ends of the arms and legs.

So I say to new comrade, 'Ivanovich, you sure that is vodka you been giving me?' And he say kind of sheepish, 'Yeah, or maybe I started the paint stripper by a time you arrive here . . .'

Hmm.

It is middle of afternoon before Ivanovich and me can get out from under that bench, after being kicked by several dozen of babushkas and pissed on by even more number of stray mongrels, leading to my happy mood being evaporated just like those end dreggings of liquid (whatever it is) in Ivanovich bottle.

And big problems now looming. Namely I don't have no suitcase, no cloths, no place for staying, no job at Academy of Science or any elsewhere, and by now I am looking and smelling exact like inveterated Moscow tramp and complete inextinguishable from new comrade Igor Ivanovich. In summing, this is not ideal situation.

Any more nights under park bench or sleeping at Byelorusski Station are pretty inpalatable prospective, in addition to far removing from my real stations in life. This is January 1963 and snows that falling now belong to a worst winter for real long time.

All afternoon, I am seeking some strategy for extricating my predicament. But even though I rake up all my brains, no solution emerging whatsoever. As for friend Ivanovich, he is planning the pleasant evening at a tramp soirée with degustation of aftershaves and meths de cologne, but I am politely refusing this invitation and wandering off by my own.

After some couple hours walking, nearly at evening time, I find myself in a different large gardens, this one named of Petrovsky Park, with a large brick building in the middle resembling old-fashion merchant palace from former Tsar times, but when I arrive at the gate I see it is actually famous Zhukov Academy of Soviet Air Force. Which by strange coincidence is exact place where my Vitebsk professors been telling me top Soviet engineers all working on ideologically correct socialist fighter jet and hydrogen bombings and so forth.

Well, if you believing in the destiny, believe in it now!

Because this sure must be hand of fate specially leading me to this place. What a marvellous chance occurring, perhaps seeming little bit like some fiction novel where unusual happenings are determining unfolding of the plot in real unexpectable directions and reader start thinking 'Hmm, maybe this is *too* much of the coinciding' but actually I can tell you such things really do happen in life and for sure they always shaping our ends.

(Anyway, that is my point of view and it up to you to believe this latest developing or not. But since this is true story, and since it me who is recounting events, it mean I am the one in charge of veracity considerations, not you. OK?)

So there I am, real luckily, standing at famous gate of Zhukov Air Force Academy, and recalling that in addition to all those supersonic aeronautics I been studying in Vitebsk, I also – very very luckily – been learning everything about advanced military engineering and nuclear physics too!

And this further fortunate coinciding is leading to whole new brilliant strategy emerging in my brain, namely immediate applying for research job at this very Academy, with consequent strong prospect of future *komandirovka* to England!

Ah-ha! Now you understand why all this coinciding been happening, and maybe also seeing how future of Zhenya story-telling going to be unfolding.

Well, sorry again, but actually you all completely wrong.

Because before I can bring this fore-mentioned plotting into life, certain incidents are happening with result that I am never setting any feets inside that Zhukov Academy ever in my life.

Instead, I am suddenly finding myself swept up and carried off in the very large crowd of peoples, which is appearing out of a swirling snowstorm and rapidly advancing through that park while making extreme loud noise of shouting and cheering.

Whoa! One more unexpected developing, taking even me by a surprise – you too?

And what is this crowd?

I have no ideas.

I am being very jostled by those fellows and strongly pushed along their chosen directions so I am complete unable of making any sensible conversing to them whatsoever.

Pretty soon these human masses are coming to edge of Petrovsky Park and starting to cross very wide busy road, which is transpiring as famous Leningradsky Prospekt (on complete different side of Moscow from that Leninsky Prospekt we been talking about earlier, so please do not be confusing them).

And so soon they start crossing, everyone begin chanting something that sound like 'This is only over turnoff!' but after listening for several times I realize they actually chanting, 'There is only Vova Smirnov!'

Aargh and double aargh!

Even here in middle of Moscow, hundreds of versts away from Vitebsk, it seem those Smirnovs still chasing me and haunting me. With such crazy noise going around my ears, I am desperate trying to understand why these people all chanting for some little fellow from down in Byelorussia, when we arrive in sight of very large footballing ground with floodlightings all illuminated and I realize, with strong sickness in stomach pits, this got to be CSKA stadium and these people all football fans chanting name of my eternal rival, denouncer and archy type nemesis!

It mean Vova Smirnov is here! He about to be playing big time match.

And I am not!

My whole life is looking sick.

I am getting swept into stadium with those crowds, following one group of lads who are jumping over some couple of walls and therefore entering by not paying, and once inside, we all quick dispersing around the tribunes for avoid getting spotted by militias, and I find myself in front row right behind the goal postings.

Well, this is turning out to be CSKA crucial league encounter with big enemy rivals Dinamo Moscow (they got their stadium just on other side of Leningradsky Prospekt, like you know, right next of that Petrovsky Park I previous been standing in) and it is transpiring to be pretty exciting game between two powerful selections.

In first half timing CSKA are making most attacking, with Vova in vanguard, but not managing to put any ball in the enemy gates.

Then just after intermittal, advantage is switching to Dinamo who rapidly marking two goals and CSKA finding themself striving to make equality.

By ten minutes remaining, they already scored one goal, but needing real big efforts now for one more to make the draw. Vova is leading such efforts.

Last minute is approaching and arbiter is checking up his watch, but Vova is gathering a ball and running clear of all Dinamo defences.

Now he only got Dinamo kipper to beat, but this kipper is great Lev Yashin his self, so not very easy task.

Except, look! – Yashin is diving to incorrect side, and Vova running round him with open gates for scoring.

But at such very moment, all my righteous anger with those sneaking Smirnovs is sudden boiling over. I am standing up in front row right behind Dinamo gateposts and agitating with both of the arms and yelling to Vova, 'You cheating cur, Smirnov. Never I forgive you for all that blight you been putting on my life', and I see Vova spotted me and get so surprised that instead of shooting into Dinamo gates, he actually shooting right into row Ya of upper tier.

Then arbiter is whistling end of time and instead of chanting 'only Vova Smirnov' CSKA crowds now shouting 'what for loads of rubbish' and other such things. Which is bit satisfying for me because, like you know, I still believe it should be me shooting goals, not him. But I am also feeling some stinging by remorse for my action and thinking maybe Vova not such the bad fish after all; maybe he just been young lad under influence of bad-intention parents and maybe he still can be my friend.

Actually, for being frank I got some material consideration for hoping these things, largely because my current predicament situation is leading me to a desperate plan, namely going to find

Vova after end of match and plead him to help me for sake of olden times.

At end of game, I am walking round that stadium to official team door and awaiting exit of CSKA players, but these fellows all being escorted by militia guard who keeping fans away and not allowing me to approach Vova or even shout him.

So what I can do?

I don't got no place for going, nor any bed for sleeping in.

Floodlightings all gone dark by now, so I am just wandering round back of stadium, where they got all those training ground and practice pitch, and lying down by a perimeter fencing.

Despite of snow and coldness, I am falling straight into deep exhausted sleep.

And next thing I know, I am awaking by very hard blow in the buttock region from some flying object which turn out to be leather soccer ball, despatched at me with lethal speediness and accurate.

And, guess what? dispatcher of that ball transpire to be Vova Smirnov, who is now standing over me and laughing real loud.

I am so dazed and surprised that I not even sure what is happening. For some moment it seem I am back on a muddified kolkhoz football ground with my leg all broken up from Vova tackling and he standing over me sneering how he just extracted his righteous revenge.

But this time I see Vova not laughing for revenge. He is laughing because he just whacked my butt with a football, which I guess is pretty funny when you think about it; and maybe he also laughing because he is happy to see his old schoolfriend from back in Vitebsk.

And when I struggle up on my feet, he gives me friendly thump in the stomach and say, 'What a devil you doing in Moscow, Zhenya? You look like some tramp just arriving after big vodka drinking competition in the Gorky Park. And don't go thinking I not been seeing you last night when I been shooting for a goal: it pretty nice of you to be cheering me, but I made the real hashes of that shot. Oh well, it is not always possible to be victorious. Good to see you, old comrade.' And he give me one more thump, which is getting somewhat annoying habit but also indicating he don't hold me in the wrong feelings.

Then loud voice come shouting in our directions, 'Smirnov! What you doing with that dirty tramp fellow? Get back over here and start work.' And I see this is famous coach of CSKA, former Soviet star Konstantin Beskov, who is holding player training session and therefore getting impatient with Vova being absent.

So Vova smile to me and say, 'Come back at six and we go for some drink, OK?' and off he run.

This good news, of course. After all that bad luck I been having, maybe things looking upward now.

Naturally, I am reflecting this is bit strange of Vova being so helpful and welcoming me into Moscow after somewhat straining relations in Vitebsk, but I am certainly not poking in throat of this gift animal (sorry for any confusion in this expression: I not complete certain of authenticity).

I am passing rest of that day pretty relaxed, picking up bit of food from trash can at *pelmeny* stall and hoping for tastier eating that evening with Vova.

And when we do meet up, it seem at last that my fate is working out to the better. For some reason – maybe he pretty lonely here in Moscow and missing old Vitebsk, or maybe he not such the bad guy after all – Vova is transpiring real friendly.

After several vodka glasses in bar of Sportivnaya Hotel, he is getting even friendlier. We are discussing old time schooldays and Vitebsk kolkhoz and all those adventures we been having in soccer team and Young Pioneer and elsewheres, except we never mentioning any broken legs, political jokes, kulaks or denouncing session, seeing as this being real bad taste and probably leading to violent punching-up right there in hotel bar. So whole evening seem flowing with the friendliness in between us, except for somewhere in my drunk brain I always remembering Vova is big soccer star and Zhenya is homeless tramp and this is real unfair and all his fault that things not complete the opposite.

After midnight and some more vodka glasses, we are arriving at the Red Square in middle of snowstorm and singing songs under Kremlin wall when along walks one real fat militiaman dressed in big thick greatcoat and waving his stick in the menacing fashion, 'What you two drunkens doing here with such caterwauling? Don't you know Comrade Khrushchev got whole country to run and don't need you *chornye lyudi* keeping him awake!' (which is not too friendly expressing).

And he already extracting out the handcuffs ready to arrest us, when Vova is reaching in his jacket and pulling out what I expect to be large amount of bribing, but actually turning out as some special pass card which he is showing, pretty in secret, to militia fellow.

Well, this got to be real powerful pass card, because militia guy is suddenly becoming height of respectfulness, including politely propping both us up while waving to nearby Moskvich police car for come and give these two distinguished comrades ride back to their apartment.

And when we arriving there, they all saluting and helping us up a stair and wishing us the pleasant nights. Which is pretty unusual behaving for Soviet militia.

After Vova and me alone in his apartment, I am asking him what such special pass card is denoting, and is it just from being famous footballer?

But no, he start boasting it is much more than that, and not even connected with footballing; and although he is not telling exact what that pass is, I am pretty sure it mean Vova is working for the competent organs, namely in 1963 being KGB.

Next day when I awake with somewhat aching head, Vova already gone out to early training session and I am just sitting there taking the stockings off all that been happening to me, namely that my life story seem to be turning into some sort of *podvig* quest of old time *byliny* folk hero.

While Vova is absent, I am prevailing myself of his apartmental facilities, which are turning out real luxurious, including private inside lavatory, central heating where radiator actually gets warm, and bath with faucets producing hot brown water as well as cold brown water.

I am using Vova shaving razor, toothbrush and tooth powder, sitting in warm bath for over one hour, on lavatory for half-hour, and getting dressed up in some of Vova spare cloths, which he having lots of in his wardrobe.

And by time he is returning home, I already eaten all the *tvorog* in his larder (Nikita not been managing any fridges just yet), all the bread in his basket, five cups of his strongest coffee and I am feeling much better.

Vova seem pretty pleased of seeing me, although pretending he is not recognizing me now I no longer look like the Moscow tramp. Straightaways he say me to put on my coat and again we go out for little drinking, this time also walking up famous Gorky Street to Aragvi restaurant where Stalin always been eating and where only top-up fellows from Party and government getting bookings . . . except that Vova is producing his magic pass card and we immediate get escorted to nice basement table right next to sealed door which old folk say lead to secret tunnel connecting direct with Stalin quarters in Kremlin, although this probably just one more myth, like all those others Russia is full of and no one can tell which one is true and which complete nonsensical (maybe you even noticed some such in my own story up to now: what I can say? – I am Russian fellow).

Anyway, that Georgian food is first category and so also Tsinandali red wine, just like Stalin always been drinking and which we are consuming in *bohatyr*-size quantities and consequent staggering home again through now obligatory snow storming, reaching Vova apartment well after Kremlin bells been climbing midnight in Moscow and dropping straight into sleep without even taking off any cloths.

And in such ways we are falling into pretty pleasing lifestyle pattern which is continuing for many weeks, without him or me ever really notice how this been coming about.

Each morning Vova is going out to trainer session, coming home in evening, going drinking with me every night when there not any football game, and enjoying me being there because he been pretty lonely before, I guess. I am spending most days visiting Moscow, seeing tourism sights and vague thinking what will be next move in that quest which is lying ahead of me.

But certain things starting to intrude in this pleasant life. For instance, I got no official papers for actually being in Moscow.

So after couple months, I ask Vova maybe he can help me get official registered and he is laughing and say sure, that is piece of pie for him, but problem is I also need some job in order to avoid being judged as social parasite (which is what he say I am anyway, although he is pretending this just the little joke).

We are pondering what sort of job I can be doing and this is not so easy question. After misfortune with Academy of Science, no possibility of pursuing further studies or engineering career, and if I am not finding some suitable profession it mean I got to report for military conscripting by end of year. Vova is suggesting few jobs, including footballing, although he is laughing when he mention this one and say I am much too fat slob for such calling, and I have to restrain myself pretty hard from replying it all his fault I am not top footballer and his foul act back in Vitebsk ruin my life, and real anger is bubbling under surface of my cordial relation with him, and – who knows? – probably also under his relation with me, so our living together is somewhat fragile.

Anyway, we decide we better postpone official registering me as Moscow resident, and I just go on being so called shadow person and living 'by the left', which mean not ever being official part of Soviet economy or society, but doing all things secret unofficial and by the *blat*. And Vova carry on food and lodging me, probably because he feeling pretty guilty over the broken leg and denouncing incidents – I hope so.

And this is how things look like continuing.

Except for some big changes which are happening in our lives. First such changes occurring at CSKA and concerning Konstantin Beskov, that trainer fellow who been calling me tramp when he see me talking to Vova during his practice session. Beskov is CSKA boss man who been recruiting Vova three year earlier from junior Byelorussia league. Vova been his protégé ever since and consequent always getting picked for playing in first team.

But one day Vova is coming home looking pretty glumly and tell me Beskov soon be leaving CSKA. New trainer is being announced, but not anyone Vova is knowing and he therefore feeling pretty worried about future directions of his career. And also no indication what departing Beskov going to do in future either.

Second big changes concern me and relating to one newspaper article I been reading in *Moskovskaya Pravda* about upcoming concert at Moscow Conservatoire by big new star of Soviet piano, name of Vladimir Krainev.

How something such small as piano concert can be changing Zhenya life you maybe asking?

Well, life gets changed by real small things; I already been telling you this.

And concert of Vladimir Krainev is looking like one of them. Because actual reason this fellow becoming such music star in 1963 is that he just been winning big new piano competition . . . in Leeds, England!

OK. Please excuse me, but this time I am not bothering with all that exclaiming stuff we been having on previous occasions (such as I am surprised and excited and making big new scheme for getting to England and so forth). Because I guess you understand pretty well by now what is going on and also what fore-mentioning event is meaning for future directions of this story. You probably also guessing already what strategy is emerging in my brain, especially as you now remembering all those piano lessons I been having with Mr Abel and how good pianist I always been (. . . OK, OK, maybe you *don't* remember, but for sure I am not giving any further damns about this!).

So for cutting short the long story, I go straightaways to Krainev concert at Tchaikovsky Hall of Conservatoire, hang around in corridor for meeting him and I explain him my own piano abilities, how I must get to Leeds competition for finding long-lost aristocrat father, rescue my mother and triumph over banality of reality . . . and can he please help me for doing this?

And he just look at me kind of strange and say, 'Keep practising and maybe one day you can be top pianist', and off he walk into the Moscow night.

Can you understand this?

Maybe.

None of the less, some things are actually happening in consequence of this concert. For a starting, I am asking Vova if I can fetch one old piano into his apartment, which I found in the Moscow flea market and bought for ten rouble, and he just shrug off his shoulders and say OK.

From then onward I am spending most daytimes practising and only going out on few evenings with Vova, who is also pretty busy with footballing affairs now, needing to impress new CSKA coach.

But one good news in middle of 1963, fate of Vova's old trainer Konstantin Beskov is finally being announced, namely he getting appointed as chief trainer of Soviet national team. This is great help to Vova, of course, because now he is dreaming of following same path as Beskov and becoming international star for USSR.

So pretty soon both of us are not drinking quite so much like we used to, Vova because of footballing ambitions and me because I am formulating my new plan, namely for enrolling into graduate music class at Moscow Conservatoire and acquiring status of piano teacher for students there.

Well, part of this plan is coming true, namely I am becoming real good pianist once again and also giving secret music lessons 'by the left', so earning useful amount of roubles for first time since coming to Moscow. But second part of my plan is not coming true, because it turn out you cannot enrol in Conservatoire without having Moscow residing permit. And you cannot get residing permit without having official job position in Moscow: what a viscous circling is this!

So I just remain the shadow person, living by the left and keep practising like Mr Krainev been telling, in hope of becoming such big piano star that one day Soviet Union will be begging me to go as national champion to Leeds, England and next international piano competition in 1966, three years later from now.

Meanwhile, Valentina Tereshkova, very beautiful Junior Soviet Lieutenant, is becoming first woman up in a cosmos, song about her entitling 'Valya my love, you are higher up than the Kremlin . . .' is topping the pops, and I am turning to twenty-two.

And this is moment when I start working on yet one more strategy of getting to England, this time connecting with the chess (real lucky that I been getting so expert at playing chess, like *I* am remembering, when I been young child sick in bed with broken up leg and luckily being tutored by top students from Vitebsk Gymnasium chess society). From reading *Izvestiya* sporting page, I discover that big international chess congress is being held every year at some place called Hasting, on southern shoreline of England and even closer from London and Belgravia than Leeds is.

So, guess what? I am reviving my chess prowessing and becoming real proficient in that field too.

In a meantimes, Vova and me continuing our friendly and not-too-friendly coexistence in his luxury apartment in Moscow Gorky Street (right next of that famous Post Office building where Great Lenin been posting off his socialist manifestos and also maybe birthday cards and so forth) and both of us abiding our times until respective dreams can come true.

For Vova, this is now distinctive possibility since he been scoring dozens of goal for CSKA and also becoming a darling of trainers and fans.

For me, this mean hanging around Moscow Conservatoire getting friendly with students and eventually also with couple of piano professors. These guys are real brilliant musicians, top in whole world. If they are tutoring me, for sure I can become great star and get sent to England.

But how I can achieve this?

I cannot enrol there because of aforemention document deficit.

But do not forget! this is Soviet time and even top genius music guys are not earning too much money . . .

. . . which is pretty helpful affair for me.

Subsidiary problem – I don't actually got any money for offering them, but please remember what I been telling you earlier about *blat* and how that system is working. Main task is to find one piano professor who need something I can supply. And that professor turn up to be real top dog, name of Lev Oborin. Lev Oborin been outstanding Soviet pianist for so many years, friend of great composer Dmitri Shostakovich and professor at Moscow Conservatoire since before Patriotic War. Lucky for me, in 1963 he is about to retire; even luckier for me, he is looking for private students; and luckiest of all, this guy is big football fan! Which is making *blat* dealing real easy for you to imagine and real easy for me to arrange. OK. For every CSKA match, all players – including Vova – getting four complimentary tickets in VIP seats. Vova never using more than one or two tickets and therefore pretty happy for handling over remaining ones to me.

Professor Oborin is real delighted.

Maybe you asking how come these top cultured guys getting so excited about football? Well, do not forget football is culture, too, and greatest composer of twentieth century, Dmitri Shostakovich, is also fully qualifying football referee, writing one whole ballet about football and being biggest soccer fan in USSR, although infortunately supporter of Zenit Leningrad team, who are height of hopeless. For me, this *blat* affair is bringing top piano learning every week and therefore big progress in playing. Lev Oborin is highly evaluating my skills and we get on together just like two burning buildings.

But when I tell Vova, he just look at me and say, 'Who is Lev Oborin? Who is Shostakovich?' But guess what! I just got the phone ring from Konstantin Beskov inviting me to come and try out for Soviet national team!' And he open up the bottle of Moldavian pink champagne, which we soon drinking to the bottom, and then one other one and one other too, meaning that my left-hand fingering turning out pretty sloppy next day when I am trying to play tricky Paganini Étude Transcendante of Liszt.

But Professor Oborin is remaining overall happy with me and after few more lessons he get me playing real hard stuff from composers not using much popularity in Soviet Union of those days such as Busoni, Alkan, Arensky and even decadent guys like Schoenberg. This is official dangerous music and we pretty much got to play it in secretly, but Oborin tell me some stuff about Schoenberg philosophy of music, including his defining of Art, which I been writing down and keeping with me even to this day, namely that 'art is cry for help on part of those who have first-hand experience of fate of humanity. Inside them, within them, the world is stirring and only the echo – work of art – finds its way into outside reality.'

Which is pretty much summing up what my mother been teaching me all those years ago about how Art gets you into different worlds and so forth.

Many more pages are being torn off our *bloknot* calendar and year is turning to 1964. Which is transpiring as big significant year for Vova, for me and also for Nikita.

First for Vova. Ever since he got that telephone ring from Beskov, Vova been making extra special effort for being top footballer and get into USSR national team. Couple of times Beskov been calling him up for training with national squad, but always being kept in reservation and never getting any actual playing. So in 1964 he is pushing for make the breakthrough and finally this is happening on 20 May.

Match taking part on that date is actually pretty unimporting affair, being only some friendly encounter with the Uruguay at Lenin Stadium of Moscow, but do not forget this all happening just one month before upcoming finals of 1964 European Championship and therefore presenting great chance for Vova to impress selectors and get into big times.

First half timing is ending at the nil–nil, but after fifteen minute of second timing, Vova is making fantastic breakaway down right wing and crossing a ball to Eduard Mudrik, Dinamo Moscow player, who gets soaring like the mighty Russian eagle and heading past Uruguay kipper for only scoring of that game.

Vova is coming home real late and somewhat influenced by the alcohol, but in mood of high euphorics and telling that Beskov been assuring him of getting selected if Soviet team are qualifying to Spain for next month European finals.

But he also recounting some other facts that he been learning from new team-mates, not so happy news, concerning strange absence of regular centre-forward, Eduard Streltsov, which I mentioned you earlier. This guy is legend of Soviet football, known in whole world as Russian Pelé and renowned by favourite manoeuvring, which is smart little pass from back of the heel still known even today as 'Streltsov feint'. Well, Vova team-mates been telling him he never got to repeat this, but Streltsov – who Vova been replacing in national squad – is in a gulag!

And when Vova is asking how come, they all shrug off their shoulders and say from some little argument he been having with Soviet authorities, namely they been demanding him to transfer from Torpedo Moscow, which is workers' team, to Dinamo Moscow, which is KGB team, but Streltsov been stubborn refusing to do this.

So, even though this guy been voted top player in USSR and constant member of international team, authorities decide they going to teach him a lesson, namely seven years in the labour camp.

I tell Vova this is real unfair and pretty repressive, but he just say, 'What you can do? Streltsov better been doing that transferring if that what the authorities are demanding.' And then he make the little laugh meaning, 'Get to the real, Zhenya: reality life is tough, so you better just accept it and do anything what get the best results for you self.'

And, actually, this is Vova speciality in life and soon you be seeing how he continue to get those best results, like he always do.

Later that month, Vova get picked for real important game, against Sweden in crucial last qualifier of European Championship. This time, Lenin Stadium is full of 100,000 fanatics and atmosphere is raising up the roof (there is no roof back then, of course, but you understand what I am saying).

Right through first half, Vova is shining bright like a red star and nearly scoring two or three times.

After seventy minutes, it is pretty clear that USSR getting the victory, because we in the lead of three goal to one, but then Vova is falling victim to clumsy tackle by big Swedish defender (although not deliberate like Vova been tackling me all so many years ago) and soon he is feeling the ankle little bit sore for running on.

Back in those day no substituting being allowed, so he got to play on till final whistle-blowing, but he is limping pretty bad by now and Beskov decide he better go top hospital, namely Botkin Clinic, for immediate X-ray.

Well, those X-rays show Vova ankle been broke. And only one month left until European Championship in Spain. No way he going to be fit for playing there.

Over next couple of week, Vova is getting real dejected and also pretty puzzling by such bad luck against him, which he never been used to having in his life.

Only, guess what? this breaking ankle is turning out not as bad luck at all, but actually as very big stroking of usual Vova-style good luck!

How come?

Explanation is connecting with events of European Championship. USSR team is big favourite to win again, just like we been doing in 1960.

And at first things all going well, with easy victory above Denmark and passage into final. But then hand of fate is intervening once more and final is transpiring to be repeat of that controversial match from four year earlier, namely USSR opponents turning out as host nation, Spain.

And this causing panic in Moscow and in Madrid.

Whole world is waiting for Franco to announce another withdrawing of Spanish team in repeat protest against Soviet socialist system, but no: that dictator obviously been doing the calculation and reckon that his fascist boys can triumph in battle of the social orders and therefore sensing handy opportunity of inflicting humiliation on our fellows.

So now it up to Nikita in our Kremlin to decide what to do.

And Nikita being pretty bumptious Ukrainian, like you know, so he just send short telegram to Konstantin Beskov along such lines of, 'Kostya! You show those fascists Kuzma's mother!'

Whoa!

International battle lines are drawing up, and two mighty ideologies preparing for mortal combat on field of foot.

Maybe Vova starting to think his broke ankle is actually better than being in such battles after all. And if he not thinking that now, he sure must be thinking it after that final match is being played.

Because it is complete total disaster for ours.

Date is 21 June 1964, Estadio Bernabéu is record full with 120,000 fanatics and whole world is watching on TV, including me and Vova in communal recreation room of CSKA social club in Moscow and also Nikita who probably got his own private TV room at home in his Kremlin.

First goal is thundershoot from fascist guy name of Jesús María (!) Pereda, but two minutes later socialist attacker Galimzyan Khusainov, little Muslim fellow from Spartak Moscow, is making pretty sharp equalizer with the left foot from a free kicking, and all our CSKA comrades – and also for sure

Nikita – are jumping up and shouting, 'That does for you, fascist hyenas! We sure settled your hashes!' and such like.

Infortunately we all wrong.

Because in second half timing, those hyenas are attacking and attacking. Rain is pouring like out of a bucket and Spanish fellows are all kicking and thumping ours – in particular great Lev Yashin our kipper gets punched on the nose but still performing like his nicked-name of black panther – but eventually even he cannot prevent one more fascist goal, with Spanish attacker Marcelino Martínez stooping low and heading past our Lev six minutes from end of time, and fascism is thus gaining bitter revenge for Communist victories of Stalingrad, Kursk, Berlin and other places.

And worst thing for us, TV coverage is being provided by fascist Spanish television corporation, so straight after final whistle-blowing, cameraman is cutting to dictator Franco and his bloodthirsty clique all celebrating and kissing each other like as if whole socialist world order just been shattered and trampled into a trash can of history.

And our fellows in Ostankino TV headquarter in Moscow are obviously too upset for thinking straight or maybe been having couple of vodka glasses for sorrow drowning purposes, because instead of immediate stopping this transmission and showing a test card with patriotic martial music, they are continuing to broadcast such shameful pictures of fascist revanchist celebration.

Well, Nikita sees this on his private TV and suddenly realizing that triumph of fascism is being beamed through fifteen Soviet republics and eleven time zones to two hundred and fifty million loyal Communists who must be getting pretty irate at seeing such a *bezobraziye* on their screens.

But not as irate as Nikita his self! Because he is personally picking up the special red telephone and yelling down it to head of Soviet television to get this broadcasting suspended at once and also informing him that he has been fired with immediate effect, and without pension.

And even two days later when Konstantin Beskov and USSR team are flying back to Domodedovo Airport in Moscow, Nikita is still not calming down and insistently inviting Beskov and players straight to Kremlin for the man-to-man talking, as result of which a special edict is appearing in name of all-Union Soviet footballing presidium making following categorical declaration: 'In connection with failure of national squad to fulfil its allotted task of defeating Spanish team, and thereby conceding Soviet possession of European Championship trophy through impermissible errors, decision has been taken to immediately relieve Konstantin Ivanovich Beskov from his duty as senior trainer.'

When this news is announced, Vova is reaching straight for vodka bottle. On the one hands, he is pretty relieving at lucky being injured and therefore untarred with any brushings of shameful defeat. But on other hands, his patron saint now been fired from command of national team after Vova only been playing two matches and certainly not established in the squad and who knows who next trainer will be and what he be thinking and who he is selecting?

But if Beskov getting fired is big surprise, even bigger one is soon following: guess who getting fired next?

No, not Vova.

And for sure not me – I not even got any job for firing from.

No, this time it is Nikita getting the firing!

And how this is happening?

In October, Radio Moscow is announcing out of white daylights that Nikita Sergeyevich Khrushchev been removed from post of First Secretary of CPSU and President of Council of Ministers 'due to many hare-brained schemes, half-baked conclusions, and hasty decisions' that he been implementing over past ten years.

Well!

Instead of getting us all TVs and fridges and dishwashers, it now seem Nikita actually been spending most of his time undermining Soviet agriculture, missing production quotas, putting missiles in dangerous locations and cutting Soviet armed forces. Consequently he been summoned back from vacation down in Ukraine and issued with a pension book.

Oh, boy!

One more fellow making big failure of being top boss!

In place of Nikita, Radio Moscow say we now got whole collection of new fellows including Brezhnev, Kosygin, Podgorny, Gromyko and few others, all of them looking like pretty mean, old-style Communists, not being too much in favour of any *ottepel'* thaw or any relaxing in field of artistic freedom and international rapprochement.

So, coming to me now, 1964 is consequently not turning out such a great time for any piano players wanting to get out of USSR and go West, like I been planning under my latest strategy plan.

But fortunately I am stubborn fellow and therefore continuing with the music training, still with old Lev Oborin as tutor. And soon afterward, Soviet Minister of Culture, lady bureaucrat by name of Ekaterina Furtseva, is announcing some piano trials at Hall of Columns in Kremlin, with specified intention to identify top Soviet young pianists for receiving bursaries and maybe also progressing to international competitions, such as Tchaikovsky here in Moscow, Reine Elisabeth in Brussel, Chopin in Warsaw and, most important for me, Leeds in England.

For this event, Professor Oborin is suggesting me to prepare Shostakovich *24 Prelude and Fugues*, which to my ear enshrine whole mental sound world of all our Russian life stories and provide magical spiritual bridge into deep other world of Russian soul, just like Bach *48 Prelude and Fugues* are spiritual bridge into soul of all mankind.

When I arrive at Kremlin on day of piano trials and walk up to Spassky Gate, I am picturing how quarter of century ago my mother been driving up here with Marshal Voroshilov and right into Stalin quarters, with fateful note from a handsome Englishman hidden in her left pocket, and for sure I am feeling her spirit pushing me onward in quest for transcendence, art and glory.

But when I step onto stage and begin playing, in great Hall of Columns where bodies of Lenin and Stalin both been lying in state, I feel another spirit guiding my hand over those notes, not my mother, not Mr Abel, not even Lev Oborin, but spirit of my absented father Lord Gore directing my fingers to fulfil my destiny of coming to England and reunion with him. I feel like Gherman in Pushkin's 'Queen of Spades', staking everything on skill of my hands at this gaming table which is piano keyboard.

At end of my playing, there is some applause and judges are scribbling down notes.

But then, disaster.

Professor Oborin been telling me earlier that he got couple of other students entering these piano trials and one of them playing next after me.

So soon this guy start playing, Beethoven 'Hammerklavier', I know for sure I am dead: he is making the music like angel from Heaven, his fingers breathing with harmony, his soul pouring into Beethoven sound lines and his genius bringing that dead composer right into life in the hall.

After he finish, I am not even waiting for results. I know for sure I can never play like this guy and however much I am practising will make no difference – I can never be great pianist, so my dream is dead. I am leaving Hall of Columns, running back to Vova apartment and drink several vodka bottles without any herring whatsoever.

Next day, article on page four of *Vechernyaya Moskva* is reporting Moscow piano trials been won by young Jewish player from Gorky, name of Vladimir Davidovich Ashkenazy. And at bottom of page is report from Municipal Hygiene Department, announcing that black Siberian crows which been introduced to Moscow under Stalin to control excessive sparrows and rodents have bred to such massive numbers that they now become a plague themselves. So city officials will be shooting them.

Ever since that day I never played piano again.

Even now I am old and living here in this place, I cannot look at a piano without the cold shivering and feeling of deep inadequate failing gnawing on my heart.

After such humiliation, I been feeling more and more desperate and consequent throwing myself into chess strategy, which is now remaining as only route out of Moscow. I already been enrolled in chess school of grandmaster Mikhail Botvinnik (more of usual *blat* dealing, of course, but now being three way *blat* involving Botvinnik granddaughter getting piano tutoring, Oborin nephew getting on trial with CSKA and me getting unofficial chess lessons: such is way that Soviet Union works).

Now I am pouring all my energy into chess practising and becoming pretty good player.

In spring of following year, 1965, preliminary first rounds of USSR Championship are taking place and I am signing up for entering. This time I am competing with young kid of fourteen year old so I pretty sure of going to beat him.

But kid's name is transpiring to be Anatoly Karpov!

After humiliating me in fifteen moves, this boy is playing simultaneous exhibition matches with grandmaster Korchnoi and Spassky and drawing both.

I feel so destroyed I want to climb in the bed, hide under blankets and never come out again.

And that is when Vova, whose ankle all fixed up now, is coming home in big rejoicing mood and telling how new USSR trainer – fellow called Nikolai Morozov – been calling him up and ask him to play in Soviet Union team battling to qualify for next year's World Cup, to be held – can this be true? – in England.

My God!

This cannot be!

How can it be that I, who so desperate need to get to England, will be remaining here in Moscow? And Vova Smirnov, who hardly know where England is, will be going there without me? This is too cruel!

Life is playing its worst bad joke on me. In that very instance, crushing *toska* is seizing me in its grip. Big flapping wings of the black crow are beating round my head and I am yelling and screaming out loud.

I am striking at Vova with mighty blows full of the anger and despair within me, all that rage against Vova who destroyed my leg and destroyed my career and destroyed my life, all that bitter bile of failure that has been growing and consuming my existence for so long. I am hitting, hurting, hitting. Hard knuckle punches rattling off his bones. But for some reason he is not hitting back, only lifting his arm to protect himself, not saying a single thing.

Still I am not stopping. Still I am lashing and shouting and raging.

His face is covered in blood. My fists still flying.

And then, all at once, it is over. My strength is gone; I am sinking to the floor; sobbing in a corner.

Vova is holding his eye, with blood trickling through his fingers. And he just says real quiet, 'I am going out, Zhenya.'

For one hour, maybe two, after Vova left and closed that door, I am sitting there not moving, not even thinking what I have done.

Falling under evil spell of the magician.

Then stirring, as if from deep, deep sleep.

The crow squawking and voices are in my brain.

But now the life around me has become so quiet as if I am listening through many metres of water to a glass smashing in tiny little shards, tinkling like shiny piano notes on a parquet floor.

I am throwing myself into my bed and the depths of my despair.

The crow is circling round my head.

I am watching it, and feel I am spinning, the world is spinning; and who knows where this spinning will take me.

For days, maybe weeks – who knows? – I have no clues where I am lying, what I am doing, or how I am continuing to live. Or who is bringing the food that keeps me alive.

I see things turning from day to night and night to day and day to night again. My life is rushing past me faster than the headlights of oncoming trucks flashing bright and dark, bright and dark, bright and dark between the lampposts of the Moscow ring road at night. And every flash of dark is another night come and gone; every flash of light another day illuminated, doused and flown away for ever.

Always in my head something is burrowing and drilling; always the thought I am lost to the world, I am wasting and my life is ebbing. Plunged in Ilya Muromets' deep sleep of lethargy and weakness. The days are flying off and still I have not begun my quest. Losing the chance of redemption for me and my mother, neglecting the *podvig* which is my only hope of salvation . . .

Time is running out.

But I have no strength.

And always in my brain that old song of the dying soldier comes over and over again . . . '*Chorny voron, shto ty vyoshsya* . . . you black raven, why you flying? . . . *nad moyeju golovoy* . . . circling here above my head . . . *ty dobychi nye dobyoshsya* . . . I'm your prey, you shall not have me . . . *chorny voron* . . . no, black raven, I'm not yours . . . *ya nye tvoy* . . . fly to my home . . . *ty leti* . . . go see my mother . . . *v moyu storonku* . . . tell her, darling raven . . . *chorny voron* . . . that you've seen her dying son . . .'

Toska is circling over me.

Hovering; struggling; between living; and dying.

Someone bringing food; leaving water by my bed.

Who this can be?

After days, maybe weeks, I am floating back up through the green water I have been lying under.

Feeling someone shake my shoulder.

Someone speaks in my ear and says, 'I am going now, Zhenya. You got to look after yourself now, OK?'

I am nodding.

And Vova is walking out the door once more, just like on the day of that great dislocation when I was hitting him with bitter blows and my life crumbled into the abyss. But this time Vova is smiling before he goes out, smiling to me and closing the door real quiet.

Another day, maybe two, before I am rising from that bed, dragging into the kitchen.

In the kitchen, strangely, is food and water.

And a note, it seems, from Vova: 'I am gone Zhenya. Get well. Watch me on TV.'

On TV?

But what TV?

Can I really be back in the world of TV?

Or still in the world of dreaming?

There is no TV in Vova apartment, I know for sure.

I am eating *tvorog* from the larder (still no fridges, and now no Nikita neither), drinking coffee from the pan. And returning.

I have been dead, but now returning.

And Vova?

Did Vova nurse me?

But why?

I hit him.

This is true.

But he broke my leg.

Ah.

And now he says I must watch him on TV.

Why is he on TV?

In a corner of Vova's apartment – a shock – a TV set is standing.

Brand new one.

Elektron.

Latest model; Bakelite not wood.

Brown knobs; beige hessian over loudspeaker.

Thick glass screen bulging outward like the belly of a woman who prepares to bring forth new life.

Impossible.

I turn one brown knob. It clicks.

First, silence.

Then, some crackle.

Hissing.

And the small grey dot that germinates from deep within the screen, expanding into flickering grey images with waving, tearing edges.

Now some sound.

Louder.

A voice.

Shouting.

Shouting to me.

Shouting real loud, but coming from many versts away through thick grey green water.

What the voice is shouting to me?

'Smirnov!'

'A goal!'

'A goal for Smirnov!'

And just like a secular Soviet miracle, I see Vova running out from the blurring grey ectoplasm of that mysterious TV set, waving his arms and preparing to burst into the shuttered room where I am standing, in the dark, dark heart of Moscow.

Then watery grey pictures of many crowded people all standing and waving their arms like grey shadows, looking like seaweed at bottom of the sea.

All swaying together.

And now I understand: these are souls of the dead all waiting in that ectoplasm to be sorted into category one, category two, category three.

Then despatched to a final destination.

Only Vova is alive and running through the grey sea of souls.

And TV voice is yelling, 'Greece one, Soviet Union four. Victory is safe. First qualifying game brings the harvest of two points and we set out on our great quest to England!'

And just as he is saying 'quest to England', I see Vova look right out through that TV screen and give some enigmatic wink, whose meaning is intended only for me.

At the end of time in that distant game, after all my disconcerting days and dislocating weeks, I still cannot tell is Vova my friend or my foe? if he love me or hate me?

If he hate me, how come he been caring for me while I am sick?

If he love me, how come he going to go to England and I am not?

But this last thought is too hard to bear for a single moment. I must banish it from my brain or it will stuff me back in the deep grey-green water of *toska*.

I fear the flap of the crow wing; the black raven circling.

For hours and days I am lying in my bed.

Later, I see that mysterious TV set has disappeared.

Or was it never there?

Did Vova just dream to me?

And this is how I am existing.

Knowing and not knowing, seeing and not seeing, living and not living. Always looking for signs.

If that spider in the bedroom window web eats that fly before a sun goes down, it means I will live. If I am in the lavatory and cannot piss away the specks of dirt from side of the bowl, it means I will die.

The signs are the only true guide to where life is taking me now.

PART THREE

ONE NIGHT, in the very deep dark middle of the night, when terrible dreams seize us and black screaming birds are circling, a sign is waking me from my nightmare. The sign takes the form of banging on my door.

No one been knocking on that door since Vova went away.

I stumble through the dark to open up.

'Citizen Gorevich?'

'Yes.'

It is some broad face man in a leather jacket.

'Yevgeny Gorevich?'

'Yes.'

'Get dressed, mate. You coming with us.'

And this fellow produces his real special pass card that says KGB right across it.

I am protesting and say there been some big mistake because such things like midnight arresting don't happen no more in this year of 1965 and only belong in 1920s and 1930s and maybe in 1940s and perhaps also little bit in early 1950s and now we got new fellows in the Kremlin and not old Joe Stalin any more. But leather jacket is telling me shut up, so I know there not much point in arguing.

Ten minutes later I have collected my toothbrush and bag of cloths from Vova cupboard and being gorilla handled down stairs to where the black raven is waiting.

Once in back of that truck, KGB guys are relaxing somewhat and start making jokes and talk about football, wanting to know is it is true I been living in apartment of famous striker Vova Smirnov, so I say, Yeah, this true, and how come I been arrested like this when I am top friend of Vova Smirnov? And do they not know Vova Smirnov is also member of competent organs same as them? But they just shrug off their shoulders and say they got no idea what my arresting charge will be; their job just to locate correct arresting target and sling in the black raven.

All this time, we are rattling and bumping along in potholes and I am rattling and bumping too, but I know for sure where we are going, namely Lubyanka Square, just past Bolshoi Theatre, round back of Dzerzhinsky statue and into courtyard of that place where people been disappearing without no trace for fifty years.

And this is all so strange, I am not even sure it is really happening. Maybe I am still in bed and all just a part of my nightmare?

Maybe I am still in that long sleep of weakness and lethargy just like Ilya Muromets?

I am trying to waken up, but things are happening real fast now. We arrive in the Lubyanka courtyard and I am being pushed out from that black raven into some reception office where two guys in uniform are registering my name, address, birth date and next of kins and then confiscating lots of stuff such as watch, belt, shoes-lace and so forth. But there is something strange about this place and I am having trouble figuring out what.

Then I realize. Music.

I can barely hear it. But for sure it is there.

Music is coming from radiator pipes, through gaps in the

parquet floor, hovering in between the window panes. Hard to make it out, but this building is playing music.

Leather jacket and other KGB fellows who been arresting me at Vova apartment announce their shift is over now and they got to go home to family hearths, but first they are wishing me good luck and one of them is getting pretty emotional and kiss me on both cheeks till tears appear in his eyes. And those uniform guys behind the reception desk are joining in with some eloquent remarks; and thin little secretary woman from the next office is entering with similar good wishes.

But strange to say, the music I been hearing coming from the building walls is getting louder and these people got to talk louder to make their selves heard, till finally they are nearly shouting.

And then they stop talking and suddenly they are all singing! And what marvellous voices they all got!

Old leather jacket KGB is most lyrical *Heldentenor* I ever heard, singing some aria of love and affection (all in Italian, but strangely I can understand every word). His comrades from black raven are providing him with basso continuo, which is rumbling along and involving some refrain about unhappy lot of a policeman; while the secretary is transpiring to have a very thrilling coloratura soprano, soaring high up to the ceiling rafters and to top C. This ensemble is filling the whole reception office and probably whole of Lubyanka too, because uniform guys are stepping forward with some lines of apology for inter-rupting, but also singing, that *Signor* Gorevich got to come along with them now and everyone else got to leave.

So after couple more exchanges of lyrical emotion, those tenor, coloratura soprano and basses exit through a back door and I am grasped by very cold hands of some uniform jailor fellows and led into the corridor to round of applause from all over Lubyanka, and especially from behind long line of doors leading off this corridor and all got bars and locks on them.

This is getting somewhat puzzling. I want to question these jailors what is lying in store for me.

But when my mouth opens, I realize I too am not talking, but singing. And actually I got a pretty good baritone, which I never been aware of whatsoever before.

I am trying to say stuff like, 'Where you are taking me?' and 'There been real big mistake here', but keeps coming out as, 'You tiny hands all frozen' and *Oh mio babbino caro* and other such nonsense.

And, surprisingly, whatever I sing is immediately picked up by everyone else in that building, including all those prisoners behind closed and locked cell doors, as if some magic choir-master is conducting the whole building in one vast and perfect chorus. But this is strange, because for one thing, how come all these criminals know such arias from Puccini and Verdi?

And how come they all singing in such perfect Italian?

OK, maybe some *zeks* – political prisoners – know such things because they mostly all intellectuals and probably including several members of Bolshoi chorus and even famous conductors and composers. But what about all those crooks and underworld villains from Yugozapadnaya and Timiryazevsky and other such Moscow places? How come they suddenly turning into opera stars?

And just when things cannot get stranger, I am being marched across that big Lubyanka courtyard and guess what? all round me, from hundreds of windows on four walls and six storeys, prisoners all leaning out their cells, gently waving off hundred of arms dressed in identical prison costumes, all

moving exact in rhythm and singing prisoners' chorus from
Fidelio . . . in excellent German!

And then for capping all off, some large patrol of MVD
militiamen is marching toward us, perfect in the step and
perfect intoning 'Chorus of Hebrew Slaves' from *Nabucco*! And
when they get level with us they are doffing off their helmets
and executing couple of synchronized pirouettes before carry on
marching on their way. This is hardly what I been expecting
when KGB come banging on my door to arrest me! In fact, it
somewhat jollier than I been expecting.

Infortunately, though, jailor fellows are now doing their
more usual things, such as throwing me in the deep and dark
dungeon cell with few rats in it and only naked light bulb for
illumination, and slowly those sounds of grand opera start
fading away.

While things are quiet, I try to take stockings off what been
happening to me and what more surprises maybe waiting in the
store. For the one thing, it pretty clear to me that it is Vova
who been tippling off KGB cronies about my forgery document
business: nobody else been knowing of this affair, so I guess it
turning out that Vova is my foe after all and revenging his self
for me shouting and hitting in his apartment before I fell sick,
just like he been doing back on that football field in Vitebsk.

But then I am thinking: if this is so, how come he been
letting me live in his apartment and showing me all that kindness while I been sick?

Soon I am so agitated from thinking that I cannot sleep.
And anyway, such disturbing sounds are coming from neighbouring rooms, including loud thumping and screaming noises,
that I am trying hard *not* to fall asleep just in case such things
being planned for me too.

I am not having long to wait.

Around 4 a.m., key is grating in my door, which is swingeing open with necessary dungeon-like creak, and in walk some uniformed KGB fellow who open up his mouth and start singing 'None Shall Sleep' from *Turandot*, but quickly coughs and clear his throat like he is embarrassed by such inappropriate musicality and instead he growl: 'Wake up you *svoloch*' (not very nice terming) and 'Come with me for special treatment.'

Uh-oh.

This not boding too good, especially in country like great USSR, where special treatment not usually involving the pleasant treats. I been hoping maybe we will waltz down that prison corridor, but no: music stuff seem all finished now infortunately, and instead I get dragged along by two big gorilla types and thrown in some interrogating room where extreme bright light is shining right in my face.

Behind the spotlight I can see outline of some peoples in dark uniforms with roll-up sleeves and green eyeshades looking real menacing in my directions.

And before I can say anything – or even sing anything – these guys all shouting and abusing at me such as, 'So here is *svoloch* Gorevich! Thinks he just come to Moscow and live like some tsar! Thinks he don't need no papers or job or registration document or permission from no one! Maybe he think he better than all us rest; maybe he think Soviet rules not applying to him; maybe he think Soviet reality not good enough for him!'

I am trying to retort something, such as pointing out that not having no residence document is not such serious offence that they got to arrest and torture and beat me up, especially now in year of 1965, but these guys are top professionals at they jobs and they not letting me get any words in by the edge.

Instead, they all making mocking imitation of my protestings and pronouncing me as the bourgeois remnant and people's enemy, and one of them pulling out that forged internal pass-port I been acquiring back in Vitebsk and asking, 'This yours, Gorevich?' and I say, 'Well, maybe so, but for sure this is not such big crime, is it, comrades?'

But interrogator fellow is placing his indexing finger on that document and indicating me to read out one passage just above forged signature of old man Smirnov.

So I start reading out, 'Bearer of this document herewith authorized to travel between town of Vitebsk and city of Moscow, following specified itinerary of . . .' and so forth, when suddenly something strange is happening and printed words of this document all start melting right before my eyes like the dripping black treacle.

And then this treacle is reforming into new and very alarming words which I am reading out with growing forebod-ingness: 'Bearer of this document, citizen Yevgeny Gorevich, hereupon pronouncing guilty of serial disrespect for laws of Soviet reality, and of repeated attempts to escape from fore-mention Soviet reality, and therefore sentenced to supreme punishment, comprising forfeiture of his worldly existence by means of electric prayer, sentence to be carried out with no leaves of appeal.'

Whoa!

This is pretty bad news and real puzzling development of my story.

But wait! because strangeness still continuing to grow.

I see those interrogator fellows are not turning their atten-tion to anything I been saying, but instead they all directing away their heads to some large TV set which no one previously been noticing (including me) in very far corner of that room.

And guess what? this TV set is preparing to broadcast

another football game, this time in between USSR and Denmark. It seem to me this is all much too much of a coinciding and everything now starting to have some not very hidden meaning for me and my future fate. Including that TV is just announcing the two teams and precisely pronouncing name of Soviet captain Valery *Voronin* from Torpedo Moscow.

Which is striking cold fear in my heart!

(You understand why if you been paying attention previously, because you know that Voron is name of raven or crow.)

Omens are looking black for me and I am awaiting for further bad developings. But ever since that moment of being woken by KGB knocking on my door, things just been getting stranger and stranger. So maybe I better not be too surprised that next development is not downwards at all, but actually pretty encouraging!

First, good news is coming from that TV set, namely that Slava Metreveli, Josef Szabo and Eduard Malofeyev are all scoring second half timing goals to make the USSR victory and therefore certainty of qualifying to World Cup finals in England.

And those interrogator fellows behind the spotlight are drinking several beer glasses for celebrating and getting pretty merry, and humanitarian impulses start taking over and making them very expansive in the friendliness and humour department until they all start telling jokes, including one about two footballers with wooden legs which I cannot repeat here as some ladies maybe reading.

And finally when they recall me still here on other side of their spotlight, they are being much more comradely and not calling me *svoloch* any more but actually laughing over my document forgery crimes and saying these are pretty darn serious of course, but they been thinking of some helpful way for getting round them.

And when I ask them what they got in mind, they say they going to offer me a deal. On the one hands, they going to forget all about my anti-Soviet escape attempts and false documenting offences; and on the other hands, I am going to come and do some little bit of work for them.

Well, in case you not aware, this is phenomenon pretty well known to all inhabitants of Soviet reality, namely those competent organ fellows are always finding citizens with couple of minor infringements on their account and then indulging some blackmailing to make them come and cooperate with KGB.

So I am pretty awary of what they proposing.

But these guys carry on talking and getting real persuasive, mainly by some repeated mention of four years in the labour colony with hard regime if I am not agreeing.

At the end, though, it is not the sticking but the carrot which is winning me over, and I got to tell you this particular carrot is pretty tasty and juicy, namely that they heard how I am top guy for English speaking and therefore they proposing special KGB mission for me, involving cover-up story of becoming official Soviet interpreter.

And guess what? this interpreter cover-up involve working with Soviet football team, travelling with them to England and carrying out KGB spying duties during next year World Cup finals!

England! Whoa!

I guess I must be looking pretty taken abackwards by this, because those interrogator fellows are laughing out loudly and nudging each other ribs and pointing at me. And so I am amazed by this developing that I am looking round for someone telling me it is the big joke being played against me.

But no one is telling this.

It seem the hand of fate really is reaching out and making my life dreams come true. I am rubbing out my eyes to be sure I am not dreaming and when I open up again, I see that TV screen has become very large and close to me, and filling up the screen is face of Vova looking real triumphing and giving the large wink of his right eye, and his mouth making the words 'Vo-o-o, Zhenya, vo-o-o!', which is Russian way of saying 'Way to go!'

And those KGB guys are standing up and clapping too and then filing out official contract between Zhenya Gorevich and Soviet state and signing and stamping it and even making me some jokes about how this is much better document than those previous ones I been getting forged down there in little old Byelorussia.

And they tell me where I got to go for collect my special pass with KGB written right across it and also when and where I got to report for interpreting duty at All-Union Soviet football presidium. And I stuff that contract document in my left pocket and go running out of Lubyanka building, past statue of Iron Feliks, past Bolshoi and statue of Karl Marx, past Gosplan building, along Gorky Street past Lenin Post Office and upstairs into Vova apartment.

Oof!

At last I am safe after all those weeks of turmoil and dislocation and madness. I thought my life was finished and my *podvig* quest doomed; I thought I was condemned to live forever in petty realm of Soviet reality, forever exiled from other better world. But suddenly things are looking to the upwards.

And who to thank for this?

Maybe Vova!

Maybe.

Maybe me?

Maybe fate?

Am I really going to that other world? Or just my dislocated nightmare?

Next day, when I arrive at all-Union Soviet football presidium, I am half expecting to get told I am false imposter with no business here.

But no. They are expecting me and show me into office of political adviser (meaning KGB fellow who check that everything hunky and dory with USSR footballing from ideological points of view).

I can see from large size of this office (bigger even than chief trainer Nikolai Morozov office) that he is pretty important big wheeler here. Behind a desk he got the resplending portrait of President Leonid Brezhnev (month is October 1965 and Leonid already decided cult of personality – meaning lots of his portraits, banners saying he is real good guy, poems and novels about him, top awards, decoratings, prizes and etc. – all OK again now, despite being sharply condemned when they previously been applying to Stalin). And sitting on this fellow desk is gold letter nameplate saying 'Mikhail Yu. Smerdyakov, Chief Political Adviser, USSR Football Presidium'.

I introduce me to him and make the friendly smile, but this guy just like some iceberg with complete unscrutable face and frowning brows.

And first thing Smerdyakov say to me: 'So, comrade. Tell me about such *bezobraziye* that been taking place during art competition final in Minsk involving pornography of Trotsky, Krupskaya and haystack.'

Oh boy, this guy going to be real bundles of laughing!

And I am right. Because whole meeting is devoted to him

telling me every bad things he know about me and about my past (which is quite a lot actually, and some of them I not even been knowing myself), about my mother and about Masha (seem she been involved with dissident samizdats and social undesirables since I been leaving her in Vitebsk) and pointing out how all this is directly my fault and I am reprehensible individual, complete unworthy of belonging to competent organs and will immediate be brought to accounts before strictest Soviet justice if ever I am not complying total and absolute with every command of KGB superiors whenever and wherever I get called on to do so.

Well, I am pretty acquainted with such blackmail affairs, of course, so I say, 'Sure, commander. I obey', even though my intention, like you know, is for getting to England and then pursue my own quest, not quest of KGB.

For next three months, I am being accommodating in the secret KGB training centre at Zagorsk, small beautiful town with ancient monastery about two hour driving from Moscow. Infortunately, I am not getting much change of admiring this scenery, because KGB training turn out to occupy twelve hours of every day including Sundays. We are studying real hard, learning political realities of modern world, namely that Communism is good thing and capitalism not (although maybe complete the opposite, I guess), practical intelligence technique such as recruiting foreign agent in foreign country, assessing about information they are providing and transmitting back to Moscow, as well as ways for entrapping and blackmailing the foreign targets and sowing stuff called disinformation information in capitalist circles.

I am staying in that KGB place for rest of October, November and December, and therefore not contacting with

Vova, who been returning in triumphant from qualifying games and now preparing for World Cup finals in England next July.

During my training months, Smerdyakov from All-Union Football Presidium is frequent visiting me at Zagorsk and checking me up, and sometimes also bringing message from Vova who is training real hard himself, although more in footballing department than anything connected with intelligence.

Then, on 7 January of 1966, which actually Russian Christmas Day (another strange date affair, sorry), Smerdyakov is arriving in Zagorsk and telling that he got Christmas present for me, and he is handling me envelope containing brand-new Soviet passport (external!) bearing my name and photograph.

'This for you, Gorevich. Prepare yourself. Next week we go to land of capitalists.'

And that is all.

No further explaining.

For next few days I cannot study, cannot sleep and cannot barely eat.

On 14 January, Smerdyakov is sending official KGB black Chaika (car name meaning a seagull, so not quite so worrisome as black ravens and crows) for collect and drive me to Domodedovo Airport, where he is waiting together with one other fellow who is introducing as Valentin Granatkin, President of All-Union Football Presidium and senior Soviet representative on UEFA executive committee.

Only now these guys are explaining purpose of our mission, which is for Granatkin to scout around England and locate correct accommodating and training facilities for Soviet team in next summer world finals.

My duty is to interpret and translate for Granatkin. And Smerdyakov duty to make sure Granatkin and me both doing our duty and not contemplating any treachery or anti-Soviet activity such as defecting to capitalist false-paradise.

On board of Tupolev from Moscow to London Khitro, we three all sitting pretty much in silent, looking each others and wondering what everybody else thinking and planning about this mission.

I am worrying what I will be finding when arriving in land of my father, and also worrying if my English language will be sufficient for carrying up official duties. Granatkin is worrying about his own mission and responsibility of finding necessary right places for our team. And Smerdyakov is worrying that maybe land of capitalists will not be turning out quite so repulsing like he always been saying and hoping it will.

Problem of these KGB fellows is that they got real big investment in historic inevitability of capitalism downfall and for sure don't like anything whatsoever suggesting it not down-falling quite so fast like they been telling people.

And probably he also worried in case me and Granatkin actually do decide for going off defecting, which for sure will be curtain closing of Smerdyakov KGB career.

So there we are. Three Soviet fellows sitting in Soviet aircraft heading for same place but each having real different and secret personal agenda.

I am enjoying first ever flying in aeroplane.

Granatkin shuffling through big pile of papers with listing of English hotels, restaurants, training grounds.

And Smerdyakov showing he is boss of all of us by insisting nobody got to drink any vodka since it is well known that capitalists immediately throwing inebriated peoples in jail, and also by requisitioning all three plaster busts of Lenin we been gifted by air hostess in souvenir of Aeroflot journey.

And when we arrive at London Khitro Airport, he is hiding

these souvenirs in false bottom of his suitcase since it is well known that capitalist custom officers immediately confiscating any socialist ideology symbols and probably also directing socialist owner of such symbol to nearest capitalist jail.

Soon as Tupolev is touching up at Khitro, Smerdyakov look out the window and start drawing attentions to rain falling outside which he is negatively comparing to traditional sunny climate we been leaving behind in Moscow. And in claim of baggages area he is looking somewhat contemptuous at his watch and mentioning that under socialism all suitcases for sure been delivered by now.

In line for passport stamping he is warning me and Granatkin not to be conversing with capitalist officials and also reminding that if we getting arrested and even if we being tortured, we must not reveal any state secrets; but me and Granatkin just looking at each others as if to be saying 'What state secrets we all knowing?' and Smerdyakov getting so nervous he got to leave that passport line and run to toilet couple of times but always warning us not to be talking to any capitalists while he away.

At the end, no one is getting tortured or even arrested, and fellow at capitalist customs desk just stamp our visa and say 'Hello there' and showing us where is exit, which is pretty relieving outcome for me and Granatkin, but pretty disappointing for Smerdyakov who for sure been hoping of somewhat more drama and class conflict.

In Khitro arrivals area, things looking pretty smart and futuristic by comparing with Domodedovo, namely no puddles of the stale beer lying around, no drunken fellows urinating in any corners and ceiling lights all working too.

But Smerdyakov is noticing couple of old chewing gums stuck to marble floor and pointing this up to me and Granatkin for blatant evidence of capitalist decadence, which for sure you never seeing anywhere in USSR (me and Granatkin looking at each others and not saying nothing, but both privately thinking that reason for this is you can't get no chewing gum whatsoever in Soviet Union, just like you can't get no jeans or biros or other such decadent items).

Anyway, we all looking round that arriving hall for fellow who supposing to come and meet us, but we not seeing him.

Smerdyakov has letter from the English saying we will be greeted by 'man from British FO', which not meaning much to him or to me, so we all just standing there and waiting but not getting approached by anybody of such description.

Pretty soon Smerdyakov is becoming height of anxiety and therefore deducing this got to be some capitalist entrapment, so he ordering us to sit real quiet in smoker section seats (me and Granatkin don't smoke but Smerdyakov does) until he determined coast is clear and we not being targeted by capitalist provocation.

After fifteen minutes and fifteen cigarettes, Smerdyakov decide we got to make some positive action, but also for safety purpose got to avoid revealing that we all Soviet citizens. So he order me to approach one English fellow sitting right opposite us smoking pipe and ask him what is time.

So I say very friendly to this gentleman, 'Excuse me, ser, what is time?' And he is replying most alarmingly, 'Ah, there my friend you have posed a deep and imponderable question.'

Hmm. I am taken *vrasplokh* by this (meaning pretty perplexedly), and Smerdyakov is saying 'Tell me what Englishman been replying' and I got no idea so I just say, 'Er, half past three' and Smerdyakov looking pretty suspicious, like my answer been much too short, which of course it is, but no way I going to be explaining what these English are talking about, since I don't understand it myself, by the way. This transpiring to be even more crazy country than I been expecting.

Well, Smerdyakov is doing more strategic thinking and decide that politically correct course is for making further positive action to foil capitalists' plot, so he instruct me to approach certain fellows who been standing around in Khitro arriving hall for past half hour and challenge them if they are British FO making covert surveillance on us.

So I walk up to one large fellow wearing clever disguise of builders' overalls with paint smudgings on hands and cigarette in corner of the mouth and say him in very best English, 'Hey, you British FO?' and he look me with somewhat angry face and reply, 'No, mate; you bloody foreigners FO!' which is making no sense whatsoever and once again I am unable of translating to Smerdyakov, who is beginning to look somewhat suspicious at my English language ability.

Luckily, just at that moment British FO fellow we all been awaiting for comes running up and say, 'Are you from Moscow?' and I answer him, 'Yes', and he is making complicated apology about big tube strike on London, which I am thinking got something to do with major military attack on English capital city, but I am not translating this for Smerdyakov mainly because English fellow – who is revealing his name to be Tompkins – is not looking too disturbed or worried like he would be if there really is being some nuclear tube attack.

And when we are leaving that Khitro Airport, it is clear that nothing wrong at all because we four just taking a taxi (which is some real strange black car not looking like any ZiL or Chaika or Moskvich and therefore proving that capitalists are many years in arrear of latest automobile designs) through streets containing hundreds and hundreds of little dachas, some joined together in group of two and some joined in long line of dachas all looking exact the same.

And Granatkin and me are starring out of this taxi in great amaze, because everything look so clean and well maintaining and trees growing alongside of roads and dachas all looking spickly span and all got large patch of tidy grass with people pushing lawn mowing machine upwards and downwards or standing outside their dachas and washing shiny new automobiles, which it seem every citizen is privately possessing, and we can see Smerdyakov also noticing this phenomenon and looking pretty annoyed by this and also pretty annoyed by me and Granatkin admiring such things, so he is saying us real loud, 'Comrades, do not be fooled by this! These capitalists are driving us through special constructed route of fake affluence in order for falsely impressing us, just like Potemkin been doing many years ago for Catherine Great.' But me and Granatkin are not completely convinced by this explaining, especially as fake affluence is continuing for many versts and not actually looking very fake at all.

So I ask Mr British FO, or rather Mr Tompkins, what all these people with green grass and shiny cars are doing in order to acquire such wealth, but Smerdyakov is sternly interrupting and suggest in somewhat forceful Russian expressions for keeping my mouth shut until he is telling me to open it.

But actually, something then happening which is making my mouth fall right open, although not for speaking, and also making Granatkin mouth fall open and even Smerdyakov mouth, although he is closing it pretty prompt afterwards.

What this thing is? It is group of young women walking along London street and not wearing any skirts! Or if they are wearing skirt, it so small we can see all their legs and also large part of bottom region, which is producing extreme pleasing effect on me and Granatkin and serving to highly increase our admiration for values of capitalist system.

And guess what? it is not only one group of women practising such delightful fashion ideology; it is every women on every street we driving through!

What for amazing place this London is turning out to be!

Soon it seem we are arriving in centre of city, because large red bus vehicles, very long and very high with at least two and probably even three storeys, are driving beside us full of passengers reading newspaper and carrying the black umbrellas. And hundreds of similar taxi vehicles like we riding in are also appearing with driver always using the klaxon horns and some hand-gesturing signals which involve use of two fingers. Streets are getting crowded with traffic and also with people on sidewalks looking at shops with actual goods in their windows, unlike Soviet shops which usually just having a sign saying shoes or hats or herring, without having any of actual things inside them.

Tompkins of FO, who is turning out as pretty quiet fellow and just listening to us conversing and therefore, according to Smerdyakov, probably intelligence agent of Britannic Majesty, is telling how he going to take us for registering at hotel where we are staying that night and this hotel is transpiring right next of Kensington Parking in the Bayswater, and opposite to Soviet Embassy in London.

It seem British FO actually having good senses of humour, because hotel is located on corner of road called Moscow Street and St Peterburg Place (which Smerdyakov is denouncing as one more capitalist provocation seeing as real name is now Leningrad, but actually me and Granatkin not taking too much noticing of his remarks any more).

Tompkins is telling that we all got free time now for freshing up and relaxing and that he come to collect us at the 7 p.m. for going to reception dinner at his FO, which is actually turning out to be name of British Foreign Ministry.

So me and Granatkin starting off to hotel bar, but quick as a flashing, Smerdyakov is spotting this and diverting us to our bedrooms. And while we two taking the showers, Smerdyakov say he going over other side of Bayswater Road to Soviet Embassy for official informing of our arrivals and also receiving formal instructions for further continuing our mission.

That evening, we are driving with Tompkins to reception at FO in the Whitehall street, together with footballing representatives of many other nations qualifying for World Cup finals, eating dinner and drinking some large wine glasses (including Smerdyakov who seem to overcome his alcohol interdiction rule quite easily as it turns out), and then we all listening to some long and boring speeches from Englishmen of the FO, the FA, the BEA, the BBC, the GPO, the ITV, the BR, the ZZZ (OK, this last one I been making up, but actually quite accurate representing of sound that is coming from mouth of one old English fellow with white hair and white moustache sitting next to me at table and heroically overfulfilling his quota for wine consuming within about half hour of dinner commencing).

My only problem is that Smerdyakov insisting me to interpret all those speeches into Russian, which make the rather tiresome undertaking, but after first few speeches and first few wine bottles, he is becoming less keen on this and instructing me instead to help him with conversing to our pretty young waitress wearing very fashionable meanie-skirting like all other Englishwomen and constantly leaning over and bending down to serve soup, which is very attractive spectacle for us Russians who never seen any such things in our life before.

And, for being fair, after undertaking some drinking practice, Smerdyakov start to become little bit more human fellow and loosening up his tongue to explain what mission is lying ahead of us. First thing, he say, we got to go up to some town called Dooram, where Granatkin got to find suiting hotels accommodation and trainings ground for use of Soviet team in forthcoming July.

But according to Smerdyakov this is just our clever covering-up story for real mission purpose, which is actually for fomenting revolution and bringing down capitalist state.

Hmm.

I understand Smerdyakov been drinking the large quota of alcohol, of course, but when I ask him just exactly how we planning to do this, he is taping on side of his nose and reply, 'Music, young Zhenya. Music is our revolutionary tool!' and then he too is falling asleep with head on a table and only waking up when banquet is over and time for returning to hotel.

Next day, while Smerdyakov and Granatkin still sleeping, I am arising real early and go to hotel reception.

At receiving desk is sitting very large African native, deep black skin colour, fuzzy hair, and real pink tongue and shiny white teeth like no one in Russia ever seen before. So I walk up to him and smiling, then speaking with extreme slow English so he can understand and making many hand gestures for explaining that I – am – guest – at – this – hotel – and – would – like – for – you – help – me – with – something. So imagine what surprise is coming when he reply real quick and snappy, 'Yeah, all right, man, watcha need?'

I am telling how I actually need of finding address for Lord Edenby-Gore who is famous English noble Lord and also my father. African fellow look at me little bit strange, but nonetheless reaching under receiving desk and taking out very thick telephone directory (something that not existing at all in Moscow, where you can only ring people you already know because it is obviously top important issue of state security for people not to find out anybody else's telephone number) and flicking through it with big black fingers and I am asking if maybe he cannot read and maybe I help him, but he just look at me and say pretty quiet '82 Belgrave Square', and I am so exciting from finally finding address of my long lost father that I am jumping some way in the air, and before returning in my room I ask that fellow if it all right to touch his fuzzy hair and he just give the little sigh and say, 'Yeah, I suppose so.'

Well, lucky I am running quick back inside my room because one minute later come the knocking on my door and it is Smerdyakov looking real suspicious and say, 'You OK, Comrade Gorevich? Seem I been hearing you door opening and closing and maybe someone going out' but I tell him that must be chamber maiden or else fellow next door and Smerdyakov look at me and say, 'Well, make sure I am not catching you talking to anyone, Gorevich; we all surrounded by capitalist provocateurs, OK?'

And I just nod.

After breakfast, Tompkins is arriving and tell us that we got to get ready because we all four catching up a BR train to Dooram town, where he got several appointings for us to see hotels and such things.

And while we travelling on that BR train, Tompkins is explaining that Dooram is exact halfway in between Middelsburrow and Sanderland, where our footballers going to play group stage of World Cup in July at footballing grounds of Hairsome Park and Rocker Park.

And Tompkins is adding, 'One more thing I got to inform you on behalf of Her Majesty Government, gentlemen. While you in this country, you all guests of Her Majesty and therefore must not be making political activity of any description. Is that perfectly clear?'

I translate this for Smerdyakov who look at me with very straight face and says, 'Please reply this gentlemen that he is capitalist *svoloch*' and then give the little wink so I know I really got to reply, 'Yes, ser. Of course we understanding this.'

But while Smerdyakov been speaking, I spot the look of surprise in Tompkins' eye, which suggest me that maybe this FO fellow is actually understanding the Russian after all and just not telling us or maybe keeping it secret in order to spy on us.

And later when Smerdyakov go into train corridor for smoking cigarette, I am also going out and mention him this phenomenon, and Smerdyakov is making face expression as to be saying, 'Hah! What I been telling you about such capitalist dirty tricks!'

But when we get back to compartment, I see Smerdyakov being more careful and also more friendly to Tompkins fellow, politely asking about him family, background, education and interests and also – somewhat surprising – ask him about him tastes for music, such as is he knowing famous groups as Loving Spoonfuls, Freddy Dreamers, Tremberlos and Yardiebirds; but Tompkins wrinkling up his nose somewhat and say, 'Actually, I am more of Mozart and Buxtehude man myself', which is bringing rapid end to this conversing.

When we arrive in Dooram, it is raining of course and no

taxis waiting at station, so we must to take number 9 bus to town centre. It look like Tompkins already been here before because he is pulling out some special plan and inviting us to follow him round several hotels which are on Granatkin list of accommodation places for Soviet team. Infortunately, these all turning out dirty and noisy with wallpapering peeling off walls, holes in carpet and strong odour of fish and chippings coming into bedrooms, so Granatkin is saying 'Sorry, no', 'Sorry, no', 'Sorry, no'. And I can see Tompkins getting little bit worried about proceedings and finally he say, 'There only one place left for showing you now, and this right on edge of town couple of miles away', so Granatkin say, 'OK, let's go', and Tompkins then revealing somewhat his true occupation status by waving at passing police car, showing some secret pass that we not allowed to see, and police driver agree to take us all to edge of town, to little place called the Grey College.

Well, Granatkin look much happier by seeing this location, which is consisting of some collection of buildings resembling red brick monastery, surrounding by greenery and trees and all very quiet. The Grey College also got proper playing and trainings field, nice fresh airs and pleasant setting with view of hills and Dooram Cathedral. So Granatkin say OK, and Tompkins take us inside to meet college principal, who expressing his delight to have Soviet footballers here and those two start discussing details of contract payments and so forth.

Then Tompkins ask us Russians to wait outside some minutes while he talk to principal fellow.

And while we waiting outside, Smerdyakov is spotting tall red box structure making out of iron and glass, which is what English telephone kiosks all look like, and he is pulling up my sleeve and ask somewhat urgently for us go and make a telephoning.

Uh-oh! This is pretty big challenge to me, mainly concerning with technical aspects such as correct selecting of completely incomprehending English coinages, extreme complicated instructions about pressing the button A and pressing the button B and also decision about dialling a trunk or not dialling any STD and other crazy stuff. And this all such a big palaver that I am failing to make any connections whatsoever, so I just tell Smerdyakov the telephone system not working today, which he is accepting OK because this often usually the case in USSR, but also telling me we got to find another calling box so soon we get back to London.

Then Tompkins is reappearing, Granatkin is concluding a dealing with Mr Grey College and we all heading backward to the Dooram station. BR train is arriving and we all catching it up to London, but ten minute later train is stopping and sit still for real long time with no heating working and we all getting pretty cold. I see Smerdyakov got the secret vodka flask and begin frequent sipping this, but not offering to us comrades or to FO Tompkins.

After half hour, train guard is appearing and announce apologies for delay which is being caused by wrong sort of leaves on the train line.

When I am translating this for Smerdyakov, he look at me with little bit drunk eyes and demand me to translate again because he never hear such a ridiculous thing before and it obvious I just being the linguistical nincompoop.

But I check with FO Tompkins and he confirm I been translating everything correct, so Smerdyakov sip another vodka flask and tell me I got to inform Mr Tompkins that this BR is complete load of *govno* (OK, you been hearing this word for several times now and you know what it meaning – shit. Sorry).

When I interpret Smerdyakov analysis, Tompkins is getting

bit red around the choppers and reply that BR is excellent service and everyone know Great Britain is home inventor of railway, as well as inventor of postage stamp, football, radio and whole other list of things.

Well, I know this not true because these all been invented in USSR, so I just say to Smerdyakov that Mr Tompkins not agreeing with his assessment.

But Smerdyakov is pretty intipsicated by now and keen for pursuing constructive exchange of views, so he instruct me to tell Tompkins that Soviet trains always running on time despite of leaves, boulders, two metre of snow or even capitalist sabotaging; also, they all got top class heating system, television screens and beautiful *devushkas* serving coffee and tea from onboard samovar.

I am looking little bit questioning when I hear this, but Smerdyakov issue the categorical order for translate everything, so I do so.

Tompkins' face now turning to the deep purple and he reply, 'If Soviet trains always running on time, please answer me this: how come you fellows got this following Soviet joke which I now recount you? "Stalin, Khrushchev and Brezhnev travelling by Soviet train but suddenly it come to a halt. Stalin give the order: 'Fix it!' and engineers try, but train is not moving. So Stalin say, 'Shoot everyone!' and all engineers get shot but train still not going. Then Stalin dying and Khrushchev give the new order: 'Rehabilitate everyone!' So engineers get rehabilitated but train remain broken. Then Khruschev being removed and Brezhnev say, 'Close up all curtains and everybody pretend we moving!'"'

And Tompkins is giving little chuckle at him own knowledge of Soviet humour.

Smerdyakov not looking too pleased by hearing this, and I

am getting pretty worried, but Smerdyakov just sit there glaring and say nothing, and later he is over-fulfilling his vodka drinking quota and falling to sleep.

Our train finally arriving in the London King Crosses very late that night. Since this much too late now for making any telephone callings, we all going to bed, and real early next morning I am contacting my African native friend again and asking for detailed instructions regarding English phone boxings.

Idi (which turn out to be his name) is writing everything down for me real careful in very beautiful handwriting script and also providing large selection of coins out of hotel petty cash-in draw, such as thrup-any-bit and tanner and bob and two-bob and florin and halfcrown and other such confusing stuff.

So when Smerdyakov is knocking real quiet in my door just after breakfast, I already and prepared for telephonic mission.

Outside, on opposite sidewalk of Bayswater Road from the Kensington Parking, is row of three telephone box, so Smerdyakov is looking all round to ensure absence of capitalist surveillance and then selecting box number two. When we inside, he hand me the list of numbers and tell me get dialling them.

First number get no reply.

Second number get no reply.

But third number is ringing and ringing and then voice appear and says, 'Hey, man, Marquee Club here. What's the deal?'

I am so surprised at getting any answer that I am in a confusion for knowing what to say and I look at Smerdyakov but he is yelling out real complicated instructions to me so I cannot figure up what he talking about at all, therefore I am not saying anything and voice on line is saying something like 'Hrrrmph' and line becoming dead.

When he hear this, Smerdyakov is getting mad and blaming me for such mission failure, but I tell him we got to coordinate our strategy better, namely he got to tell me what is purpose of this calling so I can conduct sensible conversing when anybody answer.

Smerdyakov look pretty warisome about including me in secret of his operation, but even he eventually realizing he got no choice, otherwise no communication going take place whatsoever, since Smerdyakov not speaking English and Mr Marquee Club for sure not speaking any Russian.

So he say 'OK' and tell me I got to ring same number once more time and when fellow is answering, I got to tell him we need three entry placings for the Rollings tonight. Well, this all sound pretty cockanbull to me, but he the boss man and maybe this is some secret KGB password or something, so I am dialling once more time, press the button A, drop in the thrup-any-bits, press the button B, and same voice answering again, 'Marquee Club. What's the deal, man?'

And I recount him exact what Smerdyakov been telling me, namely we need three entry placings for the Rollings tonight.

And it seem that guy kind of understand what I am asking him because he give the little laugh and say, 'You want three tix for the Stones, man. Is that what you saying?' And I look at Smerdyakov and see he got no idea about anything, so I just say, 'Yeah, man, it is precisely for sure what I am saying.' And that guy laugh one more time and say, 'What name is that for, man?' I translate this real quick for Smerdyakov who starts looking pretty panicky so I can see we don't got to give any real names, and Smerdyakov is saying, 'Tell them some English name . . . get making something up!' but all I can think of is Shakespeare and Dickens, which is sounding ridiculous, so I am hesitating and then say, 'Er, it for Mr Tompkins.' So guy on phone say, 'That's cool, man. Get here by eight. I keep you tix at the door.'

Phew! Mission success!

I am looking real proud at Smerdyakov and recount him all this, but he don't look too pleased, actually, and say, 'Why you not get address of this club? And why you not find out cost of these entry placings?' and other such questions.

But I say him, 'Don't worry, everything will be cool' (new phraseology which I just been learning from any telephone conversing and now planning of frequent using for giving my English authentic touch from this onward).

Rest of day is free time day, so me and Granatkin tell Smerdyakov we planning to visit famous sights of London such as palaces, towers and Madam Two Swords (although in reality I actually planning further actions in my own quest for Lord Gore of course), but Smerdyakov is looking real disapproving and informing that in fact all three of us are going to High Gate to visit grave of immortal Karl Marx (which seem to me like some bit of linguistic contradiction going on here, but never mind) and later as special treat we all going to the Grove and Ore Square for big surprise that Smerdyakov will not tell us about.

This is real annoying, of course, because we only got couple more days left on this visit and time is running out for my *podvig*, but what you can do? Smerdyakov is boss, he is KGB, and no good quarrelling to him now or for sure he disqualify me from coming back here with Soviet team for July World Cup.

So we all taking London tube (name affair explaining that

strange apology by Tompkins for late arriving at Khitro Airport) to High Gate, lay some flowers on grave of immortal father of world revolution, visit house in Primroses Hill where other German fellow, Engels, been living, and later return south on the Northerly Line (do not ask: I not understanding either).

Then Smerdyakov is taking us on visit to famous British Museum where Great Lenin and Karl Marx and probably also Great Stalin been sitting and reading some books.

And when we find precise seat where Great Lenin been sitting, I am feeling the strange presence as if His immortal spirit is still with us in this world and actually keeping watch over me and knowing and judging all my words and deeds and sending me some important message from wherever He is now.

When I mention this to Granatkin, he just laugh and tell me, 'You know what they say: Lenin always with us!' and maybe I am mistaking but it seem to me like somewhere far away I heard Lenin laugh, too.

Later that afternoon Smerdyakov tell us it is time to go to Grove and Ore Square, so we walk down the Tottenamcort Road and the Regent Street and the Oxford Street, all of them full of great department stores big like palaces and containing real goods for sale and windows all illuminated with bright shining lights and decorations and odour of beautiful perfume wafting into the sidewalk and anyone can enter them even if you not the top-up party official, and Granatkin and me wanting to go inside, but Smerdyakov warn us not to neglect the patriotic duty which apparently mean keep walking and follow him.

In ten minutes more, we are approaching this Grove and Ore Square and hearing loud noise of many voices shouting and singing and also people clapping and chanting and some horses neighing, and me and Granatkin looking puzzled, but big smile is starting up on Smerdyakov face and look of rightful socialist triumph in his eyes.

And reason for this soon becoming clear, namely all that noise is coming from big manifestation of popular sentiment outside fascist US embassy with five, maybe ten thousand peoples directing popular sentiments against American imperialism in People Republic of Vietnam and neighbour Laos.

Straightaway, Smerdyakov is joining in that crowd and shouting him own slogans such as *Doloi Amerikanskim fashistam* (you can guess this) and *Smert' Dzhonsonu* and other stuff highly bemusing to everybody else in manifestation, most of them being fellows with very long hairs and wearing beads and embroidery and maybe velvet jackets and also young ladies with flower on the ears and sunglasses looking very lovely and also mainly wearing those meanie-skirts we so highly appreciating or otherwise yellow pants with very wide bottom legs.

And real strange smell is in the airs, not being perfume and not being tobacco, but actually being quite sweet and fragrant and after you been breathing in for some time, whole world is seeming much happier and nicer place, which is probably a reason why those manifesters all remaining largely unagitated and not actually storming US embassy like proletariats been storming Tsar Winter Palace back in October (later becoming November) 1917.

But capitalist polices are doing very utmosts for provoking this peaceful crowd by walking among them and keep saying 'Move along there, young lady' and 'Come on now, young sir, let's get home to Mummy, shall we?' and other such harsh repressive things.

Smerdyakov is telling how popular manifestations like this provide complete irrefutable proof that whole capitalist system on a point of collapsing from weight of its own internal contradictions, and historic inevitability of triumph of socialism is now assured.

And I see Smerdyakov is getting carried away by force of such sentiments but soon also getting physical carried away by force of large crowd sweeping him toward far corner of Grove and Ore Square, and me and Granatkin are making out like we trying real hard to follow him and not lose the contact, but actually we both pushing somewhat in an opposite direction and soon we are complete lost and he also complete lost, and me and Granatkin are looking at each others like naughty schoolfellows who somehow managed of escaping from their teacher.

Aha! Now we are free.

Granatkin is immediate suggesting we pay the visit to famous London Soho area where very beautiful girls are located offering special services not usually available in Vitebsk or even in Moscow. But I say, 'No, you go Soho, Valentin; I got some other thing I got to do', so Granatkin say, 'OK, Zhenya, but problem is I am little bit short of the sterling pounds. Maybe you got some left overs from daily allowance they been giving us?' And I say, 'Sure. I don't need no sterling pounds for place I am going', and I handle over all those ten bobs notes what I got in my pocket.

Half hour later, I am walking in the Belgrave Square, which is very unlike Grove and Ore Square because it is complete absent of any manifesters and real quiet and even seeming empty of people whatsoever. OK: for us Russians, such place as Belgrave Square is pretty hard to imagine. Maybe you thinking of Lenin Square or Pushkin Square or Mayakovsky Square, but this not helping you even one little jotting.

In centre of that square is beautiful, luscious green garden, full of trees that been grazing down on human lives ever since many centuries; ground covering with sweet smelling flowers; splendid blooming bushes lining all it pathways; and glimpses of calm shady corners where tormented humanity may lay down in peace and find rest. All round this square, magnificent tall houses are looking immaculate like white palaces, all with marble steps and carved front doors with shiny brass knocking handles.

I try to glance inside one of them but instead I see myself reflecting in its sparkling bright windows and all around me in that window is the golden halo of bright shining light.

My heart skips its beats. House number is 82 . . . my father house!

I cannot stop; cannot pause.

I just keep walking.

Round and round.

And maybe I still be walking today, except that people are appearing at several houses window and pointing at me somewhat suspicious and soon I see the bobby (English name for people's militia) walking at other end of that square and coming in my directions.

I got to decide what to do.

I cannot flee because this where my future and my happiness is containing. But I must not get arresting. Only solution – get into that garden in middle of Belgrave Square and hide there. Garden is behind tall black railing with spiking on top and notice saying 'This garden reserved for only chosen people who holding special entry pass and key. No ordinary people allowed in.'

But such I am desperate that I take my life into a hand and

climb up the railing, resulting in torn pants and scratched bottom, but nonetheless clamber inward and gain safety from threat of the laws in world outside.

And inside that garden, I am feeling in paradise. For one half hour, I just sitting there grazing through those garden railings at house 82, waiting for anyone coming out, maybe Lord Gore his self.

But no one is emerging.

House 82 is real quiet. Maybe deserted and everyone gone away.

But then, basement door is opening and two ladies walk up steps to the sidewalk, one of them old and one young and beautiful. Maybe that old person is false Lady Gore. Maybe. But beautiful young person with brown hair all tied up in elegant hair net contraption with cylinder roller things in it and overcoat looking somewhat shabby but obviously this is noble style of great aristocrat family, and carrying some parcel wrapped in newspaper . . . who can be this lovely maiden?

These ladies are linking up the arms and walking together and – now my heart is fainting with joy – coming toward me!

I can hear their talking – something about fish and vegetables and soap – but guess what: old lady is addressing that young girl as 'princess', saying, 'Come along now, princess' and, 'now then, princess, don't forget the carbolic'.

I am calling through the railings, 'Ladies! I am here! Look at me!'

And both those gentle ladies start screaming and run away.

But I call out again, 'No! Ladies! Stop! It is me, your long lost Zhenya! True heir of Melvyn Lord Edenby-Gore!'

And I see that old lady hesitating and turn to beautiful princess and tell her to wait.

And old princess come to the railings to see who is in her garden.

I see her face; not exactly like wisewoman Mavra been describing – namely not real beautiful and smooth and delicate, but actually somewhat rough and red and maybe little bit dirty – but for sure this is great lady from world of high aristocracy.

So I say her, 'Lady! This is Zhenya here. This is son of the Lord!'

And she look somewhat strange at me and say, 'You're foreign, ain't you, dearie?'

And I say 'Yes, noble lady, I am Russian foreign, but also your related, and I am loving all of you.'

And that fine old lady give the genteel little laugh and say, 'Well, bless me, dearie, I ain't knowin' nuffink about that.'

And I say, 'Yes! You got to believe me, noble lady! And please to tell me, for sake of all archangels, who is that beautiful young person? For sure she is lady?'

And old princess just laugh again, very noble sort of laugh, and say, 'Oh, that's Susie, dearie. And she's better than a lady. She's a lady's lady!'

Oh! Now I am in paradise for sure!

Even better than just lady! This is lady's lady!

All my dreams coming true and all at a very same time!

I am smiling to that old lady and ask her name, and she say to me 'Liza, dearie, that's my name', which I know to be real noble aristocratish name . . . Lady Liza . . . !

But just then there is sudden male voice emerging from a bushes behind me and shouting somewhat gruff, 'So there you are! I've been watching you, sonny Jim!' and I am thinking that fate is now making my cups run over because this for sure must be my father who come for me, so I say, 'Not sonny Jim, my father. This is sonny Zhenya . . .' but then I realize it is not my father after all but actually that bobby (people militia) I been mentioning you, and this bobby is not being friendly English copper (militia) but actually adopting similar fascist tactics that been deployed against those manifesters in Grove and Ore Square.

So I inform Lady Gore I got to be going just now but will return so soon as possible, and then I turn to my heels and start scarpering, but bobby militia is scarpering after me and we both scarper together through that beautiful garden and fortunately he is transpiring as not so top of the fitness brigade because he get puffed off after couple of minutes running which give me the chance to reach a railing gate and climb sharpishly over (although tearing my pants once more) and jump promptly back into outside real world and rapid depart in the northern direction back through Grove and Ore and onward toward the London Soho and never even stopping or looking backward in case bobbies all pursuing behind me.

It is only when I reach the Oxford Circus that I am slowing down and look around me, and actually it getting pretty dark of eveningtide by now and my watch saying seven-thirty which is sharply reminding me of important forgotten rendezvous.

Ah, you forgot also?

Well, it is that rendezvous I been making earlier by the telephone, namely 8 p.m. at Marquee Club for watching the Rollings with Smerdyakov and Granatkin. Problem is I got no idea where such club is located, except for knowing it is on the Voordoor Street of Soho.

And time start pressing now because any lateness probably arousing suspicions by Smerdyakov, so I am resolving to over-come natural socialist distrust of fascist militia bobbies and enquire directions from two of them which are standing there at that Circus.

But strange to say, those bobbies transpiring to be height of hopelessness because they both scratching on their heads and shrugging off their shoulders and say, 'Voordoor Street? Voordoor Street? No, never heard of that one. Have you, Bert?' and other such mutterings, and even when they both looking in a special AZbookh which they carrying for such occasions they are not finding anything and even show me in the indexing where they been searching in vain, but for sure those fellows must be illiterate *muzhiks* because it transpiring that they been looking under letter V!

Immediately I look in correct place – namely under letter W – I am finding that address straightaway and consequent departing up the Oxford Street and turning to Voordoor Street just before Smerdyakov get there looking real pleased with his self following dialectical satisfaction of anti-fascist manifestation and Granatkin also looking real pleased with his self following dialectical satisfaction of visit to London Soho.

And this general satisfaction is positive element as far as I am concerning, because no one is raising any questions about my were-abouts during that afternoon, but simply concluding we all got accidentally separated in shared ardour of proletarian manifesting.

We are locating Marquee Club pretty quick because outside it got the large stripy awning looking like marquee tent and even larger crowd of young peoples hanging about talking and smoking and drinking beers bottle.

Only thing, I am thinking we three maybe look somewhat out of places here because we all dressed up in standard category Soviet suits (namely grey, with stitching falling apart from most seams) coming from GUM department store on the Red Square, in specific socialist style that is not using much popularity in capitalist West, and we also having standard Soviet haircut, meaning pretty short hairs, which is not matching prevailing style of other peoples here (namely long and not being combed).

Smerdyakov also notice this and instruct me and Granatkin that we all got to blend in with native locals and not get identified, which is not real obvious how we going to do this, but anyway we all trying.

I am approaching fellow at Marquee Club door and speaking with very natural English expressing such as, 'Hello cool man. This here is cool party of Mr Tompkins, Mr Dickens and Mr Shakespeare come for collecting they tix and also watching those Stones, man', which seeming to do the trickery because fellow is producing three scrap of paper with 'Three Pounds' writing on each of them and therefore demanding nine pounds sterling off us. Smerdyakov, who control the financial affairs, is getting out the ten pounds note, which I am handling over and therefore expecting changes of one sterling. But that fellow on the door just wink to me and instead of produce any money, he is handling over three cigarettes, all quite long and not too well rolled up, but he is smiling and say, 'This is real good stuff, man. Have a groovy time.' And we three all saying polite thank you and descending into Marquee Club, which is actually downstairs in basement of some clothing shop warehouse, name of Boorbery, along narrow corridor leading into pretty dark and sweaty rectangle shape room with sticky floor and strong odour similar of what we been inhaling earlier in Grove and Ore Square.

At that moment, stage is empty and everybody just standing about talking and smoking, so Smerdyakov is getting real nervous, like as usual, and ordering me and Granatkin to act natural, and when I ask him exact how we got to do this, he say, 'Just do same as all others people', and he start lighting up one of those cigarettes which door fellow been giving us.

Ten minute later, Smerdyakov is not so nervous after all. In fact, he is leaning up against a wall and wearing the real big smile and completely stopped issuing any orders whatsoever.

By time of those Stones coming up on stage, Smerdykov already smoked all three special cigarettes and got so relaxed that he is laying down in corner of the room together with couple dozens other people all staring in the space and really digging the vibes that are going down (meaning they like Stones music, including even Smerdyakov who keep waving and saying 'Vo-o-o! Vo-o-o!' and other such positive expressions).

Granatkin and me, who not been smoking any special cigarettes, are also quite enjoying Stones music, especially such combos as 'Let us spend night together', 'Not fading away', 'Wish to be your man', 'Get off of the cloud' and real top tune of 'Not getting any satisfaction'. We are highly evaluating performance of Michael and Keef, leading cadres of that ensemble who keep running up and down stage, sometimes removing their cloths, which is highly evaluated by female audience who are also removing some of their own cloths (which is highly evaluated by me and Granatkin and most other male gender fellows there).

But we cannot figure out at all why Smerdyakov been bringing us here and why he been getting so interesting in this capitalistic music which is not having any place whatsoever in socialist culture and certainly being much more endangerous and formalist than any Shostakovich symphonies, and just think of all the negative appraising which Shostakovich been getting!

So when he is emerging somewhat from his relaxing state, I ask him what this mission actually all about and Smerdyakov look at me with very wise expression on his face and say, 'Reflect about this, Comrade Gorevich. What these English people are most caring about in whole world? For sure it is not worthy goals of Soviet revolution and noble socialist cause. No, it is football and also this pop music phenomenon', so I say, 'OK, maybe this true. But is what interest for us, comrade?' and he is taping the finger on side of his nose with very cunning look and say, 'CPSU know best, young man. You remain with me on this pop mission and you soon be understanding wisdom of the Party', and then he is collapsing into corner again and not waking up for some time following.

Meanwhile I am highly enjoying being on KGB pop mission and also using new acquired English colloquialness for making acquaintance with other audience members, including some guys who are offering me a beers bottle and questioning about foreign nature of my accent, and since Smerdyakov is sleeping, I tell them Yeah, I am Russian fellow actually, so they start enquiring about Moscow and Yuri Gagarin and Brezhnev president, although no one of them ever been hearing about Vitebsk or even Minsk, so no points whatsoever in recounting about these places.

Anyway, those guys inform all their colleagues about Russian presence and straightaway everyone start approaching and wanting to meet real Soviet fellow, since no one ever seen any Russians before.

Pretty soon, whole of Marquee Club is getting real friendly with me and Granatkin (Smerdyakov still sleeping) and gathering round and questioning about our haircuts and our cloths, and then remarking on torn nature of my pants, which been ripping up on Belgrave Square railing as you remember, and I guess those guys are thinking this is kind of new fashion ideology, because one of them says, 'Cool, man. Dig those groovy torn pants', and proceed to make similar tear in his own denim jeans, and then his friends also doing the same and eventually everyone start copying this new idea, and guess what? trend for torn jeans is becoming big fashion estatement in whole of capitalist world and pretty soon clothing enterprises such as Leewize and Rangulers start selling new denims already pre-torn in exact same way of my old pants which actually been the original starting of this whole global phenomenon.

But this is digression. Sorry.

When Smerdyakov is waking up, those Stones nearly terminated the playing and already walking off stage and Smerdyakov start getting agitated and worried again (i.e. back to normal state) and he say me, 'Zhenya! Quick, before those fellows all leaving, we must to get talking with them!' And I just look at him and say, 'No way we going to get conversing with Rolling Stones, comrade. They all going to leave now and get whisking away in some Chaika limousine.' But Smerdyakov is real insisting and start issuing orders again (I was liking him better when he been forgetting about that stuff) such as 'Comrade Gorevich! I order you to make English language contact with musician personnel!' and also informing that whole of my KGB career and future possibility for return to London is depending on me making this successful mission, so I go to my new English friends and ask what is best way of acquainting with those Stones and they all say, 'Hang about, man. See that slim guy over there with glasses and smart outfit? This is Andrew. Come on and we introduce you!'

So they take me over to this fellow and it transpire he is trainer of those Rolling Stones by name of Loog Oldham and real friendly guy with interest in Russia and pretty much supporting proletarian efforts of Kremlin in struggle with Yanki imperialists. So I say him, 'Look, Andrew, I must meet your Stone fellows if this anyhow possible', but he is just laughing off his head (meaning real loud) and say, 'Look, man. You see all those cute chicks lining up by exit door? These are only folk that Stones interested in meeting right now!' and he is making the winking gesture so I can understand reason of this and I also understand that me and Smerdyakov will not be fulfilling our mission tonight.

But with benefit of KGB training, I am rapid thinking on my feets and tell Loog Oldham, 'OK, man, I dig what you saying. But maybe me and my comrades can meet your Stones some other time soon, like maybe in July when we all coming back here with Soviet team for World Cup?' And he say, 'Sure, man. Mick is big fanatic of the soccer', and he give me his official visitcard saying, 'Andrew Loog Oldham, entrepreneur and representative of stars'.

Well, Smerdyakov is pretty unhappy of not meeting Rolling Stones straightaway that night, but he is taking Loog Oldham visitcard in the pocket and say, 'OK. At least I succeeded in opening the contacts', which actually appear somewhat the exaggeration seeing as it been me doing any contact opening, but I am not saying nothing and only making little grunt.

And just as we leaving that Marquee Club, I catch a glimpse from cornering of my eyes of one fellow I been noticing several times during that evening like as if he been secret observing me and Smerdyakov and even taking some notes about us in the little book. This is tall fellow, dressing in embroidery shirt and kaftan with bell pants bottom, but not having any long hairs and somehow not looking real comfortable in such attire and such location, like maybe he preferring to listen to Mozart and Buxtehude instead of Rolling Stones, and guess what? it look to me like the guy who been spying on us all that evening is Mr Tompkins of FO.

*

Next day, we got more Granatkin business for dealing with, namely he must to find extra hotel here in London in case of Soviet team winning through group stage matches up in Middelsburrow and Sanderland and therefore coming down to Vemberley Stadium for contesting World Cup final. So most of that morning we get taken round more hotels by Mr Tompkins of FO, who is never mentioning anything about Marquee Club or Stones or any such things, but only saying 'You gentlemen all OK this morning?' while looking particular close at Smerdyakov who is now wearing dark sunglasses and not moving too quick.

By lunchtime we been concluding the hotel location affair and Mr Tompkins is offering us chance of visit to Vemberley, but Smerdyakov instruct me for declining such offer and inform the FO that we going to have real quiet afternoon and not doing anything much at all whatsoever in any sense.

I see Tompkins not actually believing in this, but he say, 'Very well, gentlemen. I come to hotel tomorrow after breakfast and accompany you to Khitro Airport for catching up the Aeroflot flight back to Moscow. Until then, fare you all well.' And he jump into waiting taxi cab and drive off.

Meanwhile, Smerdyakov is saying that actually we not really having any free time at all, because we got more mission tasks to accomplish and I got to accompany him to several pop record shops where we must buy all latest music of certain groups which are interesting KGB and Party leadership.

Well, this sound pretty strange, because I am having big trouble to imagine that Leonid Brezhnev is wanting urgent copy of 'Hippy, Hippy Shake' or 'Boots Made for Walking', but even when I press him, Smerdyakov will not reveal any more about pop music operation and merely say I must to wait and see.

So for next few hours, me and Smerdyakov and Granatkin

are walking up and down Kings Road in the Chelsea and visiting groovy record shops, such as Island, In A Groove and Needle Spin, where we are purchasing large pile of 45 rpm singles. And then Smerdyakov, who got the long list of special Kremlin requests, say there are two rpms he cannot locate anywhere, therefore we got to go to the Whitechapel and find top record shop by name of NEMS run by fellow called Epstein, which is involving very long ride on London tubes.

And whole this time I am desperate hoping we soon be finishing so I can escape and return to Belgrave Square.

But it only at the 6 p.m., when shops all closing and eveningtide becoming dark that Smerdyakov is finally satisfied with shopping mission and therefore announcing official business terminated for today.

He tell me and Granatkin we must return direct to hotel and wait there while he report our mission progress to KGB controller at Soviet embassy, and we both say, OK we do so.

But so soon as Smerdyakov departed, I am straightaway scarpering back to beloved Belgrave Square and native home of number 82.

This time, I am not hiding in a garden, but walking up to front door with firm resolution of presenting me to father Lord Edenby-Gore.

I am making the bold knocking and await for reply.

But no reply is emerging. I am knocking again and feeling little bit of the anxiety coming in.

Again no answer and I am getting preyed on by trepidation.

Only this time come creak of a window opening in basement below and when I look down I see wondrous sight of that young Princess Susie leaning out and looking up to me, and in real noble voice she say, 'Oh, it's you again. What you after?'

And such is her beauty that somehow I cannot prevent myself replying, 'Oh, my darling, I am after you!' but she give the little noble laugh and say 'Gertcha!', which is not very understandable to me, and she is closing up her window and disappearing. And even though I am waiting and knocking and knocking and waiting, she is not reappearing whatsoever.

What I can do? Only solution is write her the loving letter. And lucky I still got paper receipt from NEMS record shop in my pocket to write it on. Soon my letter is all composed in finest poetry like I been learning from my mother (and also from Aleksandr Sergeyevich Pushkin), recounting true story of my birth and noble English pedigree, and expressing my true passion for her.

I am closing it by the loving kiss and asking beloved Susie to give me some sign because now I will be waiting in paradise garden opposite her house and keeping all-night vigil like Slavonic knights of old or holy lover proving his unflinching constancy. And then I tie my letter to large stone and drop it down that basement area where Susie been leaning out her window.

Now I guess you wanting to hear if Susie been receiving this letter and giving me the sign?

Well, actually I am never knowing this.

How come?

Because so soon I am climbing into those garden bushes, I am rapid and complete falling asleep.

And already it is the 7 a.m. when I am awaking, and only because some kolkhoz milk delivery truck is arriving and making the loud bottles rattling.

Whoa. This is bad news.

Last night Smerdyakov been insistently telling that we must gather in hotel lobbying at 7.30 a.m. for return to Khitro Airport and immediate flying off to Moscow and no one whatsoever got to be late for this.

I must make a rapid deciding: should I go or should I stay?

Wait here and therefore get severely judged by implacable Soviet justice for defecting? Or abandon princess Susie vigil and scarper back to hotel?

After intensive debating, I decide I got to scarper.

Only if I go back now to Moscow and proper official return in July can I succeed to woo Princess Susie and reunite with Lord Gore, present beautiful bride and her family to KGB (namely Smerdyakov), convince Soviet authorities that I been acting with due spirit of socialist integrity to reclaim English birthright and therefore convince them of allowing me to stay in England and also bring my mother to share this paradise with me.

With heavy heart I write one more PS letter to Susie, this time not being in poetry but actually hasty and scribbling, maybe even with English grammar mistakes, explaining that I got to leave now for important reason of international socio-politics, but she just got to remain constant in her burning love for me, and soon I return to marry her, namely in July when Russians coming to London to conquer World Soccer Cup.

As final thought, I add short verse of famous Russian song, '*Zhdi menya i ya vyernus*' . . .', meaning 'Wait for me and I return, Only very much wait and wait . . .'

Then I drop this also into Princess Susie basement and go running off real fast cross Hyde Parking and Kensington Parking back to hotel in Bayswater Road, just at time to find Smerdyakov, Granatkin and Tompkins of FO standing in hotel lobby awaiting me for imminent departure to Khitro Airport.

As we boarding our Aeroflot Tupolev, Tompkins is shaking off all our hands and telling that he hope to see us again in July when he can again be our guide and helper on behalf of Gracious Majesty and I say this is something I am also highly desiring, while glancing with strong facial meaning at Smerdyakov.

Four hour later, we are back in Domodedovo Moscow Airport and also back in laws of Soviet reality. Noble beauty of transcending world of London is seeming real far away.

PART

PART FOUR

Moscow in January is full of dirt and grey brown snow driftings. Filthy pothole road from airport to town leads through muddy fields and crumbling housing estates, over frozen river with thousand of hopeless footprint not leading nowhere, past rusty old anti-fascist tank defences and ugly chemical plant, and I am thinking, How a man can live in such a world like this?

After debriefment at Lubyanka headquarter, me and Smerdyakov and Granatkin all saying *do svidaniya* and departing for few vacation days before resuming KGB and footballing duties.

And as I am walking out from that Lubyanka, past statue of Iron Feliks, past Bolshoi and statue of Karl Marx, past Gosplan building, along Gorky Street past Lenin Post Office and up stairs again to Vova apartment, I am wondering what will await me from now on.

Vova is not home when I get there, but I still got a keys which are turning and opening that familiar door where Vova been walking out of my dream and where KGB been knocking in middle of a nightmare to come into it . . .

Inside that apartment, I am searching real careful everywhere but no signs existing of any latest model Elektron, nor any TV set whatsoever.

But hanging on a wall is very large blow-up photo of USSR football game in which Malofeyev just been scoring a goal and

Vova Smirnov wheeling into camera with the large grin and the big wink on his face.

And hanging next of this on thumb tacks is three USSR football jerseys with number 10 on back, number belonging to Vova Smirnov, as everybody know.

I place my baggages on Vova floor, sit down on his sofa and look around.

And things feel pretty hard.

Hard for being back in Moscow, hard for being back in Soviet reality, hard for being so far distant from father Lord Gore and beautiful Princess Susie and also far distant from beloved mother. Now that I been tasting that other world world, how I can be settling back in this one?

Just then, door is opening and in walk Vova carrying three vodka bottles and large jar of pickle herrings and he look at me somewhat surprised and say, 'Zhenya? You come back again? So you been cured now?'

And I look at him and not understanding what he is meaning, so I just smile with somewhat straining smile.

But Vova laugh and say, 'Oh well, never care! Let us open first this bottle and then we open up this one and later we open up this one!'

And that is exactly what we been doing, and only finish off drinking each and every one to very bottoms when it is long past midnight in Moscow and maybe even chiming thirteen or fourteen!

And when I awake next morning, Vova already left off to training session, so I am sitting in that apartment and reflecting on all that been happening to me.

On the one hands, I been glimpsing into other better world and seeing lights at end of a corridor.

On the other hands, here am I back in Moscow, exile from

that paradise, and thoughts are circling round my head like black ravens trying to plunge me back in the *toska*.

That night, when Vova return home, I try to question him about the strange events that been happening to me. One thing especially puzzling me: that nightmare visit from KGB and how come it happened for me to get recruited by competent organs?

What been the cause of this? Is it doing of Vova and his KGB comrades?

But when I ask him these questions, Vova just look at me like I gone mad.

So I smile and ask him again.

But Vova just shrug off his shoulders and say, 'Look, Zhenya, I am not knowing anything whatsoever about all this. And anyway, how come you think I been involving with competent organs? I am just simple footballing fellow. And KGB team is Dinamo, not CSKA, which is army team like you know.'

Well, this is somewhat strange reply, but I guess it must be necessary subterfuging by Vova, who been strictly enjoined always to deny true nature of his intelligence activities.

Then we are discussing what will happen next in our lives, and Vova tell all about forthcoming training period for World Cup in July. But something strange, because he make no mention whatsoever of my role as top interpreter for USSR team, like somehow he doesn't think I am coming to England at all.

I keep telling him that for sure I am working for KGB and I already been in England with Granatkin and Smerdyakov and I recount him all my adventures there.

But Vova is not replying and just look at me somewhat strange and dubious about everything I been saying.

And things stay this way between us for next few days with nothing being resolved and all questions remaining open.

After a week, I tell Vova I soon got to report back for KGB duty at Lubyanka and he say, 'Look, Zhenya. You sure about all this? You sure it true that you are working for KGB and got go to Lubyanka?' And I just say, 'Yes, for sure I got to go, Vova. KGB awaiting for me and depending on me for success of Soviet team in World Cup', and Vova is shrugging off his shoulders and says, 'OK then, whatever you saying.'

But that night all my old nightmares are dreaming back to me again and I cannot keep them out of my brain.

And after midnight I hear real loud knocking on the door and at first I am sure it is the black crow come for me or maybe leather jacket KGB with a black raven outside.

And in fact it really is KGB fellows, although not come for arresting me, thanks God, but actually come to take me to Lubyanka for important top level meeting with my KGB comrades.

I am getting up and getting ready, but when we are driving on the Gorky Street, I see I am still wearing my pyjamas and no shoes, and the fly of pyjama pants is open so I am trying to hold it closed but it keep opening and making me feel embarrassed.

And when we arrive in Lubyanka courtyard, KGB fellows in uniforms are all drawing up to attention and saluting real respectful and I realize it is me they are saluting and all of them trying to ignore my pyjamas and open fly because it is rude and insubordinate to laugh at me.

Inside Lubyanka, I am being led into the large conference hall with marble pillars and red velvet curtains.

When I enter, all KGB top bosses are there and all clapping

and making real low bows to me. I see they are holding some red velvet cushion with pair of black spectacles on it, and KGB Chairman is making polite speech saying what great honour to be bestowing this award today to KGB operative Yevgeny Gorevich, young man who distinguish himself in many field missions and therefore being specially entrusted with this very valuable pair of KGB spectacles. But maybe I am looking bit surprised at this, because KGB boss is smiling and explain these are not ordinary spectacles but actually containing extra special powers and only very few people ever considered worthy for receiving them by Soviet leadership.

Then whole delegation is clapping and I am about to put on the spectacles, but KGB Chairman give the nervous laugh and say, 'Maybe you better not put on those glasses while you still inside here, Comrade Gorevich, because for sure you do not want to use your new powers on us loyal comrades!' And whole room is laughing now and laughter is getting louder and louder and gets so loud that I pick up those spectacles in one hand, holding my flies together with other hand, and start running real fast out of that room, out of Lubyanka and onto the street.

And I am so scared of being in Lubyanka Square and only wearing pyjamas that I put on those magic spectacles in a hope that maybe they make me invisible.

But they don't do this at all.

In fact it seem every people is now looking at me, and strangely I can read precisely what is going through their minds, namely they thinking 'What for idiot and madman that guy must be, walking round in pyjama with flies open.'

So I hurry into nearby shop and pick up the jar of pickled herrings and when I hand over ten rouble note, shop assistant returns me only two roubles so I say, 'You been short of changing me' and shop fellow say, 'No, you only give me five rouble note', but because of magic spectacles I can read in his mind, namely he has the deep black heart and always cheating customers and hoarding money gains in secret chest made of sandalwood with large copper lock which he keep under his bed, so I say him, 'You better return my money, comrade, and also illegal roubles you got hidden in that sandalwood chest under you bed', and this guy is so shocking by this that his mouth drop right open and quickly hands me twenty rouble note and run in back of shop shouting for militia to come.

But I already left that place and now entering nearby Bolshoi theatre where *Sleeping Beauty* is performing and I sit in the circle looking down on parterre just as voluptuous, gorgeous evil black fairy Carabosse is entering and she look right at me and sweeps her long fingernails across her breast and straight-away I am looking round that theatre and I have the gift of seeing all women there as if they are naked to my gaze and furthermore can tell exact which one will love me and come to my bed and which one will not, such is power of magic KGB spectacles, but also – real scary – I can see who in this auditorium will die before the year is out and who will be crushed by trolleybus and who expire from infarct and who from cancer of epiglottis and who from overeating at Kropotkin-skaya restaurant and choking on the big fat chicken bones. I can see who will murder his neighbour, who will run off with Mrs Nekrasov and who be sent to *psykhushka* (psychiatric hospital) for crime of protesting against reality of Soviet life.

And all sorts of knowledge is vouchsafed me by these spectacles, including knowledge I do not wish to know, so I am reaching to remove them, but – horror, horror, horror – they are glued to my nose and my ears and I cannot take them off, so I am condemned forever to the unwanted gift of clear sight and knowledge . . .

And then I awake.

Ookhty, bookhty! Thanks God! I been daydreaming.

I am not in Bolshoi at all. But actually in some boring meeting at my office, discussing department budgets and new quotas for paperclips, so no wonder I been dozing away! I am so relieved to wake up from my nightmare that I am even pleased to see Smerdyakov there, taping with his finger on the desk and looking annoyed.

And I realize the reason I just been awaked is that Smerdyakov has been turning on me to address that meeting and it probably his finger banging which been sounding in my dream like KGB door knocking and he been calling out my name and getting angry, so now he is saying, 'I repeat: Comrade Gorevich will now report about successful music mission of SMIRD operatives to London. Comrade Gorevich, floor is yours!'

Phew!

Thanks God nightmares all ended and I am back in reality life, and only task I got to perform is simple report about our trip to Chelsea and Whitechapel for purchasing KGB 45 rpm records.

Quick as a flashing, I am listing all those rpms we been purchasing, such as Herb Alpert, Beatles, Troggles, Kinkles, Sneekers, Hollies, Mannfreds and many others which giving the accurate musical picture of UK political consciousness and class struggle in conditions of bourgeois democracy.

At end of my report, Smerdyakov turn to other KGB fellows and say, 'So, colleagues, from report of Comrade Gorevich you see full powerful potential of forthcoming revolutionary actions. Now task of Secret Music Ideology Research Department is to study these rpms brought back by Gorevich and by myself and work with Stakhanovite rhythm to complete necessary tasks before our mission continues in London in July. Comrades of SMIRD! Let us complete our mission with revolutionary zeal and ideological commitment! Let us work in name of Lenin. Lenin lived, Lenin lives, Lenin will live! Everybody go to works!'

Well, now I wish I still got those magic spectacles with special powers of understanding, because none of this is making much sense. What is all this music revolution mystery? And where is this SMIRD department suddenly appearing from?

But when I ask Smerdyakov for further explanation, he just say, 'Be patient, comrade. So far, you been carrying out a successful mission. Now duty is to stand ready for aiding SMIRD colleagues with necessary linguistic undertakings.'

During following weeks, those SMIRD fellows are coming nearly every day with requests for translating phrases into popular English idiom and Smerdyakov is coming and going for top levels meetings in Lubyanka and pretty soon also in Kremlin, which just over the other side of Marx Prospekt like you know. When I ask who he been meeting there, he is taping on side of his nose and making face of the fattish fellow with slitty eyes, so I know he actually referring to top boss, namely Comrade Brezhnev.

But that night when I am going home to Vova apartment and telling how President Leonid turning out as big fan of Cilla, Lulu, Dusty and Moody Blues, Vova just make some snorting sound and say, 'Don't be crazy, Zhenya. Now for sure you gone mad!'

Well, maybe so. And maybe not.

Because work of SMIRD is continuing at Stakhanovite paces (meaning fast and furiously) and plans for toppling over British capitalism making such progress that quotas all being fulfilled and overfulfilled every week, with some KGB operatives even receiving commendation for Lenin Prizes, so for sure this must be top operation we are working on and destined to hasten historical inevitability of triumph of socialism through spread of Marxist-Leninist revolution.

Meanwhile, Vova also training extra hard and overfulfilling all his quotas too, although I not too sure what exactly these quotas consisting of. And one day early in June, just around three week before schedule departure for England, he is returning home and waving about some piece of paper with great excitement which turn out to be final list of players selected by trainer Nikolai Morozov for Soviet team squad in World Cup finals, and list is:

Lev Yashin, Viktor Serebryanikov, Leonid Ostrovsky, Leonid Ponomarev, Valentin Afonin, Albert Shesternev, Murtaz Khurtsilava, Josef Szabo, Viktor Getmanov, Vasily Danilov, Igor Chislenko, Valery Voronin, **Vladimir Smirnov (!!!!!!!!!!)**, Aleksei Korneyev, Georgi Sichinava, Galimzyan Khusainov, Slava Metreveli, Valery Porkuyan, Anatoly Banichevsky, Eduard Malofeyev, Eduard Markarov, Anzor Kavazashvili and Viktor Bannikov.

Such announcement calls for immediate celebrating, of course, so Vova and me open several bottle of Georgian Tsinandali followed by several bottle of vodka.

And from this moment onward, things all starting to move forward with sudden increase of velocity as last countdown commences to final struggle of Vova and team-mates to conquer World Cup, final struggle of KGB and socialism to vanquish evil capitalists, and final struggle of Zhenya to redeem downtrodden sufferings of mother, me and all mankind.

*

At end of June, several Tupolevs and whole fleet of Ilyushins is taking off from Domodedovo with destination of Khitro Airport, London. Inside is USSR soccer team, All-Union Football Presidium, high number of officials and political advisers (meaning KGB fellows), big group of journalists and TV, and also any top Party guys who happen to like football or enjoyable few weeks in decadent capitalist West. And when we all arriving in London, whole regiment of reporters and photographs is coming with flashing cameras and shouting questions at us and I start to translate, but Smerdyakov look sternly at me and say '*Ty – zatknis!*' which is pretty vigorous way of requesting me to quietness.

If you think there been plenty of formalities such as banquets and speeches and things last time we been in London, you better see what happening this time! For next couple days, it seem like we all living in endless rounders of eating, drinking, speaking, toasting and – for me – translating. Mr Tompkins of FO is accompanying us again, like he been promising, and seems he is paying particular special attentions to me and Smerdyakov, such as following us right to door of hotel bedroom and even to gentleman lavatories, as if he suspicious of what we getting up to (not anything in lavatory of course, but maybe he think we are using such opportunity to make contact with progressive revolutionary elements of English society, which FO supposed to be repressing).

Pretty soon, all footballing parts of Soviet party, including Granatkin and Vova, are departing out of London and away to Grey College in Dooram town to prepare for upcoming World Cup games. I been expecting to go with them, but Smerdyakov is taking me apart and tell me that him and me actually staying in London to carry out special KGB mission, which is major good news of course because it mean I am remaining here close to Belgravia and objects of my own mission.

But actually it look like Smerdyakov doing the very utmosts to ensure I don't got any spare times whatsoever for independent activities. So soon as footballers all left, he is taking me with him to top level meeting at Soviet embassy, where we are sitting down with Second Secretary (one more KGB fellow, obviously) and they give me real long lecture about importantness of this mission we embarking in and how it got to be kept complete secret from outside world and if it succeed then we are striking major blow for cause of socialism and maybe even altering international geo-political realities such as East–West balances of powder.

And it take these guys maybe thirty or fifty minutes of talk about Soviet values and noble Lenin and so forth, before they getting to any real information whatsoever. And even then, they not explaining much, but just telling how I will be crucial element of this operation and get informed of my role on the strict needing-to-be-knowing basis, meaning I get ordered about for doing things without never understanding what they actually for.

And first such task, they say I got to sit down right now in top security room of Soviet embassy and translate some vital documents into correct English.

At last, I am thinking, now we getting to the chasing, so I am expecting maybe top secret military plans or shocking revelations about capitalist iniquity to translate, but no! what they actually giving me is some big pile of poems. And not even any good poems such as Pushkin or Lermontov or Tyutchev or Fet or even such as Balmont or Blok or Mayakovsky or even Khodasevich, but actually just some doggerel poems like any idiot can be writing so long as it got the true revolutionary sentiment (which, to be fair, actually account for pretty large proportion of all Soviet poetry).

Anyway, I am sitting there in top security room and diligent translating these poems, and they all similar of this following one, which goes a little bit like this:

> I hear a noise of the revolutionary feets
> Which are walking up and down through all our streets.
> Summer weather is warm;
> Just right for socialist new dawn.
> Now is dialectically proper time
> For constructing barricades all in a line.
> But what a poet can do?
> He must join a revolutionary crew!
> And his singing must drown
> Bourgeois apathy of London town!
>
> Harken to me, comrades! We need palace revolution!
> For people's ills this is only true solution.
> Well then, is anything what poor poet can do?
> Oh, yes! He must join the revolutionary crew!
> And his singing must drown
> Bourgeois lethargy of London town!
>
> OK! So my poetry will cause disturbance;
> It will raise a cry for deposing the king and also
>   condemn his servants.
> But what a poor poet can do?
> He must join a revolutionary crew!
> And his singing must crown
> New socialist order in London town!

After few hours, I emerge from that room to unveil such top English translating to Smerdyakov and other KGB fellow and they are scratching on their heads and say, 'Mmm. Pretty good translating, comrade, but what about maybe change this bit or that bit?', but I say they better just mind to their own affairs since neither ones of them understanding English whatsoever, so they actually just being typical bossy KGB types like as usual, and how come they would know anything anyway?

And this seem to do the trickery because those fellows both meekly shutting up, and later when I ask them again what is strategic purpose of this translating operation they finally letting some beans out of the bag.

In fact, Smerdyakov seem real proud of his self and start boasting about brilliant ingeniality of this mission which he invented. And those two fellows are getting carried up with enthusiasm and posing me questions such as, 'What is your information about proletarian consciousness of English pops music, comrade?' and 'Who is most revolutionary pop ensemble in whole of England?' and I say actually I got no ideas at all, so they somewhat smirking at this lack of knowledge and proudly announcing, 'Top scientists of Soviet SMIRD department, which we been especial creating for this mission, been deploying latest research and analysing methods for dialectical surveying whole of UK pop culture scene and now they objectively concluded without any shade of doubts that most revolutionary ensemble in whole of United Kingdom is for sure: the Dave Dee, Dozy, Beaky, Mick and Tich!'

Well, I am pretty surprised by this conclusion, because this is pop ensemble which been producing such top hits as 'If music be food of love, prepare for indigestion', 'Touch me, touch me' and lyrics resembling 'zabadak, zabadac, zabadac; karakakora, kakarakak, zabadac; shhai, shai, skagalak; zabadac, love can reveal us all', which to me is not sounding too revolutionary or imbued with burning sense of class consciousness and indignation at fate of working peoples.

But Smerdyakov is waving round some piece of paper with

algebra looking signs and very long scientific calculations and declare, 'Look! This is dialectical analysis by SMIRD computer, so no point you arguing whatsoever, comrade', and from then on I just shutting myself up.

Next day, Smerdyakov and other KGB fellow say I got to come with them for real important meeting with manager of the DD, D, B, M and T and maybe we even going to meet top revolutionary man, Dave Dozy his self.

But before going to this meeting, which is taking place on the Compton Street near to Soho, I ask these fellows what exactly is real nature of our mission, because if I am not knowing, then for sure I will make cardinal errors in my interpreting. And those two bosses look at each others and then nod, and Smerdyakov make the little speech of explaining. 'Comrade Gorevich,' he say, 'this is mission of vital importance for world revolution. You remember we been discussing what elements are playing central role in life of English peoples, and we been concluding football, beer, bingo and pops music? OK, well KGB been scientifically evaluating all these possibilities for revolutionary exploitation and they given us the mission to infiltrate one of them – namely the pops music. Goal of our mission is no less than covert infusion of Marxist-Leninist dialectics into English pops world, with same effect like we are infusing special socialist ideology drug (which not actually existing, infortunately) into universal drinking water of whole English nation. Today we are making historic link-up between people's dictatorship of USSR and top revolutionary pops ensemble of UK in order for planting seeds of subversion, sedition and revolt in minds of the English classes! This is master stroke of socialist ingeniality!'

I am replying of course this is great idea, but secretly I am maintaining doubts about any wisdom of such a mission and especially about level of revolutionary consciousness attained by ensemble of Dave Dee, Dozy, Beaky, Mick and Tich.

And when we arrive in the Compton Street, these doubts are complete bearing themselves out, because Mr Dave Dozy is not even coming to meeting and that manager guy is taking one look at our proposal of lyrical material and bursting into the loud laughing.

Ten minutes later, we three revolutionary poets are back in the Piccadilly tubes station and all arguing about what are reasons for such conclusive mission failure.

Smerdykov claim this must be solely fault of my unsuccessful translating, because he know for sure that SMIRD scientists been constructing objectively perfect song lyricals for accurate matching with music and ideology tastes of English pops market and also been scientifically choosing Dave Dee, Dozy, Beaky, Mick and Tich as perfect ensemble for covert placing of such lyricals.

And he get pretty enangered and looking right at me while saying that further failure to implant KGB lyricals – we got six or seven more such poems – will necessitate abandoning of whole mission and therefore immediate return to Moscow.

Next day is coming some better news, this time connected with footballing affairs, namely that Soviet Union is triumphing in first league group game against Democratic People Republic of North Korea being played at the Hairsome Park of Middelsbur-row FCs. Those Korean fellows all big ideological soulmates of Soviet people, of course, and for some reason they get to be wearing the red outfitting while ours got to wear white and blue. But this is not impeding socialist momentum of our side and Malofeyev is scoring from out on right hand touching-line after thirty minutes, followed by goal of Banichevsky just two minute later.

Vova is also having storming game and making the big pressing on Korean defences, which are getting pretty tired up by end of ninety minutes, so allowing Malofeyev to score one more just before end of the match.

Afterward, I am ringing up the Grey College to talk to Vova and congratulate him on victory. After dropping in the thrup-any-bits and pressing button B, it is actually friendly Granatkin fellow who is answering and make couple of chattings with me and then passing over telephone line to Vova who sounds real excited.

He say trainer Morozov been congratulating all our guys, but also predicting big team changes for next game, against Italy, and I guess Vova even thinking he got the chance of becoming Soviet team captain, although he not saying this.

Eventually, Vova ask what been happening in London and I tell him that things not doing too good, mainly due to continuing failure of pops lyric operation and also failure so far to fulfil my personal mission.

This last bit seem to interest Vova because he start asking questions, like what is my intentions for this personal mission and what my exact plans, and after I explain him everything he is saying, 'Well, Zhenya. You mean you actually planning to go defecting?'

And I say, 'This not defecting, Vova; this is reclaiming true birthright and heritage.' But Vova not sounding too convincing by this and we are saying farewell with somewhat subdued atmos-phere and promising to speak again after Italy game in four days later.

After this telephone call, something strange is happening, namely every morning during breakfast meeting, Smerdyakov

starts handling me complete official timetable for that day with
exact details where I got to be located for meetings and eatings
and even for sleepings at all times, and also stressing any changes
in official plan got to be notified to him or to Soviet embassy,
and I am thinking, Hmm, looks like Smerdyakov not trusting
me too much whatsoever any more.

One good thing happening that week, though, and this is
involving the musical subversion manoeuvres. After considered
reflecting – meaning he don't got any better ideas – Smerdyakov
is agreeing that my suggestion of maybe contacting Rolling
Stones fellows is not looking so bad one after all, especially now
that Dave Dozy and Tich been turning out as unprincipled
bourgeois stooges.

So he is handling me back that visitcard of Stone manager
Loog Oldham and I am ringing up and reminding of our
agreement we been making six month earlier at Marquee Club.
Loog say Yeah, he remember me. He not real sure when we can
get conferring with Michael and Keef, but maybe if we come
to revolution later on, he will see what can be doing. So I
say, Yeah man, see you at the revolution and I put down that
telephone and immediate run to African friend Idi at hotel
receiving desk in order for finding out what is this revolution;
and fortunately Idi is laughing and say, 'Revolution is top night
spot, Zhenya, locating on the Frith Street. But you guys better
get preparing for pretty long night, because Revolution action
usually going on right through to dawning times', which quite
good news for me seeing as I am still young man at this period
and pretty interesting in these sort of affairs (night clubs, not
revolutions).

When we arrive there, I explain to door fellow that we are
invited guests of Mr Loog and Mr Michael and Mr Keef, so he
allow us inside.

Inside is pretty strange place indeed. It look just like some dark chambers out of reign of Henry Eighth, with wood panels on walls and one room with signs of zodiac all painting on the ceiling, but with loud music playing such as the Trex and the Whose and real bright lights flashing on and off which is making Smerdyakov feel nauseating, but I quite enjoying it.

Meanwhile, Mr Loog is spotting us and indicate to join him in a side room where things is somewhat quieter and dining table laid over with food and – especially – drinks.

Smerdyakov is adopting his frowning KGB look and instructing me to ascertain were-abouts of Michael and Keef, and Mr Loog reply, 'Oh, Mick is in the cupboard', which I understand as some slanging expression meaning he is drunk or something, but actually turning out to be literal describing because pretty soon Mick is emerging from secret concealed door in a back wall together with some real foxy chick (meaning attractive young lady) and both of them still adjusting their cloths which is giving good indicating of what recent activity been going on in there.

And actually it seem this activity been going on pretty well and most likely giving Mick that satisfaction he previously been lacking, because when he find out that we are Soviet fellows, he is appearing highly amicable and talkative, first asking about World Cup prospects and highly appraising performance of Vova Smirnov, which I am greatly appreciating and recount him that Vova is my best friend (and also best enemy, which I am not recounting).

Then Mick say maybe it going to be USSR playing the England in final match of World Cup, since group tables looking toward such likelihood, but first Alf got to get his wingless wonders going, which I am not understanding and therefore not translating, and Smerdyakov is smelling some rat here so he demand me to immediate propose SMIRD invented song lyricals to Mr Mick.

Hmm.

Following Dozy Dee experience, I am somewhat dubious of this idea.

But actually it is OK because Mick just take one look at these lyricals and say, 'Hey man, this is cool writing operation you got going here' and he show our KGB composition to Mr Loog who is also nodding off his head and Mick say, 'Thanks, man. We can use this for sure and we gonna call it by name of "Fighting in the Street Man".'

I am pretty exciting by such mission success, but Smerdyakov is insistently nudging me and keep saying, 'Make certain you also get someone to take that "Anarchy in the UK" song we been composing', and eventually I am handling this over to very young fellow by name of Mr Rotten, but I don't think this one ever getting made into any top pops.

It is the 3 a.m. before Smerdyakov and me leave that Revolution place, and he is in pretty good mood because musical mission been accomplished and he can report back to SMIRD on successful first stage of undermining UK bourgeois democracy.

Only one thing slight worrying me: while we exiting onto the Frith Street, I catch a sight of tall fellow in hippy (meaning popular culture style) kaftan and beads looking somewhat secretive and watching us with real beady eyes and even jotting down in the notebook, and actually I am pretty sure this is old friend Tompkins of FO once again.

But when I recount this to Smerdyakov he just make little bit drunkish smile and say, 'Do not worry, Zhenya. All is well in material world and inevitable triumph of socialism approaching on horizon.'

So I guess this mean I better just shut myself up like usual.

Next day, Smerdyakov is having several meetings at Soviet embassy and returning in mid-afternoon with top enjoyful mind frame and telegraph cable from SMIRD in Moscow. Cable is written in secret language (in case MI5 interceiving it) and says: 'Congratulation on ready, steady, go of top popping mission. Party DJ Number One is thanking you lucky stars', which clearly referring to personal commending from President Leonid his self!

Smerdyakov is opening up a vodka bottle and settling down for well-deserving celebration, so I am profiting to scarper off on my own *podvig* mission and running to Belgrave Square.

This time there is happy surprise in the store.

So soon I arrive, I see objective of my passions, very beautiful and elegant Susie, right there in shady square garden behind the black railing.

For some moments, I am standing there enwrapped. Susie is dressed in the aristocratic hair net device and eating elegant fish and chippings from top people's newspaper *Financial Time*.

This princess is having so much class!

I call out to her, but she cannot seem to hear, and when I get up closer I understand why: she got the transistor radio playing real loud and she is singing along and twisting with Mr Fluff the pop picker.

So I watch her through the railing and she seem to me like some beautiful unattainable goddess, some ideal, perfect *prekrasnaya dama* on other side of that boundary between two worlds – world of us poor mortals over here and world of flawless beauty over there.

Then I shout even louder and Susie turns her noble face to me and say, 'Oh blimey, it's you again', and I say 'Yes. Please open up a door to your paradise garden.'

And Princess Susie come slowly over to those railings and say, 'Well, if I lets you in, you gotta promise you ain't getting up to no funny business', and I say, 'For sure no, beautiful lady. I only getting up to serious business.' And she look at me little bit strange but open up that garden gate and I go inside.

Straightaway I am falling to the knees and begin my passion declaration, but Susie make the gracious noble gesture for to me arise and say in beautiful voice of true love, 'Gerrout of it! None o'that stuff in 'ere or the gardener'll spot us and sling us out.'

So I sit down on a bench aside her and we both listen in silence of loving rapture to transistor radio playing the pop tops. After some minutes, Mr Fluff Freeman is introducing Mindbenders record and I am begin again with the passion declaration, but Princess Susie read my mind and say, 'Shurrup! It's a groovy kind of love.' And I reply, 'Yes, my darling: my love is very groovy and true!' And for next half hour we are listening together to tranny radio and she keep making similar exclaimings to confirm her love for me, such as, 'Oh! You don't have to say you love me!' and 'Oh! It's got to be you!' and 'Oh! Don't stop lovin' me baby!' and 'Oh! Reach out; I'll be there!' and 'Oh! Yellow Submarine!' (although I am not really understanding what she mean by this last one).

Next day is coming big footballing moment, with crucial USSR versus Italy clash in the offering, and us Soviets at hotel and embassy are getting pretty nervous and gathering in TV room for watching the BBC coverages.

Those former fascists got pretty strong stars line-up, such as Albertosi, Facchetti, Mazzola, Meroni and so forth, but Soviet

Union also having some top names back who not been playing versus Korea, such as Lev Yashin, Valery Voronin and Vasily Danilov, and also having hand of Great Lenin guiding over us, which always very helpful. Vova is playing too, although not being made captain because Shesternev is retaining in that function.

And additional lucky omen, this is birthday of USSR football president Valentin Granatkin and also of top midfielder Mr Voronin.

So combination of Lenin – who always with us – and lucky omens is bringing home the victory to team of people's proletariat.

Igor Chislenko is scoring only goal, and afterwards Italian trainer Edmondo Fabbri say he is sure that USSR going all the way into final.

Even fascist English newspapers such as *Sun* and *Daily Mail*, which previously been sneering to our Soviet team, now got to admit our guys are top fellows and calling Chislenko 'Russian Rocket' and Shesternev 'Ivan Terrible' (although not meaning terrible, but actually meaning top man).

Most important thing, victory over Italians mean that USSR now assured of passage into quarter-final knocking-out stage, whatever result occurring in our final group game against Chilli.

So Morozov announce he going to play all our reserves team for Chilli game and making nine changes from regular line-up, including to drop out V. Smirnov.

But that night when I ring up, Vova is not down at hearted and say, 'Actually, this is good thing Morozov want to get me and other fellows fit and rested for following quarter-final with Hungary' (which going to be the real needling match seeing as heroic Red Army been friendly invading their country just ten year ago in 1956).

After some more footballing affairs, Vova enquiring again about progress of my plan for reunification mission at Belgrave Square and sound very interested in hearing what next steps I am planning.

When I tell him my plan is for slipping out from hotel real early next morning, Vova just say, 'Thank you for information, Zhenya. You can trust me', and then he put down the lines without making any rendezvous for further phone calling, which is somewhat arising my suspicion.

That night, I am feeling impossible for sleeping. Whole time, I am regarding alarms clock and awaiting for silence to fall, which is sure indication Smerdyakov and other KGB fellows now dreaming sweet dreams of Lubyanka interrogations and holidays trips in their black ravens.

At 3 a.m., I am unable of awaiting any further. So I put on my cloths, place the Not Disturbing notice on my door and slip out through fire escape to Bayswater Road.

Half hour later, I am arriving at the Belgrave Square and appointment with my destination. This time, I not wasting time knocking front of the door (which seem pretty pointless anyway since no one ever open it), but instead I push that little gate in front house railings and descend down stone steps to basement area where I once seen Princess Susie.

Down there I am screwing up my bravery just like great *bohatyr* Ilya Muromets and pushing a door to see is it opening, which actually it is doing straightaway with little creak to make me jump. Inside is deep dark room where I cannot see whatsoever before my eyes.

So I am tip of the toeing forward and looking for some

Edenby-Gores, when I hear terrible loud noise like a train is thundering into that basement.

And in front of me I see whole bunch of people slumped in chairs, or with heads resting on tables . . .

And train noise is these people snoring!

Some very loud, like the big diesel express train and others – mainly ladies – rather delicate like quiet Soviet electric train that been promised under latest Five Year Plan. Loudest of all snorers is one very large fellow in waistcoat and stripy pants slumping in some old battered armchair with arms hanging down (his arms, not chair arms) and very large belly moving up and down like it trying to burst out of those stripy pants. If poet Mayakovsky been seeing this, I think maybe he re-write his great poem of 'Cloud in Pants' to pudding in pants, or maybe whale in pants. Ha, ha! This fellow got the mouth wide open while snoring, and several bluebottle flies buzzing in and out like they playing the game of who get caught and who not.

But in other corner of that room is much more attractive sight. Sleeping much more beautiful and only doing the dainty snoring is lovely Princess Susie.

I am quickly checking up my appearances, such as smartness of the hairstyle, by looking to the mirror hanging on a wall.

But this mirror is *tooskly* and *smootny* (meaning dark and dim) and I cannot see too much through it, except maybe deep within that dimness a small point of light is coming from very far away, from another country or another distant world. Just like I once been seeing in Lord Gore's silver mirror in my mother's secret chest.

And I know my destination is to wake that princess and all her courtiers.

I try coughing, but not succeeding.

Then I say, 'Excuse me, ladies and gentlemen', but again failing to wake them.

They are sleeping on like some magician's curse preventing them from returning to this world.

So I lean over Princess Susie and prepare to make the respectful but loving kiss on her lips, since this is well-knowed way for waking up from evil fairy's spell and princess will open her eye and see her beloved prince (namely me) and straightaway embrace her rescuer (me) leading to mutual happy ends.

Well, first part is coming true, namely beautiful princess awaking.

But then she is making the real loud scream, some little dog is starting up with the barking, fellow in stripy pants is standing up and seizing me with firm grip around the collar, and few moments later whole room is full of bobby militiamen rushing in from doors and windows and maybe even out of cupboards, who knows? and they all shouting different things such as 'Stop thiefs!' and 'Hello, hello, hello!' and burglary alarm is ringing off and police klaxon-sirens wailing and what a poor boy can do except putting up the hands and surrender?

In half hour later, I am sitting in fascist prison cell of Belgravia police station and staring on the window with bars and walls where prisoner names all carved while awaiting hanging on account of sheeps stealing or similar offence.

Outside, dawn is raising and still I cannot comprehend how those bobby militias been emerging and doing the collaring duties or even how they been knowing I am there at all. Worst of all, I am imagining how Smerdyakov is coming to breakfast meeting about this very moment with usual time-tabling of where I got to be that day and not yet knowing I will be in complete different locations altogether!

And how surprising he must be and how even more surprising and furious when he discover what happened to me.

But then some other thoughts entering in my head. Black thoughts, mainly concerning Vova Smirnov!

Maybe it is Vova who been tippling off those English bobbies?

All the more I am sitting there, all the more I am convincing that Vova been my nemesis again, just like he always done before. All those times when he been pretending as my friend and looking after me, he actually been playing a game of stools pigeon. Now things all making sensible, such as why Vova been taking so great interest in my Lord Gore plans and why I am falling victim of fascist English justice and probably also of socialist Soviet justice too, so I guess he will be happy.

Hours are passing by and fascist English jailors throwing slops of the stinking food in my cell and I am pacing upwards and downwards and beginning to slide into deeps of the *toska* with black crows about to appear and I cannot keep track of events, and time and my life spinning into the blur of gloom and dislocation.

And then cell door is opening and in walk ... Mr Tompkins of FO!

Mr Tompkins is wearing usual grey suit again, not any kaftan or beads, and got three big jailor fellows with him all doing what he tell them and treating him respectful, which make me think Mr Tompkins is big wheeler round here, and also getting me worried about impending fascist torture sessions they probably preparing.

I am recalling Smerdyakov warnings about not revealing any state secrets to fascist torturers, but actually desperate trying to remember any state secrets I can think of so I can reveal them all pretty sharpish and get these fellows off of me.

Infortunately, not too many state secrets coming into my head just now.

Mr Tompkins and his fellows are crowding into that dungeon cell, which is pretty tight fit due to being only couple metres long, and they all looking real mean and threatening, so I say, 'Mr Tompkins! I am Yevgeny Gorevich of Soviet Union and I demand for seeing official of Soviet embassy!' But this not producing too much effect on them so I quickly add, 'And I am Lord Zhenya Edenby-Gore of 82 Belgrave Square and close relative of Her Majesty, so do not be exerting too much undue torturing on me please', which is seeming to have desirable effect because Tompkins is ceasing the mean and threatening looks and showing he is pretty impressed about this royal revelation by adopting more respectful attitude, namely he start little bit smiling.

And one more step in desirable direction is soon following, because Tompkins tell his torturer fellows to leave that cell and we just remaining there on our owns.

Now Mr Tompkins is acting pretty friendly and even making apology for everything that been happening to me, including getting arrested and spending unpleasant few hours in Her Majesty prison.

But I am not being fooled by this, because I remember KGB training telling that fascist interrogators often adopt such false friendliness routines. So I repeat my insistent demand to see Soviet official (which seem more hopeful than demand to see Her Majesty), but Tompkins say, 'Actually, that may not be best thing for you at this moment, Zhenya.'

And when I ask him what is reason for this, he smile and say, 'There are one or two things I better explain you, young man. We all of us in the same business, like you know; and in this business of ours, things not always exactly what they seeming.'

Well, I tell him he can repeat that again!

In fact, not many things in my life are turning out what they been seeming for pretty long time now, and I hope this Tompkins fellow going to explain some of them.

But first I want to learn why I better not be seeing any Soviet official, and he say, 'You know, there are Soviet officials and there are Soviet officials', which seem pretty oblivious statement to me. But Tompkins continuing, 'Some Soviet officials working for Soviet Union, some Soviet officials working for their selves and some Soviet officials working for us. And you better get knowing this, Zhenya.'

Well, I am protesting that this is complete impossible because loyalty of Soviet peoples not open to any doubts, and for sure this got to be some capitalist slander and centrefuge designed to throw dust in eyes of infortunate Soviet hostage, namely me.

But Tompkins say he is not misleading me and actually trying to assist, and he promise to prove this, but first he going to explain how he can help me.

And then he is revealing how much he already know about my life history, which is quite a lot actually, including whole story of me and Masha at Minsk art competition, sad episode of my mother and *kommunalka* people's court, events surrounding forgery of internal passport and removing to Moscow, and even details of me and Vova drinking habitudes.

This all coming as pretty big shock to me, and Tompkins notice this and start laughing, 'You surprised by hearing all this, Zhenya? Well, remember what I just been telling about Soviet officials and who they actually working for. How you think I been finding out all these details? It is not from reading the *Pravda*, you know!'

So things becoming little bit clearer, firstly that Tompkins of FO is not actually of FO at all, but probably of MI5 or MI6 or MIsomething; secondly he been talking to someone or some-ones with pretty intimate knowledge of my career so far; and thirdly this someone can only be KGB official, having access to all my files.

I want to find out who been denouncing on me and also ask Mr Tompkins some important questions about what exactly been going on, but he just smile at this and say, 'Sorry, old chap. It the tea time now and I got to go on a tea breaking. So I leave you to reflect somewhat on what I been revealing, and then I come back again and we talk further. Toodle-pip.'

And out he walk from my cell, leaving me in the deep quandary of doubt and speculations.

And those English fellows must be pretty serious about their tea breaking, because Tompkins is not returning that day and not even coming back next day or day after.

And whole time I am sitting in that dungeon place and getting more and more overwhelming by worry and suspicions.

I am worrying what going to happen to me; worrying what Smerdyakov thinking about me and where I disappeared to; worrying that I will be condemned to jail sentencing and never see my mother again and she going to be sitting there in Vitebsk wrongly thinking that only son Zhenya fled to land of happiness and abandoned her to the fate.

By time of Tompkins returning after three days later, I am desperate for hearing what he got to tell me and ready to do pretty all whatever he ask me in order for getting out of there.

But Tompkins is instructing me to patience and telling that I got to follow him somewhere.

And that somewhere transpiring to be out of cell and down corridors into some room with few chairs and half dozen of bobbies all watching television set (not Elektron of course, but model name of Pye). On screen is elderly bobby man (actually resembling most of those fellows sitting there!) and he look right into camera and say, 'So, moral of this story that crime does not pay whatsoever anything, and criminals always getting caught and serving up with their just desserts. So long for now, and see you again soon in Dock's Green. Evenings all' and then some sort of whistling music, programme is ending and those bobbies all say, 'Well, that was good wasn't it? Time to get catching some criminals ourself.'

And soon me and Tompkins left by our owns and I want to ask him all my questions, but he is signalling for further patience and indicate that TV about to begin a new programme, turning out to be football match between USSR and Chilli which I been mentioning you earlier.

So me and Tompkins sit there watching football game and whole time I am desperate to learn about my fate, but he just telling some story about Sir Walter Drake and game of bowls and this meant to be explaining that never any need to be rushing things and everything going to be explained, but first you got to drink some tea and play some bowling and watch some football, and this is just English way of doing things.

In fact, I am beginning to suspect MI5 psychology ploy from Mr Tompkins, namely making me so nervous and worried as possible in preparation for final reckoning that is coming in between us, but anyway I got no choice so I just got to sit there and watch football with him. Only good thing is that USSR triumphing once again, this time by score of two-to-one, and both goals scoring by Valery Porkuyan, young striker fellow being selected in place of usual guys Banichevsky and Malofeyev.

At end of game, Mr Tompkins turn to me and offering congratulations on Soviet triumph and then he say, 'I got some

more good news for you too, young man, namely I been thinking about your predicament and been discovering real perfect
way of helping you out.'

I am almost giving Tompkins Russian style kiss on the face,
but he is signalling this is not English way of doing things so
instead we just got to smile and shake off the hands. And in
fact, this is probably better, because I am immediate thinking
this so-calling good news maybe actually just one more capitalist
ploy against me.

And Tompkins ask me, 'Tell me, Zhenya, what you desire
most in this world? What your top wish if you can have any
wish you like?'

Well, I suspect some trickery here, so I decide I better reply,
'Triumph of socialism is what I most desire in this world.'

I see Tompkins smiling somewhat when he hear this and
then say again, 'Fine. This is good answer, Zhenya. But what
you actually wanting for yourself? What you really, really
wanting?'

Hmm. This starting to get tough interrogating. So I decide
best answer to say, 'I tell you what I really really want. Triumph
of Soviet football team in World Cup. That what I really, really
want.'

And Tompkins smiling again and say, 'OK, Zhenya. But
triumph of socialism and triumph of USSR football team not
exactly something I can arrange, infortunately. Maybe I can be
some assistance, though. Maybe I suggest what you really, really
wanting is actually for get free from this police station and then
get uniting with Lord Gore and Miss Murphy.'

Well, this is somewhat perplexing because Miss Murphy is
not anyone I know, so I say Mr Tompkins naturally I wish
his assistance on the liberation issue, but the person I desire
unification with is Princess Susie.

And once again, Mr Tompkins give the little smile and say, 'You mean Susie Murphy?' and I say, 'Maybe that what you calling her, but in fact she is Princess Susie. And how come you knowing so much about all these secret things that are only knowed by me?'

But Tompkins just smile once more and say, 'It is my job to know these things. So tell me, you wanting my assistance, or not?'

And of course I got to say affirmatively, yes I do.

And this when Tompkins is offering up that bargain deal I been expecting ever since he first mention me about mysterious good news, and which KGB training rigorously instructing all agents strictly to refuse even if it is highly tempting bargain deal and sounded like a good idea at the time.

'Zhenya,' he say in real friendly voice, 'for getting assistance from me and desired unification with Lord Gore and Miss Mur ... er, Lady Susie, all you got to do is make me one little favour ...'

And when he say this, there is completely no way whatsoever I can even think of refusing, because he just summed up those things I always been desiring and only outcome in my life that can bring me happiness and sweet revenge over so many bad things material existence been throwing at me and my mother for so many years.

So I just say, 'OK, Mr Tompkins. You win. You tell what I got to do and I be doing it.'

And Tompkins smile one final time and pats on my back and say, 'Very good, Zhenya. Now I going tell you some things that maybe of interest to you.'

And for next half hour he is recounting whole improbable truth of what really been going on for past months in my life and also – this really important – in life of Mikhail Yu.

Smerdyakov, so-calling political adviser to Soviet footballing presidium and so-calling loyal member of KGB.

And how different this new truth is from previous truth I been believing in! According to Mr Tompkins, person who been informing to him is not Vova Smirnov, but that very same Smerdyakov who been constantly reminding me, every single morning and every single night, about stern responsibleness of loyal KGB operative and strictly warning against any contacts with strange English people.

Now it transpire that man with all the strange contacts is Smerdyakov!

And chief strange contact is Tompkins of the MI5!

So I say, 'You mean you telling me Mikhail Yu. Smerdyakov is traitor to USSR?' and Tompkins smile once extra time and start telling how this not so easy thing to be assessing who is traitor and who not traitor, who is patriot and who is villain, who acting for correct reasons and good of all humanity and who not, and other difficult stuff.

At first, these ideas seem all wrong to me. But then I am thinking about my own duties and loyalties and actually reach some strange but also useful conclusions, namely that I myself got several patriotic duties and several necessary loyalties.

How come?

Because I also got several countries and several realities I got to be loyal to.

On the one hands, I am Yevgeny Gorevich, Soviet fellow and KGB operator (although I never really been too keen on this last bit . . . but never mind, this not the key point here), so these two things I got to be loyal to, for sure.

But I am also Lord Zhenya Edenby-Gore, important member of British aristocracy class and therefore Englishman.

So two more elements (capitalism and Englishness) I got to be loyal to.

And finally there is one loyalty area more higher and more important than any preceding ones, namely loyalty to mother and my own selves.

So all in all, this can give me pretty wide range of choices, and in fact there not too much problem for accepting any duties at all which Mr Tompkins going to propose me!

But when he finally make this proposing, it is not whatsoever what I been expecting. First Mr Tompkins say that big import- ant mission is being planned and he see me as perfect person for it, and then say this maybe going to sound somewhat strange idea, but he is proposing me to play important role in MI5 operation . . . to overthrow English prime minister!

Hold about!

English MI5 planning to overthrow English prime minister? This is height of craziness.

So I ask Mr Tompkins, 'Just for checking I been hearing you right. You want me to take place in coup plot against Prime Minister Harold Wilson? This is something I expect to hear from Smerdyakov and other KGB fellows, but not from servant of Her Majesty Top Secret Service!'

But Mr Tompkins just smiling (again, sorry) and say, 'That make things easier for you then. If this is sort of work you been expecting of doing anyway, you not going to have too many sleepiless nights about it.'

And I reply him, 'Maybe this true. But can you explain me why you fellows actually wanting to do such affair? Why you wanting to do down with Mr Wilson? Seem to me like you carrying out our own KGB duties for us.'

And Tompkins just smiling (very last time, this is promise) and ask me for being patient; he going introduce me to very important fellow who confirm all he been telling and also explain reasons for this operation.

And I say OK, but please I can talk to Mr Smerdyakov in means time?

And Tompkins say he try to arrange this, but then more days are passing, I am still sitting in jail and no Smerdyakov appearing. And when I ask Tompkins reason for this, he just say we got to wait for suiting opportunity of Smerdyakov getting away from Soviet embassy and not raising any suspicion.

Finally, Mr Tompkins is announcing that very important person he been mentioning, and this fellow turn out to be MI5 agent by name of Peter Right, who is introducing by secret codename of Ratcatcher, tall thin fellow with real sharp eyes and wearing smart blue blazer with stripy tie. He is shaking off my hand and smiling just like Tompkins (I think this must be MI5 special training smile which they all got to learn), so I say him, 'Why you intelligence fellows all plotting against Harold Wilson, your own prime minister?' and quick as flashing, Mr Right reply, 'Prime Minister? Do not be making me laugh! That guy is Commie bastard!' and then he realize who he talking to (namely me) and say, 'Oh, sorry. No offence being intended!' and Tompkins and Right both collapsing in a giggle, and even I am smiling some little bit because whole situation getting like the farce of Moscow Circus.

I got lots of questions for Right and Tompkins, but those fellows doing their Walter Drake tricks again and say, 'Yes, yes, Zhenya. We explain all that, but first please come with us because the Alf's boys about to play and we got to see if they beating those Argentinas.'

So we go again to TV room with bobby militias, and watch real dirty football game of England beating Argentina by score of one goals to nil, and when dirty Argentine captain is sent away by the arbiter, all those bobbies and spies get pretty exciting and pretty unEnglish and only me is remaining quiet.

At end of match, Right and Tompkins shaking off each other hands and even slapping on the back and announcing that signs now looking good for USSR confronting England in final of World Cup and how this is combination everyone in the MI5 hoping will transpire, with USSR just got to defeat Hungary and then maybe Federal Republic of West Germany (i.e. undemocratic former Nazis) in semi-final stages.

But now my patience been completely expired so I say them, 'Look! If you wanting me to take place in your plot affair, then you got to answer my questions right now, and no more tea breaks or Walter Drake bowling matches or even football games, OK?'

And Mr Right say, 'Right', and for next two hours he is recounting whole bundles of strange things including certain facts about Mr Harold Wilson (who actually he say we got to refer to as Mr Henry Worthington due to urgent top security and secrecy reasons), such as how he been going lots of times to Moscow, got lots of Russian friends, little bit on left wing of Labouring Party and so forth.

But I say, 'OK, maybe this all true. I am just simple Russian fellow so not understanding too much about anything. But all this seem pretty thin ice for launching the coup against him.'

And Peter Right just looking at me and say, 'Mr Gorevich, you are not knowing even half proportion of it. We got conclusive information that Henry Worthington been long time agent of you KGB guys and sending top secrets direct to Kremlin, such as promising nuclear disarmings and dismantling Western defence against Communist attack and so forth, and reason he been doing this is because he is deep in pocket of Kremlin and KGB.'

This pretty surprising news.

So I ask him how exactly KGB been getting Mr Worthington (actually Harold Wilson, but we not got to mention this name) into their pockets, and Mr Right is taping on side of his nose and reply, 'Blackmail. That how they got him in there. Involving murder at highest levels.'

Whoa!

Murder at highest levels! This is something I want hear more about.

But whatever I ask further, Mr Right refuse to answer and just say all will be clear when I join their plot.

So I say, 'OK, but let me get one thing straightened off. You all declaring that Henry Worthington is Commie agent, so you going to get rid of him. KGB declaring Henry Worthington is capitalist swine, so they also wanting rid of him. So everybody agree Mr Worthington got to go, only for different and opposite reasons?'

And Mr Right say, 'Right!' and give me real meaningful wink of an eye, and I say, 'So, if I understand correct, you not actually proposing me to be traitor at all?' and he say, 'Precisely the case. Or maybe it not the case. Depending on how you looking at things. But if you help us out, you probably get the Lenin Prize . . . and maybe even get secret Night at the Garter from Her Majesty, too!'

Hmm.

All this make real good sense while Mr Right explaining it, but not making any sense whatsoever when you sit down afterward and try to figure it out!

However, something now occurring that mean everything going out of my control anyway. Namely Right and Tompkins announcing that I now know so much about their plotting plans that actually I got no choice whatsoever except join in with them, because otherwise they going to have to send me to Department of Wet Affairs (which I know from our own KGB slanging is actually special department making fatal spillings of wet blood from anybody they not too happy with).

So I just say, OK, count me up.

And they offering me big congratulations about this and welcome into plot and so forth, and they now going to transfer me to more comfortable quartering and also introduce me to other conspirators, including some Russian fellows.

That evening, I get moved out of Belgravia police cell to special safe house these MI5 fellows keep in the Pimlico, and that same night, guess who comes arriving? Smerdyakov and one more Russian, introducing by name of Anatoly Golitsyn and turning out as KGB defector to England and apparently that very same fellow who been giving top secret informations about Henry Wilson (Worthington) to the MI5!

Then Right and Tompkins say OK, we going to leave all you Russkies together in this safe house for some friendly Russkie chattering and you all pretty safe here and please discuss whatsoever you wish to.

But when those English are gone, Smerdyakov is rapidly pointing up at ceiling lightbulb and make the shushing sound with finger on his lip, so I guess he warning we got to be careful in case someone listening up.

Smerdyakov and Golitsyn are both speaking in real low whispers and confirm it is true what Right and Tompkins been telling me, namely that some fellows in the MI5 are starting the plot against their own prime minister, but these are not official MI5 policies whatsoever and actually just some handful of agents doing it, maybe three or maybe thirty.

And when I ask, 'So it true that Harold Wilson is KGB

agent?' Smerdyakov and Golitsyn both saying quite loud 'Yes, this is true indeed' while looking up ceiling lightbulb, but at same time both of them shaking off their heads and making little secret smile to me, which suggest these MI5 guys been getting some dust thrown in their eyes.

I am also asking them about murder at highest levels material which KGB been using to blackmail Mr Wilson-Worthington, and Golitsyn reply for sure it is true that KGB been helping him murder off his rivals so he can get top job as PM, but again he is winking up at lightbulb and big smiling.

And when I ask who exactly been telling those English such things about Mr Wilson-Worthington, Smerdyakov point at Golitsyn and Golitsyn point at Smerdyakov and both of them give the little silent giggles and looking real smug and pleasing of themselves.

So I am getting the message pretty loud and clear (although actually real quiet, of course, because of microphone situation).

When I ask exactly who are Right and Tompkins, Golitsyn say they are rogue elephants of the security services, which I guess mean they sort of charging through the international espionage and security jungle trampling down trees and smashing up everything round them with their big tusks and trunks.

So I ask Smerdyakov and Golitsyn, please just tell me if I actually being the traitor to motherland when I accept Tompkins bargain deal in return for helping out their plot affair, and both of them saying, 'Complete the opposite: you are national hero!'

Which is top good news for me and now look like I am in winning-winning situation at last and everything finally getting hunky and dory.

And later that same evening, which is 23 July, we are switching on Pye TV in that MI5 safe house and watching *Match-up of the Day*, showing USSR team playing at Sanderland

Rocker Park in historic quarter-final victory over Hungarians, with top performance once again by Vova Smirnov and quality goals from Chislenko and Porkuyan, following by heroic feats of kipper Lev Yashin, renowned black panther, keeping those false socialists and traitor Hungarians at bay for rest of the game.

So semi-final line-up now clear: England going to play Portugal, and USSR play not-so-former fascist Nazis, for right to meet each others in grand final match one week later, on 30 July.

And next day Tompkins and Right coming to my Pimlico safe house and telling that they just been talking to top man behind their organization network, with secret codename of Sweetie-Blunty, and real big decision now been taken, namely that plot against Henry Worthington going to reach final dramatic conclusion on very day of World Cup final, 30 July at Vemberley Stadium!

And even bigger decision, but not quite so good for my opinion, they announcing that hero of this exploit going to be me, Zhenya.

Uh-oh!

When I hear this news, my stomach gets a large sinking feeling.

But Tompkins and Right tell me not to worry, they always be protecting me, everything going to be quite safe and I can end up as hero not only of Soviet Union but also of right thinkings people here in England too, and when popular new government get instilled following removal of Henry Worthington shambles, I going be occupying real imposing position of power – along with those plotter fellows, of course – and therefore having no trouble whatsoever in regaining rightful place in English aristocracy for me and my mother.

*

That afternoon, Smerdyakov and Golitsyn come to visit me, and both repeating what Right and Tompkins been telling, namely this is great patriotic duty I am performing and great honour for me and whole Soviet peoples.

That night, I am lying awake and unable of any much sleeping.

And when I do drift to the dozes, I see visions of me and Henry Worthington locked in deadly wrestling combat and each trying to strangle the others, while Right and Tompkins and Smerdykov and Golitsyn all gathering round and shouting and cheering me up. And Mr Worthington is looking at me and say, 'You sure this what you want, Zhenya? Why you doing this to me?'

When I awake next morning, 25 July, it seem clear that things not going to the best and some large amount of betraying going on round here, and person mostly getting betrayed is Zhenya Gorevich.

I am thinking about plans for urgent escaping.

Pimlico safe house got the front door and back door and several windows. Only problem, they all got the firm lock and bolting and no way to open them.

Outside of front door is one large fellow from the MI5, and outside of back door is one large fellow from the MI5.

Couple of hours later, Right and Tompkins arrive and drop off large black suitcase. They say this is materiel for upcoming mission so I strictly not got to open it till instructed for doing so by them or by Mr Sweetie-Blunty his self.

When they gone, I am sitting there and looking at this suitcase.

It is sitting there and looking at me.

And filling me up with very, very bad feelings.

Whole morning I am walking upwards and downwards in that safe house and not feeling very safe whatsoever.

At the lunchtime, BBC TV is making football preview programme and talking for long time about semi-final of England versus Portugal which upcoming on following day.

I can see MI5 fellow guarding the back door is peering through window for trying to watch this programme, and when I look at him, he just shrugging off his shoulders and give the little smile.

I am watching because other semi-final of USSR versus Federal Republic of Germany is happening that afternoon, but not too much time being devoted to this game whatsoever.

Eventually, though, Mr Buff is introducing Mr Vulstenhome and he say that he been speaking to top Soviet football star, with aid of interpreter of course, so here now is interview . . . with Vladimir Smirnov!

But something strange is happening, because we are seeing Mr Vulstenhome asking questions to Vova and then we seeing Vova replying the answers, and Vova is speaking in the Russian of course, but some English voice saying his answers.

But wait.

Not this is strange thing.

Strange thing is when Vova moving his lips, words his lips are making never seem to be equal to words which English voice speaking. So for an instance, English voice is saying, 'Yes indeed, we going to play with two wingers and two centre halfs' but it seem to me like Vova lips in Russian actually saying, 'Zhenya! Zhenya! Quick! Listen me . . .'

And when English voice is saying, 'Lads done good in that Hungary game . . .', it seem to me that Vova lips saying, 'Open suitcase, Zhenya. Open suitcase. You in the big danger . . .'

Then English voice is saying, 'It will be tough game against

Germans, but we looking forward to winning and playing big final match against host nation England . . .' but I am sure Vova lips are saying, 'Get away from there, Zhenya. Get away right now. It is you only chance . . .', and this time Vova is not winking whatsoever, but looking real serious and real worried.

That afternoon, USSR is playing pretty darn bad against former Nazis. Chislenko getting sent off for expressing his righteous anti-fascist sentiment (in form of kicking some German fellow), and we losing by the two goals to one. Soviet hopes of finalizing against England going straight out the drains.

At end of time, poor Nikolai Morozov look real dejected on the BBC TV and all his players do too, although Vova not anywhere to be seen.

I should be feeling sad too, but I am not feeling anything, because I can only think about that secret warning Vova been sending me through the TV screen and constant worrying about what going to happen next.

That night, I decide I got to take the positive action, so I resolve for doing what Vova been telling me, namely open up that suitcase.

Inside it is full of worrying objects, including telescopic rifle with ammunitions, real long scary syringe with liquid vials and packet of tablets labelling as 'Cyanide: use only if captured'.

Whoa!

Bad news.

This is pretty desperate situation and things not looking too hunky any more.

World final coming in five days.

Five days left to carrying out the plot against Henry Worthington.

Five days left to me being the carry out.

That night I am not sleeping and not even dozing. So no nightmares, but no rest.

Next day, 26 July, I am in grips of the exhaustion and cannot arise from the sofa.

I switch on TV again and semi-final of England versus Portugal is ready for commencing.

Bobby, Nobby and Bobby (*not* people militia) are leading out the English. Eusebio leading out the Portugals. Vemberley Stadium full to the brimming and sun is shining.

But I cannot find interest for this. Only my interest now is nightmare of upcoming disaster on 30 July with me arrested and lynching for engagement in assassination of English prime minister.

Then come sudden loud knocking on the window. Uh-oh!

I look around ... and see smiling face of MI5 fellow in back garden.

He is pointing to TV set and making a look by his face which mean, 'Please, you nice Soviet fellow going to let me come inside and watch the Alf's boys on you TV?'

And I say him, 'OK. You got the key. You open door and come right in.'

MI5 fellow look real grateful and happy.

And I am starting to glimpse a plan!

First half timing of that match is pretty tense. One Bobby scoring for England, but Eusebio nearly equalizing and Portugal doing all the attacking.

MI5 fellow is getting highly nervous.

In middle of second timing he start to enlighten a cigarette, but I am rapid thinking and say, 'Sorry. I am suffering by the asthma: maybe you don't mind to go outside for smoking and I

put on a brew-up?' and he say, 'Of course. Thanks you for letting me watch game.'

When that fellow go out for a smoke, he is real careful
locking up the door and taking keys out with him.

But when he come back in, I am immediate handling him
the large tray full of teacups, teapot, milk jug, sugar bowl,
doilies, spoons, Abbey Crunch and Ginger Nobs, so he not got
any free hands remaining and just having to be nice English
polite by saying thank you and taking over tray to TV room.

And just when he get there, Bobby is scoring one more goal
for the England and MI5 fellow is getting height of excitable
and complete forgetting that he not been locking any back door
whatsoever.

So while Mr Vulstenhome is commentating over replays of
England goal, I say I just need go to a toilet and MI5 fellow
say, 'Of course', and I am rapid slipping out of unlocked back
door, into safe house garden, over couple of fences and here I
am free at last!

Well, freedom is great inalienable gift of mankind, of
course, but it only any useful if you got some place to scarper
to.

Which I don't. So I am standing on a Tems river bank
looking round and thinking that pretty soon the MI5 going to
be scarpering after me.

And KGB scarpering after them.

Metropolitan bobbies (people militia, not football) scarpering after them.

And solely God know who scarpering after them.

Position is desperate.

And who can be helping me?

Not Smerdyakov, not Vova, not Right, not Tompkins, not

KGB, not MI5, not Lord Gore or Princess Susie, not Lady Liza, not even my mother.

And so soon I think of my mother, I start with the crying. Right there in street of Pimlico.

Tears flowing on my cheek because I am feeling sad and abandoned by all mankind and whole future promising only loneliness and gloom and eternity of *toska*.

But then I spot the pub (meaning tavern) of Pimlico Arms and get sharpish running inside.

OK, consuming vodka never solve all mankind problems. But maybe it help me forget about them.

I am drinking four, then five, six, then eleven, maybe even more vodka glasses.

And out of edges of my eye, I am glimpsing once again that beautiful maiden from long ago, from dream of flying witches, and she is sitting right there in corner of that pub, smiling over me and making the friendly suggestion such as, 'Hello, dearie, you fancy a little something?' But I am recalling how this maiden been dragging me down from the sky, down from Mavra broomstick, down to death on earth and nightmare of spirits from beyond.

In my head I hear Mavra warning words that such creatures come to us with evil intent, to drag us into their world, and even though she may be beautiful, all she wants is me to keep her company in realm of the dead.

I turn my head away and close my eyes.

And the world starts to melt.

Just like treacle.

Like that document in my Lubyanka nightmare.

And looking back now, looking back in my memory, I can see this is the moment I crossed from one world to another.

Out forever from the world of life reality.

And into another reality.

But not to the world of love and beauty.

To the world of horror.

To the world I have been in for forty years now.

The world I must live in for ever more.

Right there in that pub, my whole life been conjuring up to me.

Please tell me: how can life contain so many memories? How can all these things be inside us and beneath us, so much of them that we are made of these memories and they are us? From day we are born, we are building, always building up this edifice of memories, all of them piled on top of each the other, always carrying us higher and higher on their back.

And sometimes you look down. You look from top of this memory mountain and your heart swoons. Your past life is gone and all seems empty, not holding any meaning despite of seeming so important all those year ago.

Never you can return to the time of Pavlik Morozov and Misha's cat, when green school books proved that life is happy and we only got to obey the rules of Soviet world reality and everything be OK.

But now this thought make your heart squeeze, because things did not turn out like that at all, and soon you are trying to escape from sad unhappy reality, and how come things can't be back again just like when you were reading to you mother and she put her arms around you and smile and always take you in her warm bed to protect against the mad crows outside your windows who are trying to bring cold and snow in your life?

In that Pimlico pub, I see all those white pages I been tearing every day from my life's calendar swirling like snowflakes in a dark night sky.

I am trying to grasp them again and bring them back, but every time I seize them they melt to nothing.

And all the time, more and more pages are flying off, and the snowstorm round my face getting thicker and thicker till I cannot see my way and I stumble in the night.

And then something is snapping in my head.

Loud, like the twang of cables breaking at some mineshaft, but this time very deep down inside you, so you cannot tell where it is coming from.

Whole world picture is changing now.

Something coming clear and in focus.

At last, I know who can help me.

He who see all things and know all things and loves all mankind.

Great Lenin can help me and save me.

Great Lenin knows my life from start to finish.

Great Lenin knows my reasons and my unreasons.

Great Lenin gave my happy childhood.

I turn to a gentleman at next table of that Pimlico pub and inform him that I need to speak to Great Lenin and please he can tell how to find him.

And he reply something like, 'I am not sure he is here at the moment.'

Which is disappointing of course, but I am not losing hope.

I go down a corridor, through a door behind the lavatories and at last I see a Sign . . .

And the Sign say 'Staff Only'.

So I walk in there and find . . .

. . . not Great Lenin.

Just some other fellow I am not recognizing.

But then I figure this must be Henry Worthington.

Prime Minister Worthington is in a policy discussion with

female aide by name of Marcia, and both expressing differing opinions by throwing plates and cutleries at each others.

So I tell Mr Worthington he soon will be the target of assassination attempt, although I Zhenya am refusing to take place in this and will not be shooting him or poison him or harming him whatsoever, and now I got to find Great Lenin and he better come with me too because maybe Great Lenin will also help him. But Henry Worthington does not seem too interested in this.

And I see from corners of my eye that aide Marcia is putting down the crockery and cutlery and picking up her special red telephone and making a call, but I am not hearing exact what she is saying.

I am trying to warn Mr W about danger of the MI5 rogue elephants and he got to act real quick, and he is looking kind of worried at me and nodding slowly, but then doors of that room all burst open and in rush the whole crowd of bobby policemen, just like previous time, only now they are followed by the MI5, KGB and more such fellows not seeming too friendly and certainly not look like taking me to Great Lenin.

Rapid escaping needed again!

And this time only way out is by jumping down a plughole of that kitchen sink, crawling through sewer and emerging from a drainpipe in a road outside.

If you never done such a thing, I just tell you: this is real unpleasing experience and better avoid it if you got the chance.

But once again I am getting lucky, and getting free, although once again not knowing where to run.

Fortunately, I now remember something real important: namely the visit few days previous when Smerdyakov been taking us to British Museum.

Why this is important?

You soon see.

I am running through the Victoria, through the Piccadilly, through the Soho, through the Bloomsbury, and everywhere are worrying headlines on newspaper hoardings announcing 'England Germany World Cup final souvenir special', but also announcing 'Zhenya on the run; urgently wanted for questioning on suspicion of everything'.

Only chance is get to British Museum.

So I run up front steps, past security guards, into the Reading Room where we earlier been with Smerdyakov and where Great Lenin also been some time previous (although time is pretty confusing in my head right now), and I shout out loud, 'Great Lenin! Where You are? Great Lenin, save me!' And when he hear this, museum attendant – must be agent of evil power – start making a shushing sound to me and calling for more evil guards to come and prevent me reaching Great Lenin inside high dome of the Reading Room. But when He sees me enter, Great Lenin is loosing off one small but powerful thunderbolt from index finger of His right hand and all evil agents are turning to white stone statues.

Then things go real quiet in that Reading Room and everywhere is turning to white – white tiles on walls, men in white coats, ladies in white uniforms with white shoes and small white hats pinning up the hair, and real strong white light illuminating every nook of that room and every cranny in the minds of men.

And Great Lenin turn to me, also wearing the white coat, and say in His loud booming voice which fills whole of the Reading Room right to height of its ceiling dome, 'Welcome, Zhenya! Welcome at last! All right if I call you Zhenya, by the way? Lord Edenby-Gore just sound so formal.'

So I say, 'Of course, Great Lenin. I been seeking You for so many years. How come You here in London?'

And Great Lenin reply, 'Zhenya! How you can be such doubting Tomas? Maybe you never heard, Lenin always with us?'

And I say, 'Yes, Great Lenin, but this is year of 1966 and You been dying forty more years ago.'

But Great Lenin just smile and chides me, 'Zhenya! Surely you know Lenin lived; Lenin lives; Lenin will live!'

And now things all becoming sensible, of course. Lenin is always here, always here in every place where Russian people gathered in His name, and where poor Russian boys needing His help.

A red banner is waving in my head – familiar red banner from long ago, from other world – and the banner says, 'Thank you Comrade Lenin for our happy childhood.'

This was banner on my classroom wall when Zoya was my teacher and Misha cat was still alive.

Tears are coming to my eyes.

I look at Great Lenin and I am ready to make my true confession: 'I been missing You, Great Lenin; I been missing You so much. Things were so much better when we were children and all believing in You. When Your magic powers been making our lives happy and sunny as if we are always playing in Bezhin Meadow and never any harm can come to us so long as You are with us.'

And Great Lenin just look at me and say, 'I am pleased you talking to me now, Zhenya. For twenty years we thought you never going to speak. We all been getting real concerned about you.'

I am thanking for His concern and happy someone is

turning attention to me and taking cares about me being OK. And so long it is since anyone been showing me such kindness, I am feeling on a point of crying and hugging him.

But He say, 'Do not worry, Zhenya. Everything going to be all right. All you got to do is talk to me and tell me everything. Then we going to help you.'

I am trembling with relief and joy. I want to tell Great Lenin all my life stories. Right from time of being little kid and living in petticoats of my mother and the crow is coming to smash our window and Mr Finkelstein want to shoot him but my mother falling in love for Dr Astrov so we not shooting him and he is smashing through our window into our hut and dying in pool of blood on our kitchen floor, and then my life is starting up and I learn about Pavlik Morozov and believing in the future, but soon people smash up my leg and smash up my life, and maybe Masha look like she can rescue me but this is not working out, so I seek and chase and follow my destination, and my true father is yearning for me but then he is dead and the nightmares come, and maybe glimpsing a chance of happiness at number 82, but then that get taken away from me too and never I can understand is Vova my angel to guard me or petty demon for torment me, and things all reached such desperation I cannot see a way out and the nightmare is sucking me down, just like wisewoman Mavra said it will.

'And only You got the power to save me, Great Lenin; but first I got to tell You something real important for Yourself, namely people plotting against You including all capitalists and even some Communists; wanting to overthrow Your power and leave us with no authority or justice to care for us, with no sense or purpose to guide us.

'I know I been disrespectful to You, Great Lenin. I sinned

against You in the thought, the word and the deed, especially back in Minsk with that painting turning out some stupid pornography and soiling Your holy name, for which I am sorry.

'But now I see You are great and right, and only You can save us from the world without end.

'So pardon me.

'Release me from emptiness.

'Restore me to faith, to days of Misha and Pavlik.

'Redeem and save me.

'Only You got the right and the power and the justice.

'Only You are the land lord.'

And Great Lenin is listening real careful and sympathetic to my confession and sometimes nodding and making notes in His spiral notebook and then asking extra little questions, and when I tell about the plotting against Him, He just give the beatific smile and say, 'Thank you, Zhenya. Thank you for this. Of course, I know what is going on, all the plots and resentments and people having the bad intentions to me.

'I know all this because it is my power to know everything.

'But your confession is worth more to me than anything in the world.

'Your act of faith has rescued you and brought you to my heart.

'You wanted to save me. Now I will save you too.'

And with such words Great Lenin is flinging about His arms round me and kissing me in the Russian manner of warmth and affection and asking what I am most wanting in the world.

But it seems I been hearing that question somewhere before, somewhere worrying, so I reply that since He is knowing all things, He must already know what is answer to His question, and He say, 'You are right' and, 'Just leave everything to me.'

For next couple of days, I am lying in the real comfortable bed of that place where everything is white and bright light shines all day and all night, but it is not disturbing me whatsoever because I am relaxed and happy now and no more nightmares upsetting my sleep.

And that bed reminds me of my mother's bed when I was little boy. Only difference I could always get out of my mother's bed whereas for some reason I cannot get out of this one, although I don't care too much because I am happy in here.

Great Lenin is dressed in white and always looking after me and smiling.

But sometimes doubts arise to my mind, so I ask Him how come He always been promising shining future of Communism, but that future always remaining just over the horizon.

And Great Lenin say, 'Do not worry about this, Zhenya. A lie told often enough becomes the truth.'

I say, 'But what about people not being free?'

And Great Lenin reply, 'It is true that liberty is precious; so precious it got to be carefully rationed.'

But probably I still look dubious, because Great Lenin ask me: 'So what you are saying? You say you want a revolution?'

'Well, You know. We all want to change the world.'

'And so do I, Zhenya. I want power to the people. And I mean real power, power of being a hero.'

'But how this can be? A hero?'

'Yes, Zhenya, a working class hero is something to be.'

'Well, I see You are right, Great Lenin. But all my mother and me want is a chance for peace in our life.'

'So that what you are saying, Zhenya? You want to give peace a chance?'

'Yes, Great Lenin. That is all we are saying. And only You got the power.'

And Great Lenin say, 'This is true; I am not sure who is greater power – me or Jesus Christ', and then I think I hear Him say, 'You can call me John', but I am not sure of this so I call Him Lenin.

Then He makes the solemn pledge of redemption and happiness and say, 'Just you wait and see. World Final day is coming.'

And World Final day soon comes.

Great Lenin announces we are going to Vemberley.

And when we get there, thousands of people all shouting and singing, and sun shining whiter and brighter and hotter than ever before been seen in England.

But when two teams emerge on the Vemberley field, there is big surprise.

Namely it not the Germany coming to confront England.

Instead of Germans, it is USSR team emerging next to Bobby, Bobby and Nobby boys. And leading that team is Vova Smirnov!

Great Lenin can tell I am surprised by this, so He smiles and say, 'This is my first gift to you, Zhenya. Take it and be glad.'

And I was glad.

And course of events on final world day is unfolding down sweetest possible lines, namely USSR playing best football ever seen in history of the game, Vova Smirnov scoring top quality hats trick and USSR triumphing by the four goals to two.

At the end of time, Vova lifts the Jules Rimet World Cup trophy but those England fellows not looking too angry. Instead, they just smiling and laughing and give warmest congratulation to worthy winners, and whole crowd there and whole millions of peoples round the world are standing and applauding such magnificent triumph of socialism.

And Great Lenin turn to me and say, 'This is my second gift to you, Zhenya. Take it and be glad.'

And once again, I was glad.

But third and greatest gift is still to come.

At ending of that game, Bobby, Bobby and Nobby are going to all tribunes around Vemberley and waving up to everyone to begin the special singing and chanting.

And soon one hundred thousands people all chanting my name: Zhenya Gorevich, Zhenya Gorevich, we want Zhenya Gorevich!

Great Lenin look at me again and smiles, 'This is my third gift, Zhenya. Come with me now into the very brightest spotlight and be glad.'

And when we descend to that football field, whole of Vemberley is erupting with frenzy of joy. Right there in middle of centre circle, Great Lenin takes my hand and raises it in the air, making the sign with His finger and thumb like a letter 'O' and saying 'Vo-o-o, Zhenya! Vo-o-o!' saluting the triumph of my *podvig* quest, triumph of the true *bohatyr*. Everyone is here now, everyone from my past and my future.

This is the moment of reconciling all mankind.

Of forgiveness and love.

Great Lenin has decreed it so.

Great Lenin is lighting up His pipe, with Great Stalin helping, and Marx and Engels too, puffing up till clouds of smoke are encircling like incense, covering the circle round the altar, covering the football pitch and all the tribunes.

And out of that smoke is emerging . . . my mother!

Smiling and waving to the crowd, kissing me and explaining through a megaphone that Great Lenin has flown her here especially from Vitebsk to be present at the final ceremony, at the triumph of her son.

Great Lenin begins the ceremony. His words ringing out from all tannoys and loudspeakers of Vemberley stadium, from all radio and television sets, in streets of London, Moscow, Minsk, Dooram and Vitebsk, from Sputnik in space across the universe.

Great Lenin says, 'Let us pray', and everyone fall silent.

Everyone doffing off flat caps and bonnets; everyone bowing heads in sure and certain expectation.

Lenin says, 'Let us pray for forgiveness. For well I know you have sinned against me. Well I know you plotted and connived. All things I know, for I am the power, I am the smoke maker, I am the only true land lord.'

And with those words, Great Lenin takes that Jules Rimet World Cup trophy in His two strong hands, drinks from it and raises it high above His head.

A murmur runs round the crowd.

A stillness descends upon the world.

Great Lenin looks up.

He speaks.

'Yeah, verily I say unto you: you have sinned against me, but I shall help you. You have plotted, but I shall make things OK. You have suffered, but I shall take away your pain. You have known sorrows, but I shall right the wrongs that were done you. Sadness and *toska* will end; grief exist no more. Only say you believe, and it will be enough.'

And all around that great stadium, all around the world, voices are murmuring in hushed amazement, millions of people all saying together, 'I believe. I believe. I believe that ev'ry time we hurt, Great Lenin knows; I believe that even in the darkest night, there'll be no crows.'

It is beautiful.

But getting late.

Very late.

Great Lenin is speaking still.

But something is wrong.

Other, new faces appearing round the altar.

Faces of suffering and grief.

The dead maiden buried in her wedding dress.

Mavra the witch.

Pavlik Morozov, the martyr child with bloody wounds sustained for Communism.

And a vision from the future: great Lev Yashin, lovely sleek black panther, now crippled, amputated at the knee, a one-legged alcoholic awaiting death in 1990.

The atmosphere has turned bitter.

The crowd chants *Gorko! Gorko!* but no one can make it sweet.

Vemberley is filled with foreboding.

A snowstorm is swirling in the stadium.

Snow is everywhere, falling fast and dense.

Enveloping the altar, the pitch, the crowd.

Sunlight blotted out.

I stumble and run for the exit.

PART FIVE

http://www.vitebsk.p'bolnitsa.wardsix:
Colleagues' chatroom. August 2006

Dr N. N. Pavlov writes:
I am seeking information on the case of A. A. Akakievich,
deceased.

Dr G. A. Imenko writes:
300 pages of interviews from this case are attached (above).

Dr Pavlov writes:
Thank you. Unfortunately, you have sent the file of a certain
Gorevich.

Dr Imenko writes:
I apologize. I thought you knew of the patient's insistence on using
that name.

Dr Pavlov writes:
Colleague! Please do not reproach me with negligence. This is a
clear contravention of hospital rules. Will we be allowing patients to
be referred to as Napoleon or Josef Stalin in future?

Dr Imenko writes:

I apologize for the breach of procedure. Patient Akakievich would not allow himself to be interviewed or referred to by any name other than Gorevich or Edenby-Gore. When you read the interview records, you will understand his assumed rationale for this. This patient was a particularly trying experience for me. I treated him for nearly forty years, from his admission in 1966 until I left the hospital last month. His subsequent death was most upsetting for me and for my staff.

Dr Pavlov writes:

This is of no concern to me. My duties are solely to write the case profile for the procurator's inquest. In that connection, I would welcome your comments on the notes you forwarded to me.

Dr Imenko writes:

For the first twenty years, between 1966 and 1986, the patient maintained a total silence. Attempts to address him by his real name of Akakievich were met by denial and bouts of self-harm.

It was only by chance that Nurse Chapayeva was one day bathing the patient and sympathetically muttering *O gore, kakoe gore* (O grief, what a grief) when he suddenly spoke for the first time. The Russian word for grief, *gore*, had produced a reaction which seemed to unlock his power of speech.

However, for the rest of his life he insisted on speaking only in English, a language I knew and was therefore appointed his full-time consultant. You will see from the case notes that all interviews were carried out in English (at times broken and hesitant and at others remarkably fluent).

He continued to respond solely to the name of Gorevich (when in his 'Russian' persona) or Edenby-Gore (when entering his 'English' persona). The issue of his forename (in reality Arkady, but in his own mind Yevgeny or its diminutive form, Zhenya) is something I was unable to elucidate. His mother's name was Nadya, but she had died before the patient was admitted, so we were unable to establish why he insisted on calling her Tatiana.

Nurse Chapayeva has surmised that his choice of both these names was connected with the patient's obsessive interest in the works of Pushkin. You may wish to speak to her about this matter.

Nurse K. I. Chapayeva writes:
Gennady Aleksandrovich!

How happy we – and I in particular – were to hear from you.

We are missing you, and we are missing Zhenya. It was so sad the way he died, and so soon after you had left us. Dr Pavlov is trying very hard to cope with the workload here. He is doing his best, but at times I feel he is a little overwhelmed. It was partly my fault that I did not make it clearer about Zhenya's case notes. I have recently spoken with Dr Pavlov and explained the unhappy history of this sad life which is now in the hands of the Almighty, God Give Him Rest.

Dr Imenko writes:
Dearest Karolina Ivanovna!

How pleasing it is to hear from you. I was saddened to learn of Zhenya's death. And I do hold myself partly responsible. I knew he would feel abandoned and betrayed when I retired, but I really had no choice in the matter.

Please assist the new doctor with the case and please keep me informed of any conclusions you and he reach.

Dr Pavlov writes:

I am sorry to intrude on the chitchat and pleasant reminiscences, colleagues. I was under the impression that this noticeboard was intended for the purpose of exchanging clinical data.

May we please return to the actual details of the Akakievich case?

Nurse Chapayeva writes:

Dr Imenko refers to my theory about the patient's invented names: it is just that Pushkin's heroine Tatiana shows traits of the classic self-inventing personality, living in an idealized fantasy world drawn largely from her reading of Romantic novels; and Yevgeny (or Zhenya) from the 'The Bronze Horseman' is the archetypal *malenky chelovek*, in revolt against the world and ultimately crushed by it. There are other literary echoes, too.

Dr Imenko writes:

Dearest Karolina Ivanovna!

Thank you for your fascinating and informative email.

The question of the poetry allegedly written by the patient's mother did exercise me a little, but even with my limited literary knowledge, I assume this is not the work of the immortal Pushkin!

Would I be correct in identifying Saltykov-Shchedrin as the inspiration for Zhenya's ghoulish dream tales (which he himself acknowledges to be generated by some subconscious literary memory)?

Dr Pavlov writes:

I have read Nurse Chapayeva's comments and I completely fail to see their relevance to the Akakievich case.

Also, I have checked the meteorological records and there is no record of any snowstorm in London in July 1966.

How do you explain this?

Dr Imenko writes:

Dear Dr Pavlov,

I fear you have misunderstood the genesis of these case notes. They are not a contemporary or indeed a factual record of actual events. My interviews with Zhenya were akin to an exercise in picking up little pieces of broken glass.

You might say his own life shattered into hundreds of shards following the nervous crisis he suffered in July 1966.

I have pieced them into a broadly chronological narrative, written in the words he himself employed, but I cannot take responsibility for factual inaccuracies. I am sure you will have noticed that in the latter stages, events are being reported through the distorting prism of his catastrophic breakdown and subsequent confinement in our own hospital. His mental health degenerated to the point where he saw me as Vladimir Lenin, an omnipotent being holding his destiny in my hand. I fear my leaving may therefore have left him feeling cast adrift and ultimately suicidal.

Dr Pavlov writes:

The patient was clearly a psychotic fantasist; his ludicrous 'adventures' the product of a diseased mind unable to cope with real life.

But what is your explanation for the so-called physical evidence adduced by Akakievich to substantiate his 'other world'?

Dr Imenko writes:

We always assumed that Zhenya spent his whole life here in

Vitebsk and, despite his detailed descriptions of Moscow, London and elsewhere, 'visited' these places solely in his traumatized imagination.

However, some elements left us puzzled, notably the patient's possession of a silver-plated English hand mirror (repeatedly referred to in the case interviews), a British Foreign Office visiting card personally endorsed by Melvyn Edenby-Gore, two tickets to the 1966 World Cup final and a handwritten letter of thanks – exactly what for remains a mystery – from the former British prime minister Harold Wilson.

Like all my colleagues, I assumed that the improbable construct of the patient's paternity (the mysterious, vanished Lord Gore) was an invention based on his undoubted wide reading and knowledge of historical events, and his deep conviction that he was a scion of the English aristocracy a deluded attempt to compensate for his personal failures and inadequacies.

I cannot help thinking it was the experience of watching the 2006 World Cup on television last month that brought back Zhenya's unbearable trauma from 1966 and provoked his final, ultimately fatal bout of paranoia.

Further than that, I cannot comment.

Nurse Chapayeva writes:
Gennady Aleksandrovich is correct.

We all believed Zhenya made things up to make himself feel better. He was unhappy with the reality of life (in Soviet era Vitebsk I can understand this), so he invented an idealized world 'just over the horizon'.

When I think of the constant promises of a better, Communist future we were all force-fed for so long, I would not be surprised if such a cruel deception actually produced tens of thousands of Zhenya Goreviches.

But, over the years, I spoke with Zhenya more than anybody –
including even you, Gennady Aleksandrovich – and these
conversations were for the most part unguarded and informal. With
other patients, it is at times like these that the internal contradictions
of their fantasy worlds are laid bare. With Zhenya, everything rang
true. From records in the Vitebsk reference library, I have
established that there was indeed a Lord Gore on the UK mission
to Moscow in 1939. This is not conclusive proof of anything, of
course, since the young Zhenya could easily have consulted the
same library records that I did. The existence of the visiting card is
harder to explain.

Dr Pavlov writes:
For the benefit of the procurator, I need to produce an accurate
account of the manner of Akakievich's death.

I would be grateful if Dr Imenko or Nurse Chapayeva would let
me have this information by the end of the week, confining
yourselves as much as possible to the relevant clinical details.

Thank you.

Nurse Chapayeva writes:
I know this subject will be too upsetting for Dr Imenko, so I shall
undertake the task.

In the weeks leading up to his death, Zhenya was in a highly
delusional state. He spoke constantly to himself about England
and about his mentally disabling fear of crows.

During this time, the World Cup finals in Germany were
reaching their culmination and Zhenya followed the television
broadcasts with great attention. He rose early for the
retransmission of the previous day's matches and stayed up until
2 a.m. Vitebsk time for live transmission of the evening games.
He developed a pathological interest in the fortunes of the English

team, which Dr Imenko supposed to be fuelled by some traumatic memory connected with the 1966 World Cup exactly forty years earlier. He became particularly agitated when Togo were playing (their assistant physiotherapist is a former Russian player called V. I. Smirnov).

As the World Cup progressed, he sank into a deep melancholy. Despite the efforts of the nursing staff to rally his spirits, Zhenya's condition steadily worsened. His attempts at self-harm grew alarmingly, in particular his habit of banging his head on the windows of the ward and, at times, throwing himself against the sheet glass of the French doors as if trying to escape.

Increased drug therapy was attempted, but achieved no noticeable improvement. Psychosurgery was contemplated but, unfortunately, this was not possible without the informed consent of either the patient himself (unobtainable because of his worsened mental state) or his next of kin (the hospital has no records of any surviving relatives). Plans for surgery were therefore delayed and during this period a rapid decline was noted in the patient's condition.

On 9 July 2006, the day of the final game of the World Cup, Zhenya Gorevich (Arkady Akakievich) killed himself. His body was found by nursing staff early in the morning, shortly after sunrise. He had thrown himself through the French doors with very great force. The glass had smashed and the patient received fatal injuries to the external carotid and common carotid arteries in his neck. His body was discovered lying on the patio, in the middle of a pile of glass shards, covered in blood. In his hand was a silver-framed mirror engraved with the English language inscription 'From Melvyn Edenby-Gore to my dearest Tatiana' and a programme for the 1966 World Cup final in England, personally endorsed by Mick Jagger and Keith Richards with the legend 'Good to know you Zhenya – the original street fighting man!'

I HEARD LENIN LAUGH

He was staring open-eyed at the sky. Nursing staff say his expression was one of contentment, *as if he had seen something he wanted to see and found something he had long been seeking for.*

5 November 2006.
Akakievich file closed. Subject deceased.
Relevant authorities confirm information is of no interest.
Documents to be sent for incineration.

EPILOGUE

Guardian,

London, November 2005

Sixty Guy Fawkes eves ago, the Moscow Dynamo football team arrived at Croydon airport. Almost literally out of the blue, for although the FA secretary Stanley Rous had invited them and settled the date five weeks before, there had been no confirmation of arrival. So when the US-built lend-lease Dakota, a scarlet star motif on the tailfin, touched down in war-ravaged London on November 4 1945, Rous was thrown into a tizz when out stepped 39 men (20 footballers and 19 trainers, minders or journalists) and one woman (the interpreter Alex Elliseyeva, whom Fleet Street in no time was to dub 'Alexandra the Silent').

Even after Rous and his staff had telephoned more than 100 London hotels, still none could (or would) accommodate the exotic party en bloc. After a bleak night at the Coldstream Guards' Wellington barracks, they threatened to go home – a promise doubly strong after the FA had dispersed them for the following two nights in threes or fours in various outlying dingy London B&Bs. On November 7, a desperate Rous persuaded the Imperial Hotel, Russell Square, to lease him a whole floor – 'Do Russians have sheets on their beds?' the manager asked – but no meals, and these were taken (including breakfast) at the Soviet embassy in Kensington.

Thus prepared, between November 13 and 28, playing spectacularly innovative football, a total throng of 269,600 watched them beat Arsenal and Cardiff City, and draw with Chelsea and Rangers (goals for 19, against 9) – and after a banquet with the Lord Mayor of London and a visit to Karl Marx's grave at Highgate they left on the same aircraft as suddenly as they had arrived, leaving Aston Villa with 70,000 obsolete tickets for a match the club mistakenly thought it had been promised for the following day.